# A Follow-Through in Faking

# BRIDGET L. ROSE

| JANUARY 14 - 28 | AUSTRALIAN OPEN |
| FEBRUARY 18 - 24 | DUBAI TENNIS CHAMPIONSHIPS |
| MARCH 6 - 17 | INDIAN WELLS OPEN |
| MARCH 20 - 31 | MIAMI OPEN |
| APRIL 15 - 21 | STUTTGART OPEN |
| APR / MAY 24 - 5 | MADRID OPEN |
| MAY 8 - 19 | ITALIAN OPEN |
| JUNE 17 - 23 | GERMAN OPEN |
| JULY 1 - 14 | WIMBLEDON |
| JUL / AUG 29 - 4 | WASHINGTON OPEN |
| AUGUST 6 - 12 | CANADIAN OPEN |
| AUGUST 12 - 19 | CINCINNATI OPEN |
| AUG / SEPT 26 - 8 | US OPEN |
| SEPT / OCT 26 - 2 | CHINA OPEN |
| OCTOBER 7 - 13 | WUHAN OPEN |
| NOVEMBER 2 - 9 | WTA FINALS |

# SCHEDULE

|  |  |
|---|---|
| JANUARY 14 - 28 | AUSTRALIAN OPEN |
| FEBRUARY 12 - 18 | ARGENTINA OPEN |
| FEBRUARY 19 - 25 | RIO OPEN |
| MARCH 6 - 17 | INDIAN WELLS OPEN |
| MARCH 20 - 31 | MIAMI OPEN |
| APRIL 7 - 14 | MONTE-CARLO MASTERS |
| APR / MAY 24 - 5 | MADRID OPEN |
| MAY 8 - 19 | ITALIAN OPEN |
| MAY / JUN 26 - 9 | ROLAND GARROS (FRENCH OPEN) |
| JULY 1 - 14 | WIMBLEDON |
| AUGUST 6 - 12 | CANADIAN OPEN |
| AUGUST 12 - 19 | CINCINNATI OPEN |
| AUG / SEPT 26 - 8 | US OPEN |
| SEPTEMBER 19 - 25 | DAVIS CUP |
| SEPT / OCT 26 - 2 | CHINA OPEN |
| OCTOBER 2 - 13 | SHANGHAI MASTERS |
| OCT / NOV 28 - 3 | PARIS MASTERS |
| NOVEMBER 10 - 17 | ATP FINALS |

# Trigger Warnings

Grief (death of a parent—in the past but still affects the fmc deeply and there is several mentions of it), anxiety and depression in full detail, vulgar language and explicit sex scenes, homophobia (not from the main or side characters but in the sport—it's something the fmc especially works against and tries to raise awareness on), mention of a person who did domestic violence (it's brief and neither of the main characters nor any import side character).

This book is dedicated to my younger self, to the little girl who dreamt about becoming a professional tennis player before life got in her way and made her dream slip through her fingers. I may not have achieved that dream, but now I get to write about strong, queer characters fighting for equality in the sport I fell in love with all those years ago.

Everything happens for a reason. I know now that, even if I didn't reach that dream, writing this book made another one come true, and I'm grateful for every path I took that led me here.

# CHAPTER 1
## SANTIAGO

"You're the number one tennis player in the entire world, Santiago, start acting like it," my mother, who is also my manager, says, flopping onto the couch of my hotel room. Her fingers move to her temples, which she massages excessively, a habit she has every time I piss her off.

My twin sister, Manuela, smirks to herself, scrolling through something on her phone. She's thoroughly enjoying all of this.

"I don't understand what the problem is. Athletes go partying all the time," I reply, pressing the cold water bottle Mamá brought me against my throbbing head. I may have overdone it last night, not with alcohol but with staying out late and dancing until my entire body ached. Now I'm dehydrated and sleep-deprived.

"You have to uphold a certain image, *mijo*, and you partying and fucking someone new every day is not the golden boy image the world expects of you," she goes on, and I flinch a little at her words.

"Why is that my problem? I'm twenty-four years old. I'm supposed to be a little reckless," I argue, but the glare she shoots me in response makes me cower in my seat. Manu grins even harder, so I throw a pillow at her head. As a tennis player herself, her reaction time is good enough to lift her arm and catch it long before it threatens to hit her face.

"You are supposed to be focused, Santiago. Tell him, *mi amor*," Mamá says, turning toward Papá, my coach, for help. He's been furious with me for days, has barely said a word when I'm in the room, and the frown on his lips seems to be permanent now.

My father's calculating eyes study me for a moment, not a single word escaping his lips. Both of my parents are concerned about my reputation, I'm well aware, but I don't think it's as bad as they're making it out to be. My performance isn't affected because of my habits. Alcohol isn't part of my partying behavior. I made a decision when I first decided to go pro to stay far away from it.

It's not something I need, so why consume it?

Going out, on the other hand, I need. Feeling like a normal person instead of the golden boy, as Mamá portrays me to the world, is the only thing keeping me from questioning who the fuck I am most days. The whole world knows me, has expectations of me that anyone would crumble under, but I haven't, and I won't. That's what my coping techniques are for, after all, even if they're not the healthiest.

As long as I get on the court and get the job done, I don't see why my personal life has to be anyone's business. I put on a show for them, make them love me, and win.

Almost every single time, I win.

What more do they want from me?

"The Grand Slam season is almost upon us, Santiago, and I have made a decision," Papá says, standing up and walking toward the mini fridge in the hotel room to pull out a bottle of water. He takes a sip, creating a tension so thick, I roll my eyes.

"*Papá, por el amor de Dios, dimelo sin el drama, por favor,*" I say, hoping it'll get him to speak. His two-meter body struts across the room with more elegance than a tall, muscular man like him should have, until he's right in my face and grabbing my shoulder.

"I have picked out a new hitting partner for you." My heart lurches in my chest.

"Who?" I ask, but his grip on me tightens until I wince from discomfort, and he doesn't answer my question.

"Additionally, to clean up your disgusting reputation, you will be pretending to date your new partner. She's in a bit of a situation herself, you see, so it's a win-win for all of us."

Papá finally lets go of my shoulder, and I jump out of my seat, trying to put some distance between us. My pounding head is not happy about the quick motion, causing the room to spin for a second before it levels out again.

"You can't force me to date this woman or have her be my new hitting partner, whoever she is," I reply, but Papá merely crosses his arms in front of his thick chest and watches me until I feel like running away from him. I look to Manu for help, but she's as silent as she always is when I'm fighting with our parents.

"You will be doing as I've said. You will clean up your reputation. If not, I will no longer be your coach."

As much as I'd like to keep arguing with him, the anger in his eyes makes me hesitate. Papá was the number one tennis player in the entire world for four years in a row, seven in total in his career. I've always wanted to be like him.

Losing him as my coach is something I'm not ready for, not after eighteen years of him training me.

Even Manuela looks shocked as she sits up on the couch, dropping her phone.

"Papá, you can't—," she says, but he holds up a hand to silence her.

"Yes, I can." I shudder at the determination in his gaze.

"How long do we have to keep up the pretense? My new partner and I?" I ask, all of a sudden feeling small and weak. Not like the adult man I am, but the child I used to be when we started training me to go pro.

"One season. That's all it'll take to teach you to grow up. One season sitting in her box during all of her matches and being a devoted partner will be good for you," Papá explains, and I suck in a sharp breath.

"One season, and then I want your promise that I can go back to doing whatever I want. Either this little experiment works or it doesn't. I do this once, and then you'll never get to control my life like this again," I offer and hold out my hand for my father, waiting for him to shake it and agree to my terms and conditions.

"No more parties. No sleeping with anyone. You will be training with your new partner every spare minute you get," he says, adding to the agreement.

"Okay, you have yourself a deal," I say, wiggling my fingers. He eyes my hand for a minute, mischief sparkling in his eyes before he shakes it.

"Deal."

I take a step back and inhale deeply, trying to slow my racing heart. Every fiber of my being hates having to do this, but at least having a new hitting partner isn't playing doubles with her, so it doesn't impact my ability to play singles. I'll still get to keep my number one title if I'm good enough.

And I am.

I've been going through intensive training all winter to prepare to keep my place in the world. I'm fast, know how to analyze my opponents, and become creative to win. I'm crafty when I play, it's why people adore me so much. It's entertaining for them to watch. It's also the reason why I'm so fucking glad my father isn't expecting me to figure out how the hell to play doubles now.

*I fucking hate playing doubles.*

Having a partner restricts what you can do on the court. Not to mention, having to rely on them to play well and getting angry when they don't sucks.

The only time I've ever played doubles was with an infuriating partner.

Then again, we weren't really partners. We may have played on the same side of the court, but we were rivals.

Unfortunately, we were unbeatable together, and our school knew better than to separate us. We brought them to the top in the entire country with our singles and doubles victories. Then, we both went pro, and I only have to see her occasionally for celebrations hosted for tennis players.

But every time we lock eyes...

Fuck, I almost shudder.

Catalina Sanchez is in the past and not someone I have to worry about anymore.

"So, who is going to be my new hitting partner?" I finally ask, slumping back onto the couch and letting the tension of the argument with my father leave my body.

Manu lets out a small snort from where she's sitting, so I furrow my brows at her. She's covering her mouth with one of her hands, but I see the amusement sparkling in her eyes. Papá gives me a full-faced smile, and I feel dread filling me from top to bottom.

"No," I blurt out.

"Your partner for the season will be Catalina Sanchez."

I'm going to throw myself off a fucking cliff.

# CHAPTER 2
## CATALINA

"Santiago Castillo? Are you kidding me?" I ask, but my manager and coach, Charlie, just grins at me. They know about my history with the men's number one tennis player. "Why would you do this to me?" Charlie flat-out laughs. They raise one of their trained arms to correct my position, their slender but muscular frame tall enough to make them have to bend down to help me.

"Hey, you're the one whose scandal went international. 'Women's tennis number two in the world caught enjoying herself with two men in a hot tub,'" they recite the title of a news outlet's headline, and I frown in response.

"I was not *enjoying myself* with two men. I wouldn't do that in public, only in the privacy of my own bedroom," I reply, curling the weights in my hands until my muscles burn. Charlie smiles their devastating smile at me, and I let out a groan in response. "How does my sitting in a hot tub with two strangers end up with me having to fake a relationship and become hitting partners with the man I hate the most in the world?" I ask, dropping the weights on the ground and taking several deep breaths.

"Well, image is everything, and the world seeing you date the golden boy of tennis? Becoming each other's hitting partners for an entire season while you sit in each other's boxes and watch one another win Grand Slams? It's every manager's wet dream," they say with that wonderful English accent, but all I can do is frown. Sweat drips down the side of my face, so I wipe it away and let my head drop.

"I'd rather have someone run me over several times, put me back together, and then saw me in half than spend any alone time with Santiago Castillo. He's the embodiment of my worst nightmare," I say, picking up the weights again to go through my last set.

"Well, for the next few months, you're going to have to pretend to be in love with him," Charlie goes on, hovering their hands over my elbows to spot me. I make a hurling noise, bringing a grin to their lips. "Don't be dramatic. You could do a lot worse than Santiago. He's incredibly hot." No point arguing that, but his looks don't make him any less exhausting to be around.

"Why do people care so much about my private life? Why does it matter how many people I sleep with?" I ask, my voice strained now because my muscles are protesting the curling motion. "I don't even sleep with that many! I was dating my ex-girlfriend for two years before we ended things, and since then I haven't been with anyone because of something called trust issues. Do you think they've ever heard of that?" Charlie snorts.

"You're a tennis player. Most of them get married young and start a family. You barely ever hear any of them having the kind of sex lives Santiago and, allegedly, you have." I cock a confused eyebrow. "Wild," Charlie adds to clarify. "Not to mention, you're a woman, making it even more scandalous. A man would have more easily gotten away with it. Santiago did for years and it only caught up to him now." I grunt in agreement, trying to breathe through the strain of the exercise.

"I think people need to start worrying about important things in the world instead of how many people I take to bed." My coach takes the weights from me after my last rep, and I sink onto the bench behind me with an exhausted, "Ouch."

"That's not going to happen any time soon, so you have to play house with the man whose ass has made more front pages than I can remember," Charlie swoons, forcing a chuckle out of me.

Charlie is only four years older than Santiago and me, something I've often found great comfort in because they understand me and my needs better than a coach and manager twenty years my senior would. It has also allowed us to build a friendship like no other, and I can't imagine my life without them anymore, even if we've only been working together for the last four years.

It's hard not to get attached to Charlie.

They're warm, kind, funny beyond measure, caring, intelligent, and they're not afraid to give me a metaphorical kick in the butt when I deserve it.

"His ass might be the greatest I've ever seen, but it doesn't change that he's Satan incarnate," I reply right as I move over to the bench press, getting ready to start my sets there.

"No, but it will make for a phenomenal view when you're training with him and sitting in his box, watching him play." I can't help it. I burst into laughter, which soon turns into a frustrated crying sound as I cover my face. "There are worse things in the world of tennis that could have happened to you," Charlie argues when I continue to pretend-cry into my sweaty arms.

"Are there?" I lift them to stare into their deep brown eyes.

"Yes."

The look on their face reminds me that there is, in fact, something much worse. And it happened to them.

"I'm sorry," I blurt out when I realize my mistake.

"For what, Lina? It's not your fault that they made me leave. It's their fault for still not respecting a person's pronouns, and I wasn't going to be misgendered at every turn. Plus, I enjoy being your coach far more than fighting for any title," they say, but I know it's not entirely the truth.

I know they miss the matches, the tournaments, the glory. I know because I would too, and they've pretty much called me every imaginable thing a pansexual person can be called, especially while I was dating a woman.

When you're in love with a sport, you do your best to make it better because it's not the craft itself that is the problem. It's the people. So you do your best to make them more open-minded. You fight for a change while you fight for the titles you always hoped you'd get. It's what Valentina Romana did in Formula One when she became the first female driver. It's what countless other female, trans, non-binary, and more athletes have done and are doing.

"You don't need any titles or specific rankings for everyone to know you're one of the best fucking players the world has ever seen," I remind them, and the smirk covering their face is so instant, I grin.

"Maybe not, but maybe if I had both, my parents wouldn't be such pains in the ass." That makes me laugh.

"Yeah, they still would be," I reply, and Charlie gives me an agreeing nod. Their parents love them, but they still wanted more for them than a career as my coach, not something I blame them for, no matter how grateful I am that Charlie chose me. That they continue to choose me no matter what.

We fall silent for a moment while I continue training, gritting my teeth as I push through the workout. But there is something I need to say out loud, no matter how often Charlie's already had to hear me say it.

"I want to be the women's world number one by the end of this season," I say once we're finished for the day.

My eyes are glued to my shaking hands, tired from the three-hour work-out—playing tennis, endurance training, and weight-lifting. Even Charlie's warm brown skin is glistening with sweat because of how tired they are from the day, their short, dark brown curls messier than they were when we started.

"You will be. You worked your ass off and it's going to get you to the top, Lina. I know it will," Charlie replies, taking my hands in both of theirs and flashing me an encouraging smile.

"I want to follow in Mamá's footsteps," I admit in a whisper because saying it out loud, putting that expectation out there, is terrifying. It's my dream, but it's also pressure beyond anything I've ever felt.

"Your mother currently holds the title for the most Grand Slams ever won, most matches ever won, and longest reigning number one in the world. If there is anyone capable of living up to her accomplishments, it's you." Charlie gives my cheek a small nudge with their index finger, and I can't help but smile in return.

"I think she'd have ripped the reporters a new one for writing that article about me and tainting my whole image," I say with a small shake of my head.

My fingers slide upward to the tennis ball charm she gave me when I won a big tournament at my school. It was the last gift she gave me before she passed away.

"Oh, a hundred percent. I'm surprised you didn't do it yourself," Charlie says as they hold out their hands to help me off the ground.

"I would have, but you warned me you'd fill my bed with bugs if I did." Charlie merely chuckles.

"I didn't think that would stop you."

Under normal circumstances, it wouldn't have, but I know better than to add gasoline when my career is the thing on fire. I didn't want to be kicked out of the WTA, especially not when I'm one of the youngest players ever to be number two, fighting for number one. Nothing will stop me from becoming who I've always dreamt I'd be.

It's just another thing that irritates me about Santiago.

*He's* number one in the men's ranking.

That jerk.

He's also already won three Grand Slams while I have won... none. Not a single one. I've won most of the other small ones like the Monaco Open, Cincinnati Open, and more, which has pushed me into the number two spot. But winning one of the big tournaments is something I have yet to accomplish.

I've come second twice, but I'm hungry for the win.

It'll happen this season, I'm sure of it. Even if Santi will be sitting in my box while it happens.

"You're thinking about Santiago, aren't you?" Charlie asks, and I cock my brow at them.

"Why the hell would you think that?" I ask as I grab my towel and water bottle from the ground, a sea turtle painted on the side of the bottle I take with me everywhere.

"Your cheeks are all flushed in the way they always are when you think about him," they reply, making my eyes go wide.

"That's disgusting," I blurt out, raising my hands to my cheeks to feel how hot they are. Charlie snickers at my behavior before nudging me with their shoulder. "They don't actually, do they?" I ask, but Charlie walks away, adding a skip to their step.

I run to catch up to them, jumping onto their back, but Charlie was expecting me, so their hands lift to catch my legs and secure me against their upper body.

"This season is going to be fun," they say.

# CHAPTER 3
## SANTIAGO



Today is reunion day.

Whoop-de fucking-do.

Papá is in the passenger seat while I'm driving us to the tennis court that he and Charlie, Catalina's manager and coach, agreed to meet us at. He's grinning like he's never been happier, and I feel like punching him in the arm.

"Having a great time, are we?" I ask him, and he turns to smile at me.

"If you're asking me if I'm enjoying the irony of Catalina being the one who is perfect for this ruse when you two have disliked each other since childhood, then yes. I'm having a phenomenal time," he replies.

I roll my eyes and focus on the road ahead of us to ignore the fluttering of my heart.

"You know, you have another child you could focus all this energy on," I point out, but he gives me an unaffected shrug.

"Manuela's reputation is flawless. She and her doubles partner of five years are playing well, and she's making her way to the number one spot in the women's doubles players ranking. I'm very happy with her," he explains, although he doesn't have to. I know my sister is perfect. She does everything right. "So, the only headache-inducing child I have will receive all of my attention, especially so I can make sure he behaves around Catalina."

Ever since Papá told me she'd be my "girlfriend" and hitting partner this season, I started digging to find out why Catalina would have ever agreed to this. She despises me, can't stand even being close to me for longer than a minute, and the feeling is mutual.

Turns out, she was caught "having a fling with two men in a hot tub." I almost burst into laughter when I read the article because *what the fuck*? These media empires have nothing better to do than spin stories out of nothing, and anyone with a little common sense would have seen they were strangers. Catalina was on the far end of the tub, on her phone, and her body closed off from them.

At one point, I knew her better than most people. I watched the look of desire in her eyes when she wanted someone, wanted *me* even when she hated me, and the men in that hot tub were far from being on the receiving end of her lust.

"One season," I remind myself, my hand gripping the steering wheel a little too hard.

"Unless, of course, you enjoy yourself," Papá replies, causing me to snort.

Yeah, right, like that's ever going to happen when I'm "dating" *mi enemiga*.

The rest of the drive passes in complete silence.

Minutes later, we're walking onto the indoor tennis courts, and I'm trying my best not to suck in a sharp breath at the sight of her.

Catalina is half-English, half-Spanish, and all gorgeous. She has a pale skin tone, blue eyes, and long, straight brown hair. Her face and curves are a distraction, her thighs all thick with muscle. I can't tear my eyes from the scowl on her lips, the dip of her hips, and the curve of her neck.

It's infuriating to be attracted to someone you can't stand being in a room with, but strangely exhilarating at the same time.

Catalina glares at me, her full, heart-shaped lips turning down as she watches me approach.

"I've changed my mind. You can quit as my coach. Nothing is worth this."

Papá merely chuckles as he struts toward my new hitting partner. He bends down to give her a hug, and she smiles up at him in a way she's never looked at me, ever.

"Alright, Santi, you can do this. It's just one season."

My pep-talk doesn't help me at all.

"Hola, *cabrón*," she greets me.

She's called me that for as long as I can remember.

"Hola, *mariquita*," I reply, standing in front of her with an easy smile and trying to ignore the summery scent coming off her because it's intoxicating.

It always has been.

"I hope you're able to keep up with me. I'm not going to take it easy on you," she says, throwing her large, oval tennis bag over her shoulder and moving toward the court. Catalina doesn't wait for me to follow, she simply expects it, and something about that already pisses me off.

Deep breaths.

One season.

"Nice to see you again, Charlie," I mumble as I pass by them, actually meaning the words because Charlie is really cool. I met them three years ago at a party where they were chugging down beer while doing a handstand. They told me after they had a headache for weeks to come, but that it was worth it.

"Nice to see you too, handsome," they reply with a small grin. "Happy to be here?" they add as we follow Catalina to the first court.

"Fucking ecstatic," I say and drop my bag next to Cata's black one.

She's already stretching, trying to warm up while I get hypnotized by her. Her arms lift over her head, showing off the toned muscles there before bending over to touch her toes.

Holy hell.

I quickly look away because nope. I'm not doing this. I'm not admiring her for a second longer. She's irritating, no matter how breathtaking I've always found her, every part of her.

Especially the scowl she directs at me all the time.

"Are you going to stand around all day or warm up, too?" Catalina asks without even turning around.

"Don't you think we should go over the rules of our agreement before starting our training?" I ask, rolling my shoulders to wake up my rotator cuffs. Then, I move on to my hips, arms, and knees, waiting for a response from *la reina* as she takes her sweet time.

"I thought this was supposed to be for us to bond. You know, play some tennis, have a friendly competition, that kind of shit," she says as she faces me again, seemingly done with her stretches.

"Do you honestly think we'd ever be able to bond or have a *friendly* competition?" I ask and cross my arms in front of my chest. Her eyes drift to my forearms, so I flex them a little more for her with a grin. She rolls her eyes but blushes as her gaze drifts to something behind me.

"How about this: if I win, I get to make seventy-five percent of the rules. If you win, you get to make twenty-five percent. Deal?" I frown at her as soon as the words have left her captivating mouth.

"Seriously?" A smirk curls the right side of her lips.

"Caught that, didn't you? Huh. Sometimes I forget you're not as stupid as you look." Charlie bursts into laughter before slapping a hand over their mouth to stop themself.

"Winner makes a hundred percent of the rules, deal?" I offer, extending my hand for her to shake, a mirror image of Papá's and my agreement a few days ago.

"You're going down, *cabrón*," she says, ignoring my hand and taking her racket instead.

I can't help but chuckle a little.

We've played against each other more times than I could count. In tennis, people often think men and women shouldn't play against each other in matches for money because it would be unfair.

It just shows that those people haven't seen Catalina play yet. She's quick, like me, and her serve is faster than most men I've played against. Yes, my forehand and backhand are physically stronger than hers in the sense of speed, but it's also about placement in tennis, and Catalina is fantastic at it. Irritatingly so. Not even I, who runs like my life depends on it during games, can get to her goddamn balls when she's in control of the rally.

We warm up in silence, like two players would during a tournament. We move from forehands and backhands to volleys at the net, then overheads. Serves are the last thing we warm up before it's time to decide who gets to start serving.

I'm ready to beat her in this *friendly* competition when, all of a sudden, Papá decides to interrupt us.

"Did you really think I'd let you off this easily today?" he says, causing my body to freeze in place.

Oh no.

"Charlie and I will be partners, versing you and Catalina. If we win, we make the rules. If you win, we'll let you make the rules. Don't bother agreeing or disagreeing. This is the way things will go," he explains, and I feel anger settling deep inside my chest.

And here I thought Papá and Charlie were warming up to play on the other court. I should have known things would never be so simple with my father.

"Fine," Cata says and struts over to where I'm standing. Breathing becomes more difficult when she lets her hair down for a minute to secure it in a ponytail instead of the bun she had it in before.

"Do you want the forehand or backhand side?" she asks when she's in front of me, those blue eyes sparkling with shades of brown near the pupil.

"Your backhand is unreliable, so I'll take that side," I say, and she directs the meanest glare my way. I love riling her up too much to keep stabs like those to myself.

"When's the last time you watched me play?" she challenges.

*The last game you played before the season ended. You were down by five games in the first set and managed to win it anyway. You were also wearing a purple dress that seemed to have been made for you in every way possible.*

"I don't know. A few years ago?" I lie.

"Exactly. You have no idea how much my backhand has improved." She's right, it definitely has. It's not her strongest shot, not like her forehand is, but it's annoyingly good.

"If you say so, *mariquita*," I reply with a bored shrug of my shoulders, making her face turn red with anger.

A smile crosses my face before I can stop it.

Naturally, it only irritates her more.

"Fuck you," she mumbles in Spanish as we get into our positions on the court, Cata squatting a little to get into position and ultimately showing off her ass.

Fuck me, indeed.

# CHAPTER 4
## CATALINA

I HATE SANTIAGO JAVIER Castillo with a fucking passion.

Our past is enough of a reason to, but there is also something about him, about that smug smile and those defined muscles making up his body, that irritates me. Add the man's I'm-better-than-everybody-else-at-tennis-fuckboy personality on top, and you have all the makings of a person that I, Catalina Rivera Sanchez, will never be able to tolerate. Even if his ass looks phenomenal in those shorts of his. Even if his arms are coiled with muscles on top of muscles in a way only athletes who work on them every day have. Even if his smile is as devastating as I remember it to be.

It doesn't help that his lips are full and round, that his hair is a deep brown, that his skin is always lightly tanned, and that his eyes are a beautiful amber. I could stare at them all day, which is another problem entirely.

"You know when you serve, you're supposed to aim for the box on the other side of the court," I say after Santiago misses another first serve, the fourth one since we started playing mere minutes ago.

"You're distracting me!" he complains, his voice low and full of irritation.

"How the fuck am I distracting you? I'm standing where I'm supposed to be," I say, pointing down at my feet where I am at the net.

"I'm scared I'll hit you, but never mind. I'll hit you with the ball if it keeps you from complaining," he says. When I turn back around, rolling my eyes, I notice Charlie and Santiago's father, Carlos, laughing at us.

"What?" I ask both of them, but they just shrug.

"You'll never win like that. You're not rivals or enemies. You're partners," Carlos says, spinning his racket in his hand.

The score at the moment is 30-40 for them, even though we're serving, which is bad. They have a breakpoint opportunity—a chance to steal our service game. In tennis, securing your service game is important. If you lose it, you're at a disadvantage in the set unless you can manage to win a service game from your opponent. You win the set by winning six games in total, but if it's five games to five, you play until seven. If it's six games to six, you play a tiebreaker where the first person to get seven points wins the set. Women only have to win two sets. Men have to win three during Grand Slams, two in ATP games.

"Yeah, Cata, we have to play *together*," Santiago says, and I turn to him to show him the glare I only ever wear in his presence. "*Juntos*," he repeats, my urge to kick him growing stronger and stronger.

The irony of him being the one to say that to me has more anger boiling inside of me. It spills right over the top, and I can no longer keep the angry tears at bay, since I tear up when I get overwhelmed by anger. It's one of the few things I wish I could change about myself because it's seen as a sign of weakness, not as a sign of "I'll rip your head off now." And the only thing to do to keep anyone from seeing is to leave.

"Charlie, I'd rather drown myself in chlorine than spend the entire Grand Slam season being Santiago's hitting partner and fake girlfriend. I'm calling this off," I say and walk toward my bag.

"Give us a second," I hear Santiago say. When I turn around with my bag on my shoulder, I run into his very hard, very nice chest. He's not that much taller than me, but enough so that I have to tilt my head back to look at him.

"Get out of my way, Santi," I warn, but he doesn't move. Those amber eyes of his skip over my face, studying me.

"This isn't ideal for either one of us, *mariquita*," he says, and I almost laugh at the nickname. He started ironically calling me "ladybug" when we were first paired together in school. He said it was because I was "so lucky," the words laced with sarcasm.

"Wow, that must have taken your last two brain cells to deduce. What are you going to do now that you have none left?" I ask, crossing my arms in front of my chest.

"Be serious for one moment. We're going to have to spend the next eight months intensively training together. We will both win several Grand Slams if we train properly."

I almost laugh at that.

"Oh, aiming low, are we? I haven't even won a single one, Santiago, how do you expect us to win several each just because we're training together?" I say and shake my head. He crosses his arms too, mimicking my stance.

"Because I'm amazing, and I can teach you how to win," he says, so I take a step forward, ready to kick him.

He jumps back, laughing even though I'm scowling at him.

"You're so full of yourself. I'm the one who is more consistent. I'm the one who gets the most shots in because you are always trying out new things that cost you points!" Needing to justify my failures makes embarrassment creep up my neck.

I attempt to walk past him, but Santiago lifts his hands in a pleading manner to get me to stay put.

"The fact that you don't try new things, play riskier, is the reason you haven't won a Slam yet." I open my mouth to yell at him, call him all the bad names in the world, but he beats me to it. "You're stuck in your ways, Cata. You play it safe, and when you're losing, you get frightened. Overwhelmed. Anxious. And while that's understandable, it's a phase I had to work past as well. You have to perfect problem-solving while under pressure. I can help you with that," he offers, and, putting my hatred for him aside, I try to process his words.

I've always been good at using the feedback given to me, allowing it to help me become a better player, a better person. So, I let his words sink in. I allow myself to acknowledge that he's right.

That *is* one of my weaknesses.

"Fine. I'll let you help me improve my problem-solving skills if you let me help you improve your consistency."

"You can most certainly try, but no promises," he says and smiles at me, the expression a little too handsome for my eyes to keep from dropping to his mouth.

"Are you two finished so we can get back to the game?" Charlie asks, impatiently swinging their racket around while Carlos grins at us.

"Let's kick some ass," Santi says, still smiling at me while I'm frowning at him.

"I'd rather kick yours, but sure," I say, getting a laugh out of him that I don't return.

We lose, and we lose badly against our coaches. Santi and I continue fighting with one another, so, naturally, we lose. Three games to six in the first set, two games to six in the second.

"You will be amazing hitting partners," Carlos says, shaking his head in disappointment as he turns to talk to Charlie.

For some reason, I'm exhausted. Not physically. I could probably keep going for another hour or two, but mentally, I'm drained. Being around Santi is exhausting when neither one of us knows how to be around the other person. He turns to me once we're done, his lips parting like he wants to say something but isn't sure how to phrase it, so I don't give him a chance to figure it out.

I grab my bag, throw it over my shoulder, and walk toward the door, then my car.

I should have known Santi wouldn't let me get away that easily.

"*Mariquita*, we need to talk about going out together soon to sell the dating aspect of this arrangement," he reminds me as I throw my bag into the passenger seat of my most-prized possession.

My glossy, black Ragna Velocità Rossa.

I may only be number two in the world, but I've worked my way up to being very important in the world of tennis. Velocità Rossa offered to give me this beauty as long as I wear their logo somewhere on my outfits during tournaments.

Yes, they sponsor me.

That's how awesome I am.

It's nothing extravagant in the world of Monaco, where Santi and I both live, but it's a hell of a lot nicer than the car he drives.

Santi's eyes attach to my Ragna for a moment, letting out a low whistle.

"*Joder*, this is nice," he says, walking around it to inspect every aspect.

"Where do you want to go?" I ask, leaning against the door as I slip my sunglasses onto my nose. Once Santiago is back in front of me, he takes in the sight of me and my car, taking several steps back to take a picture on his phone. "What was that for?" His answering smile is like sunshine that was bottled up for years, finally being released.

"That was for me to post on my socials. But we're gonna need something more convincing," he says, taking several steps toward me. He wraps his arm around my shoulders and pulls me to his side, pressing his cheek against mine and taking another picture with one of his big, happy smiles. As soon as he's done, I push him off me and glare at him. Santiago laughs, a deep and amused sound that makes my knees a little weak. "That face of yours, Cata, it's so beautiful when you're angry."

I might blush if I weren't so annoyed with him.

"That face of yours, Santi, I want to punch it," I reply, almost bursting into laughter when he chuckles at my jab. "Don't press your cheek against mine again," I say before adding, "Actually, don't touch me at all."

"Why? You like it too much?" I snort at that question.

"No. I don't like you touching me because I don't trust you." All of his amusement fades, his expression turning sad and thoughtful all at once.

"You know, we're going to have to find a way to change that. If we go out in public and we don't touch, no one is going to buy that this isn't more than a publicity stunt to get our reputations cleared," he says, and I hate that he's right. But I also have no idea how to keep from wanting to push him away every time he gets close to me.

"What do you suggest?" Santiago crosses those trained arms of his.

"Come to my house to have dinner with me tomorrow. I'll make you a delicious meal and then we'll discuss all of the rules and boundaries of this arrangement. No matter the deal we made with Papá and Charlie, we're the ones who'll have to agree on what exactly 'dating' will look like for us," he says, yet again bringing up such a good point that I can't argue.

And I won't argue for the sake of arguing.

"Okay. I'll be there tomorrow, but I'm bringing the food. You are useless in the kitchen," I say and open the driver's door, watching envy enter Santi's eyes.

"Fine, bring the food." He's too busy ogling my car to fight. He wants it, wants the sponsorship I have with Velocità Rossa, and I love rubbing it in his face when I let the engine roar to life, a beautiful sound that has him groaning. "I'm gonna steal it from you one day," he says, a teasing smile on his lips.

"Try it, *cabrón*, and I'll shave your head," I warn, panic filling his gaze as I drive away, my middle finger raised into the air outside my window.

The last thing I see in my rearview mirror is Santi grinning.

# CHAPTER 5
## SANTIAGO

MATTEO RICCI HAS BEEN my best friend since childhood. Ever since we were paired together for a project where we ended up doing absolutely nothing and receiving the worst grade ever, we've been inseparable friends. We've also been through hell and back together because when his dad passed away, I took his hand and we walked into the burning depths together so he didn't have to be alone. So he'd know I was right by his side whenever he was ready to walk back out again. He stayed with me when I was at my lowest point with my depression, giving me as much time and patience as I needed. We've been friends through all the silly stages of our lives too, the awkwardness, the queer awakenings, everything. It was difficult to separate us as kids because we were either too busy playing games on the video game console, being on the court to practice since we both wanted to go pro from early on in our lives, and eating our weight in chips.

Maybe not the best thing to consume when you want to become a professional athlete, but oh well.

When I look at him, I feel strangely at peace. Like not everything has to be going right in my life for him to find a way to make me laugh.

"How's your mom?" I ask him, gripping the handle of my tennis racket a little more firmly before spinning it once in my hand.

Normally, he and I would have done anything other than play tennis to spend time together, but his hitting partner has been sick for the past week, and this close to the beginning of the season, he needed someone to practice with who isn't his coach.

I'd give my life for Matteo, as dramatic as it may sound, so playing a round of tennis even if I'm sore is the least I can do.

"She's alright, but if you ask her, then she's not because she's annoyed with me for being an idiot," he replies and takes a sip of his water. I can't help but laugh.

"So, just the usual," I say and he shrugs.

"Pretty much." He lets out a sigh, and I give him a comforting smile. No matter how much he loves his mamma, she's a difficult woman, according to him. She complains a lot. He never does anything right. That sort of thing.

"And how's it going with your new coach?" Matteo cocks a brow and smirks. "No, you didn't."

"Of course I did. He wasn't a very good coach, but the rest of my team made me promise not to fire him. So, I didn't. He quit. Said it was unprofessional to train someone he saw naked," Matteo says and shrugs, and I let out a surprised laugh.

"You're impossible."

"No, I'm smart. I didn't piss my team off since he just quit and they couldn't blame me, and I didn't have to put up with a coach who told me everything I was doing was wrong because it wasn't *his* way. Plus, he was attractive. He was attracted to me. We had some fun before he went and found himself a different player to coach, one who wasn't so stubborn," he explains with a little evil laugh, and I shake my head at him.

"Okay, you're right. You're not impossible. You're a genius."

"Exactly."

Then we're both grinning at each other before we walk to the opposite sides of our court.

We spend the next half hour playing a ruthless sort of tennis. Neither one of us holds back. Neither one of us plays nicely at any point. We're pushing each other to our limits, but somehow it doesn't feel the same as when Cata does the same with me. When I play against her, it's a constant battle of having to prove who's better. And maybe it's because I win most points against Matteo. Maybe it's because I can try new things without risking losing the point and giving Cata the satisfaction. Maybe it's because I don't have to prove anything to look cooler and impress him.

I don't fucking know.

But I have so much fun.

At least until we move to the net again to get our things, and I have to poach this very inevitable topic of what the fuck is going on in my life because he asks me how I'm doing.

"There's something I should tell you."

Matteo has been laughing at me for the past four minutes without a single break. Every time I think he's done, he wheezes out words I don't understand and keeps laughing. Tears jump out of his eyes and he snorts but then covers his mouth with his hand to stop the same sound from leaving him again.

Under different circumstances, I'd join him. Matteo has the kind of laugh that's irresistibly contagious.

But not when he's laughing at me.

"My God, this is the best news I've ever heard in my entire life. Who can I pay for making this happen? They deserve some money for this wonderful turn of events," Matteo says, throwing his head back to once more burst into laughter.

"We trained for three hours. You shouldn't have the energy for all this laughing," I say and wave at where he's sitting on the other side of the sauna from me now.

The tennis club we're members of, *Lumière des Étoiles*, has everything we could ever need. Tennis courts, gyms, several pools, saunas, and enormous showers in all the washrooms. It's paradise here, one of my favorite places in the world.

"I'm sorry, but I can't help it. Do you remember how the two of you always kept score in the past? You weren't even playing each other, but every match, every game, every point you won was written down so you could keep track of who'd won the most," he says and bursts into laughter again.

"Yes, I remember," I reply as I lean back on the wooden bench I'm on, breathing in the steam surrounding us. Sweat is dripping down my body, my towel soaking up as much as it can, where it is around my hips.

"Do you remember that one time when you two were playing doubles and she served the ball right into your ass? You started fighting, her claiming it was an accident and you insisting it wasn't," he laughs the words the whole time, barely speaking at all. I'm surprised I understand him at all.

"I remember," I say through gritted teeth while he continues reveling in his amusement.

"Do you remember—" I cut him off.

"*I remember everything.* Every moment with her. Every interaction. Every word. I remember it all," I blurt out, too annoyed to keep the words at bay. "You don't have to remind me, and, for the love of God, could you cover your dick. I don't want to keep looking at it," I add when he shifts and his towel moves away from his groin.

With a swift laugh, Matteo removes the towel altogether and shifts on his bench until he's lying down, one arm under his head.

A sigh leaves him.

"There, is that better?" he asks, pointing at his naked body on full display.

"You are intolerable."

"Yes, I am, but you love me anyway," he reminds me, flashing me one of his dashing smiles. "The people I've been with loved my penis, so maybe you just need to learn to appreciate the glorious sight of it." He smirks, then turns his head and closes his eyes.

"I don't know what's making breathing more difficult, the steam or the amount of space your ego takes up," I tease, and Matteo snorts. "Plus, I've seen and had better." This makes his smile drop, and mine grow.

"Liar," he mumbles, but I cock a teasing brow at him.

My gaze lifts to the ceiling, thinking about the dinner Cata and I will have tonight. Maybe I shouldn't have gone so hard during training today. I'm going to need all of my energy for Catalina Sanchez.

"You know what your greatest obstacle will be for the next eight months?" Matteo says, his voice breaking into my thoughts.

"Trying not to stab myself in the eyeball when I'm around Catalina?" Matteo sits back up and wraps his towel around his hips before walking toward me and putting a hand on my shoulder.

"You're not allowed to have sex with anyone else, Santi, and you sleep with someone new almost daily. How will you survive eight months without your playboy ways?" He's taunting me, I can see it in the smug gleam in his eyes.

"I'll focus on my career. It'll distract me," I reply, feeling a sense of unease settling in my chest.

"On your career or Cata?" A glare takes over my face, but my asshole of a best friend laughs. "Please, Santiago, you've been obsessed with her since you were kids. You always talk about her, dedicate every win to 'rubbing it in her face,' and you always get that glimmer in your eyes when her name is mentioned. You don't hate her, you never have. You love the challenge she gives you." My lips seal shut at that.

"Are we talking about Catalina?" someone says, and I jump in my seat, my heart skipping several beats.

"What the fuck are you doing here?" I ask, my eyes drifting to the crown prince of Monaco.

His Royal Highness Thomas Crovetto.

"I went for a swim and saw you two going into the sauna. I thought I'd join you, see what's new," Thomas says as he very gracefully sinks onto the bench next to

Matteo, who jumps at the opportunity to tell our friend about my situation with Cata.

Thomas is always so calculated about his movements. I have never seen this man let loose in any way, but I wish he would. We've been friends for over five years, and I have yet to see him with a single hair out of place or hear a bad word come out of his mouth. Even around us, his friends, he thinks he has to keep up this façade that's been ingrained in him since he was a child. I wish he'd be whoever he wants to be with us instead of being who he's been told he has to be since he was born.

A king.

A leader.

An image.

A pawn.

But there's no way to allow him to open up when we hardly ever see each other. We talk on the phone, sure, but with his busy schedule and ours, it's difficult to find time to spend with one another, simply sharing a meal or a conversation.

"Is Catalina the woman you're in love with but pretend you don't like?" Thomas asks with his thick Monegasque accent, running a hand through his curls. He's very tall with a chiseled face, a million muscles, beautiful dark brown skin, and a charming smile that wins over every single person he speaks to. I won't lie. When we first started hanging out, I had a little bit of a crush on him, but that disappeared quickly.

They all seem to as soon as I start thinking about... *her*.

"I am not in love with her. What is wrong with you?" I blurt out, and Thomas tilts his head, intrigue in his eyes.

"So defensive," he states, making a *tsk* noise with his tongue. "Denying your feelings will get you as far as lying. Far enough to think you'll make it to the finish line, but never close enough to reach it. My father always says, 'One cannot reach the end when one has taken the wrong path.'"

"What century was your father born in?" Matteo says with a mischievous grin, but one look from Thomas is enough to make him clear his throat and turn serious.

The only way I can describe Thomas' expression is how I imagine he looks at his brother.

Scoldingly. Warningly. Threateningly.

"All I'm trying to say is that you can deny how you feel to me, to Matteo, to yourself, all you want, but it will not help." Thomas folds his hands over his lap, his towel snugly hugging his hips to prevent anything from accidentally slipping out. The complete opposite of Matteo, in other words.

"I'm getting irritated with both of you," I say, wiping the sweat off my forehead. It's getting even harder to breathe, and it isn't because of the steam surrounding us. It hasn't thickened. The only thing that's changed is the heaviness of the conversation. "How are your royal duties going?"

Thomas smiles knowingly at me but doesn't force us to continue speaking about my complicated feelings for Catalina.

"They are as they always have been, Santiago. Tiring." He smiles, leaning his head back to stare at the ceiling of the sauna. "But a future king must do as told and never complain."

"You're allowed to complain to us, you know?" Matteo chimes in, placing a hand on His Highness' shoulder. "We will never tell anyone what passes between us." It's a promise neither one of us will ever break, but it's not that easy for Thomas.

"You actually know how to keep that big mouth of yours closed?" Thomas teases, nudging Matteo with his shoulder.

"Depends," Matteo says with a quirk of his brow.

"On what?"

"On whether you'll finally make me a Lord. Or a knight. Lord Matteo Ricci or Sir Matteo Ricci sounds phenomenal." I can't help it. I burst into laughter at the mere thought of my best friend forcing me to address him in either of those ways because he would.

He absolutely would.

"I'd rather knight a toad," Thomas replies.

I almost fall off the bench laughing.

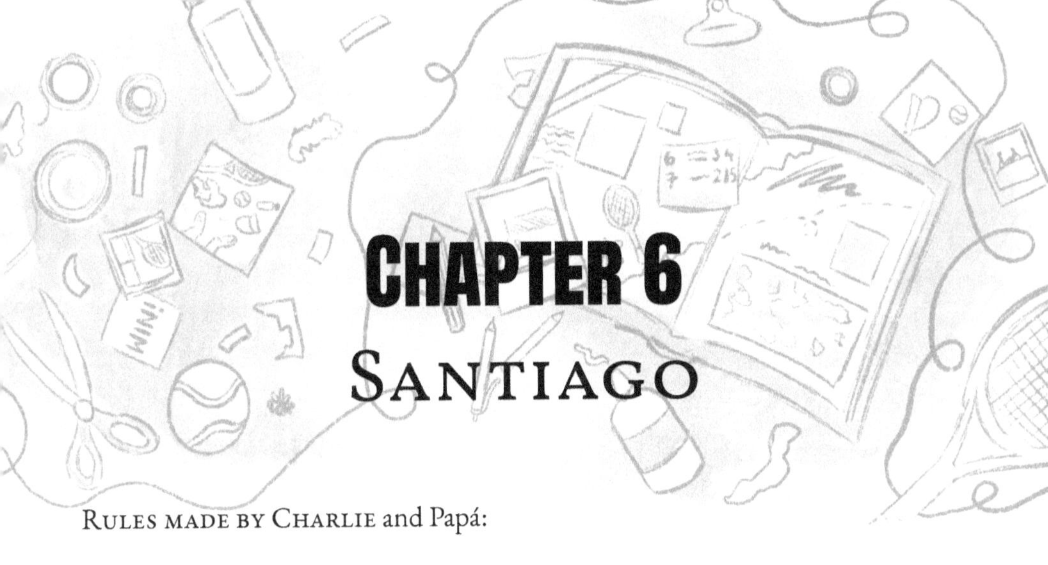

# CHAPTER 6
## SANTIAGO

RULES MADE BY CHARLIE and Papá:

1. **Convince the world you're dating/don't hate each other by spending lots of time together where people can see you.**

2. **Attend each other's games. All of them.**

3. **No fighting or bickering in public. Hold it in until you're alone and somewhere private.**

4. **Training comes first, above everything else.**

5. **Mandatory private dinners at least once a week.**

Rules made by Cata and me:

**None.**

We've been staring at each other all evening while she avoided making conversation by scowling at me whenever she caught me staring at her. To be fair, I haven't tried talking to her either. I never know how to speak to her without making her angry. I guess that comes with the territory of having despised each other for so long.

Part of me also likes simply looking at Cata. She's just so... beautiful isn't a strong enough term. Breathtaking doesn't quite fit either.

Extraordinary.

Exquisite.

Enchanting.

"Would you stop staring at me? You invited me here to talk. So, talk," she says, those blue eyes of hers searching my face as if she'd find answers there instead of having to hear me speak.

My bunny, Tornado—named this way because whenever I get home, he hops in circles like a tornado—is curled up on Cata's lap, getting petted and purring happily.

"We have to make rules," I remind her, the breath catching in my throat when she leans back against the arm of my couch and stretches her arms into the air, all of her curves and muscles displayed with the simple motion.

Exquisite is definitely the best word to describe Catalina.

She sucks in a sharp breath and lowers her arm again, holding her shoulder with a grimace on her face. Tornado looks up at Cata, so unhappy she stopped giving him attention that he hops off her lap to move to his area that I set up in the living room with his bed, toys, water, and anything else he needs.

"What's with your shoulder?"

"Nothing, *cabrón*. Let's make these stupid rules." She lets go of her shoulder and refocuses on my face.

"One rule has to be that you can't call me that in public. You need a nicer way to address me." She frowns like that's the worst idea I've ever had.

"Like what?"

"Like *guapo, hermoso*, baby," I suggest, but she makes a face at the last one.

"I'd rather call you anything else," she says and takes her glass of water from the table beside us. I chuckle at her grumpy attitude, but she flashes me another deathly glare.

"How about *bebé*?" She scrunches her nose up in disgust and shakes her head.

"No." Silence engulfs us for a moment when another nickname pops into my head.

"How about '*mi corazón*'? Since you don't have a heart, it could never be true," I offer, and, if I didn't know better, I'd think she was fighting off a smile. The corner of her mouth twitches as if it wants to curl upward, and it would if she were in the presence of anyone but me.

"Fine. What will you call me?" she asks as she picks up her bottle of water and takes a long sip.

"*Eres mi mariquita*," I reply, hoping it'll bring out her smile. I see it so rarely, but it's by far the most stunning one I've ever laid my eyes on.

She keeps it under lock and key once more.

"Okay, rule two, you can't glare at me in public like I'm your worst enemy," I remind her, and Cata gives an agreeing nod.

"I know, Santiago. We don't have to make a rule for that. I'm as likely to frown at you as I am to bite your head off, but you wouldn't make that a rule either, would you?" she challenges, crossing her arms over her chest and watching me with so much distaste, the temperature in the room cools by several degrees.

Oh, to get a full smile from Cata.

It must be sunshine incarnate.

"I don't know, maybe I should. You do frighten me," I say with a grin. That finally brings the smallest of smirks to her lips.

"Good. So, rule number three: Don't bite off Santi's head." I burst into laughter, grabbing the notebook and pen I had placed on the coffee table in front of the couch earlier. After scribbling down our first three rules, I turn back to Cata, who's already watching me with something akin to fascination.

"Why are you looking at me like that?" I ask, putting the notebook and pen aside again and leaning forward to close the distance between us. Cata watches me but doesn't move a centimeter.

"You find so many reasons to smile around me. Why? Is it to irritate me?" she asks, pointing at my smile to prove her point.

"I like smiling and laughing, whether you're here doesn't change that," I explain, moving a little closer until my hand is hovering over her ankle. Her breathing hitches a little as I run a single fingertip over the exposed skin between her yoga pants and socks. "How do you feel about me touching you now?" I ask, my heart racing as I wait for her answer.

I don't know why it races, why it hopes she doesn't feel so appalled by it.

"I'm not sure," she admits.

"Do you want me to stop?" I ask, already halting my movements.

"No." It's all the reassurance I need to keep going.

Cata watches my finger as it traces circles on the exposed skin by her ankle, not saying a thing. Slowly, so painfully slowly, I trail it up her thigh, up the side of her upper body, up her arm, before finally bringing it to her face. I wait for permission before I touch her there. She gives me a strained nod, her eyes locked on mine as I cup her cheek. She juts out her chin like she's about to protest, to argue with me, but when I caress her cheek, rub my thumb over her cheekbone, her eyes flutter shut like she's enjoying the sensation as much as I'm enjoying touching her.

Physical touch has always been my favorite way to express my feelings because I'm not good at voicing them.

As a matter of fact, I often say things and mean the complete opposite.

Her breathing hitches again, this time harder. Her chest rises and falls so quickly, the urge to run my thumb over the pulse point on her neck is too strong to ignore. I bring my hand from her cheek to her neck, pressing my index finger on it to feel how quickly Cata's heart races for me.

"Will we kiss in public?" I ask, my voice barely more than a whisper now.

Catalina's eyes open halfway to focus on my lips. She's only ever looked at me like this once when we were sixteen. It was the night I almost kissed her, a time I've done everything I could to forget.

"Is that a rule you'd like to establish?" she replies, and all I see is a red light flashing, telling me to slow down, to stop this immediately.

"No," I say and stand up, letting go of her completely to grab the bowls that our dessert—a fruit salad because that's all our coaches will allow us to have this close to the start of the season—was in earlier.

"Do you think people will believe we're dating if we don't kiss?" she challenges, crossing her arms in front of her chest again.

"I'll take the risk."

I can't kiss her. I don't want to find out what happens to me, to my traitor of a body, when I get my first taste of Catalina Rivera Sanchez.

"You're the one who started touching me, but now you can't kiss me? Where is the logic, Santiago?" she asks, cocking both of her brows in challenge. I press my tongue against the back of my teeth, thinking about what the fuck to say to that when she's absolutely right.

"Do *you* want to kiss *me*?" I ask, turning it back on her, hoping she'll drop this conversation.

"I'd rather stick my tongue into a burning hot coffee."

"Want me to make you a cup, *cariño*?" I offer, grinning at her before carrying our bowls into the kitchen and giving myself a second to breathe.

It's always so damn hard to breathe around Cata. Like my body forgets it needs the oxygen because my eyes are too busy drinking her in to remember.

"So, no kissing. What about romantic gestures? You should do at least a few publicly," she says, following me into the kitchen.

"I'll do some if you do some," I reply, placing the bowls in the dishwasher.

"Do you consider dropping a poisonous spider down your pants a romantic gesture?" she asks, dead serious as always, but I burst out laughing at her question.

"Not particularly. Do you consider throwing you into a bush of poison ivy romantic?"

"*Not particularly*," she says, lowering her voice to mock me.

"Then we should probably stay away from romantic gestures." I wash my hands before turning to her again, her brown locks all over the place because she just took her hair out of its braid. Her heart-shaped lips are downturned into a frown, and her eyes are full of hate directed toward me.

And yet, I still think she's the most beautiful person I've ever seen.

I ever will see.

"This rule thing is stupid. Can we take things as they come?" she asks, picking at a loose thread on her sweater.

"But then how do we know each other's boundaries?"

She thinks about my question for a moment, shifting her weight from one foot to the other without saying a word.

"Well, the most important thing we established is no kissing. It's not like we have to write down 'do not fall in love with each other' or some ridiculous shit like that," she says, snorting at her own comment.

"Of course not. You're the last person on this planet I'd ever fall for."

"Right back at you, Santi," she says and shakes her head, wincing when the motion hurts something in her shoulder.

Without a second of hesitation, I walk around my kitchen island to get to her.

"Let me take a look at that," I offer, but when I reach out to touch her shoulder, she smacks my hand away

"I'm going to head home. We have training in a few days. Don't be late. I can't have you slacking off on the first day." Cata walks around me to grab her purse from where she put it on the counter earlier, slinging it over her shoulder. I notice she places the weight on her other shoulder, not the one that has been making her wince all evening.

She attempts to walk past me, but I grab her arm, tilting my head down as she lifts her chin so our eyes can meet. Neither one of us says anything for several seconds, but the tension of the moment builds in my chest until even my heart forgets to beat.

Her eyes staring into mine have a similar effect to what people say happens to Medusa's victims. Cata may not turn me to stone, but she has me temporarily frozen in time and place, too swept up in her to remember what I wanted to say.

I pinch my leg with my free hand, regaining the ability to speak.

"We'll win. All of it. This season will be our season and no one can take it away from us. I'll be at the top of my game, and I know you will be, too. I have faith in us, Cata. You should have some, too."

Her eyes soften a little at my words, but when she steps away to break skin contact, I know she still doesn't trust me enough to allow me to touch her so casually.

"I would, but you've always been a little too eager to meet your goals to care about mine, Santi. Too eager to prove yourself, even if it was at my expense. There is a reason we don't get along. We'll go through this season, pretend we're a happy couple to get the media off our asses, but then that's it. You and I will never see each other again. We will be done," she says, and I hate the way my body revolts against the very thought of never seeing Cata again.

And even though I feel this way, all that comes out of my mouth is a very simple, very stupid, "Fine."

She leaves my place without another word while Tornado makes his way to the door, staring at it long after Cata is gone with his nose moving from side to side in that cute way I love. He turns to look at me before shifting his gaze back to the front door as if he wished she'd have stayed.

It terrifies me that I feel the same.

# CHAPTER 7
## CATALINA

THE DAY HAS BARELY started, but my mood's already gone from happy to fucking pissed.

My dad, two sisters, and brother invited me to go on vacation before the season starts in a few weeks, but I had to tell them to go without me since Santiago and I have to bond by going on dates and training together. It made me hate him a little more, even if I know it wasn't his fault.

Well, not entirely.

"What has you frowning so much, pretty girl?" Sage, one of my closest friends and fellow tennis players, asks right as I lower the barbell I was holding. She's the only Canadian in our friend group, but she's lived over a decade of her life in various parts of Europe.

"Yeah, tell us why the vein on your forehead is pulsing," Vanessa, everyone's favorite CEO, chimes in with her thick French accent, and I direct my full glare her way.

It's all I can do to keep from laughing.

Ness owns *Spin*, my biggest clothing sponsor. She's the designer of all of my outfits, something she only does for me, so she's responsible for always making them look like they should be worn on runways instead of tennis courts.

"She's angry at the world for making her have to team up with the person she hates the most," Charlie adds, and I nod in agreement.

"That's partially why. Mostly, I'm frowning to hide the fact that I miss my family and can't go see them soon," I admit because I've always found it so easy to tell the three of them what's going on in my life.

"Then I have something that'll hopefully cheer you up," Ness says, wiggling those perfectly shaped brows of hers at me as she steps toward where I'm jogging on the treadmill.

Not only is Vanessa the smartest woman I know, she's also the kindest and one of the most drop-dead gorgeous. She's short and super curvy with dark skin, her dark curls twisted into several braids, and light brown eyes that always reveal more of what she's feeling than words could. She's also the most fit person out of our whole group, despite not being a professional tennis player or athlete. But if we're talking endurance, this woman could outrun me any day of the week.

Ness holds out her phone for me, showing me some designs for a new racket.

"I love that one," I say and slow down my run to look at it more closely.

It's white and berry-magenta-colored with a pride flag painted on the side. The head of the racket has a striped look that I like a lot, and she's made the strings colored in a way that the letters CS are written in them. My initials. It's very unlike what other companies do, but then again, other companies don't have this amazing woman as a CEO.

"I thought you might. I'm working on the design for your new outfits too, but I'm not ready to show those yet," she says and snatches her phone out of my hand to keep me from swiping through more pictures. Ness gives me a mischievous look, and I grin at her as she walks away, back to the mat she was exercising on before.

"That did cheer me up. Thank you." She throws me a kiss, and I blush as I catch it.

"Why don't you ever cheer me up when I'm sad?" Sage asks as she starts stretching on the floor in front of Ness.

She was the number one women's player for years, but she's had a few surgeries and injuries, so she had to take a season off and dropped in the rankings. When she came back, she struggled so much that even though she returned, she didn't get back up to the top.

"Because there isn't enough time in the day to cheer you up when you're upset, love. No offense, but you're so stubborn," Vanessa replies, and Sage's mouth drops open.

"Offense taken, thanks."

They start bickering playfully with one another as I pick up my pace on the treadmill. I notice Charlie is looking at their phone with their brows furrowed.

"How's your sister, Charlie? She's getting married in a month, she must be nervous," I say because I know that's what's bothering them. Their sister means the world to them, and they told me she's been so stressed since her wedding is approaching.

"My sister is fine. Her fiancée, on the other hand, has already fired several caterers because she didn't like their attitudes."

"That's understandable. This is their special day. You don't need dickheads ruining it by giving you attitude," I reply, loving that when I say "dickhead," the first face that pops into my head is Santi's.

As it should be.

*Dickhead.*

"I guess. It just gets difficult because Jenna likes to plan everything and Dels keeps throwing everything on its head," Charlie adds, but all I can do is nod absentmindedly. I'm focused on my breathing now, trying to make it through my run without getting a stitch in my side.

But I see both sides.

On one hand, I like to plan everything to the smallest detail to make sure things run smoothly. On the other, I hate dealing with assholes. Which is why I gave up on trying to make rules with Santi.

"They'll figure it out, and if they need help, I'm here," Ness says, and Charlie offers her a grateful smile.

"Okay, who still wants to go get a tattoo with me later? I made an appointment for all of us, but I'm not sure if any of you changed your minds," Sage says after a while of all of us doing our exercises.

I slow down the speed of my treadmill, sweat dripping down my burning hot face.

"Yeah, I'm still in," I reply, walking now instead of running.

"Me, too. I've waited two years to get this tattoo, I don't want to wait a day longer," Charlie chimes in while Ness gives an agreeing nod.

Out of all of us, Ness was the least likely to change her mind. She has at least a hundred tattoos. Most of them are small and spread out, but she loves them. She's also the one who made me fall in love with getting piercings. We've known each other for over six years, and Ness and I have gotten about a dozen piercings since, nipple and clit piercings included. I also got a few tattoos, but not nearly as many as she has.

As a tennis player, I have to be careful not to have too many. They can't be too visible or people will start judging. Tennis is a prestigious sport. Wimbledon, arguably the biggest and most well-known tournament of the sport, still holds the tradition of the tennis players wearing white. They want proper, elegant, clean images. They don't want tattooed, pierced, and "tainted" ones. It's why Santi's and my scandals were judged so harshly. For athletes in general, it's dangerous not to fit the images given to us by the public. Sponsors will retract their sponsorships. You will not be invited to tournaments. They will never forget.

Especially when you're a woman. Everything becomes more heightened. They judge you more harshly. They will take everything away from you because they are *looking* for reasons to. Getting opportunities is a battle, losing them happens in the blink of an eye, as easily as breathing.

All I can hope now is that my "dating" Santiago will make them believe my scandal was just a rumor.

"Alright, that's enough, Lina. Get off and do some stretches," Charlie instructs, so I turn off the treadmill, grabbing onto the handles to take several deep breaths.

Then, I settle down on the mat in front of them, letting them stretch out my tired limbs. I love this part of my training sessions. I get to relax and while some stretches hurt like a branding iron to the skin, it prevents me from being too sore the next day.

"Fuck!" I groan when Charlie stretches my back. More specifically, my left shoulder blade.

"Been bothering you again?" they ask, but all I can do is nod as I breathe through the pain. "Alright, let me massage you and cream the sore area." One more deep breath keeps the tears at bay as the stinging sensation finally leaves.

I've had back problems ever since I was little, so this is nothing new, but it doesn't make it any more bearable when a nerve gets stuck or a muscle cramps. I've seen doctors, but they couldn't help me. They said I should come back when the pain got worse, which is fucking fantastic.

Especially because this feels like the most important season of my life, and I want nothing to stand in my way of making it to the number one spot.

Nothing.

"Shit, shit, shit," Charlie breathes out, tears streaming down their face as the tattoo artist continues to put his tattoo gun to their skin. "Ness, you did *not* tell me it hurts this badly!"

Ness bursts into laughter.

"Because it usually doesn't, you chose the most painful spot to get a tattoo," she replies, still chuckling.

"Mine also hurt, if it's any consolation," I offer, lifting my shirt as I stand in front of the mirror to admire the words now forever engraved under the sea turtle that runs from the top of my cleavage all the way down and expands under my breasts.

*La vida de una tortuga marina es una vida libre.*

The life of a sea turtle is a free life.

My mother always said, "If I'm ever reborn, I want to return as a sea turtle. I want to be as free as they are, swimming through the ocean and spending my days exploring the sea."

Mamá loved the ocean. When she was younger, my *abuelito* and her used to go sailing together.

I hope she got her wish. I hope she's come back as a sea turtle, like she always wanted.

"It looks phenomenal," Sage says as she approaches me, placing a hand on my shoulder and giving me a comforting smile.

Sage knows the story of the sea turtle and my mother. She knows why I got this tattoo, they all do, but they think it makes me sad to look at when it does the opposite. I love this reminder of Mamá. I love having a piece of her on me forever, especially because people can't see it unless I allow them to. It's mine, and I've hardly shared it with anyone. I usually wear bathing suits instead of bikinis because the media would tear me to shreds over it with assumptions and criticisms.

Only my friends know, not even Dad or my siblings. I think it would make them sad, and I don't want to be the reason for that.

"She'll be with you every second of the season. She'll give you strength," Sage says and leans her head against mine.

God, I hope she's right.

I can't do this without Mamá.

# CHAPTER 8
## SANTIAGO

FIRST DAY OF BEING hitting partners with Catalina.

First of hundreds.

My head sags at the very thought, but Papá laughs like it's the funniest thing in the world to see me this bent out of shape.

"You still want me to take care of you when you're old, so I'd be careful," I warn, mostly teasing, which only makes my father bend over at the waist to laugh even harder.

"*Mijo*, I'm rich. I don't need you to take care of me," he replies, so I roll my eyes at him. "Plus, Manuela would take care of me if I asked her to," he adds, and the mention of my sister, who's been on vacation with her girlfriend for the last week, makes me miss her even more. We're twins. She's supposed to be here so I can vent to her after every session with Catalina.

"I'll find a different way to get payback then," I say right as Charlie and Cata step into *Lumière des Étoiles'* indoor tennis courts.

Cata has sunglasses resting on the top of her head, pulling her brown hair out of her face. She's wearing a two-piece set, yoga shorts that hug her ass and a tank top in the same color and fabric that frames her chest and stops right above her belly button. Her piercing there sparkles in the light a little, and when my eyes trail up, I notice imprints of what look like piercings by her nipples, too.

I forget all about talking until she's in front of me, waving her hand in front of my face to snap me out of my staring trance.

"If you're done admiring my tits, can we get a move on? I have other shit to do today," she says, and I try to find a witty comeback, but I'm still so intrigued by the possibility of her having nipple piercings that I struggle to breathe.

My mouth opens to reply, but no sound leaves me, none other than a strange wheezing one I've never made in my life before.

"See, this is what happens when you work with men who like boobs. The faintest sight of a pair of them and all blood leaves their brain and goes to their dick. It's really no wonder then that the world is going to shit with straight men in charge, is it?" Cata goes on, pushing past me with her tennis bag slung over her shoulder.

"She has a point, you know?" Papá chimes in before walking past me too and following Cata. Charlie grins as they appear in front of me, grabbing my shoulder and squeezing once.

"I might throw myself in front of a moving train if she doesn't murder me first," I say, getting a laugh out of them.

"It'll get easier. The two of you haven't found your rhythm, and you have yet to apologize for what happened when you were both still doubles partners as kids," Charlie says as if that would comfort me.

Also—

"What the fuck did I do? She's the one who all of a sudden hated me without an explanation," I reply, taking a step back to break the skin contact between us. It's not Charlie's fault, but I'm pissed now.

Their face turns all serious, their lips parting in surprise.

"I'm assuming you don't know because that only makes you slightly stupid. If you know and are pretending it wasn't your fault, then you're not just an asshole but also the most emotionally incompetent person I've ever met."

They don't offer me another explanation, simply walk away like all of that made any sense to me.

Once I manage to catch my jaw off the floor, I start walking toward the court where Cata, Papá, and Charlie are. With her back toward me, I spot some writing on Cata's shirt.

### *Santiago Castillo Hate Club*

I almost burst into laughter.

"Where did you have that made?" I ask instead, poking Cata's back where the writing is. She spins around to get my finger off her, scowling at me like she always does.

"I had shirts made for all the members of the club," she says, crossing her arms in front of her chest. I'm convinced it's her way of shutting me out, closing herself off, and I find I hate it more and more every day.

"Even haters are fans. I'm glad I mean so much to you that you'd found a club in my name," I reply with a smirk, loving the way she almost growls at me because I twisted her words.

"Let's get on with this. What do your training habits look like?" she asks as she walks over to her bag to get some bands out.

"I work best with a reward system and lots of praise," I tell her, still smiling because I know it pisses her off.

"What, you need a cookie every time you do a good job?" she asks, her fists moving onto her hips as she watches me with a confused look spreading across her features.

"Anything you want to give me will be the sweetest reward, *mariquita.*"

She scrunches her nose up in disgust at the insinuation of my words, but I finally understand what to do. I need to win her over, charm her, flirt with her. I need to be the perfect fake boyfriend to truly get on her nerves. She's used to us bickering, thrives off it like a fire being fed with gasoline.

This? Me doing a complete one-eighty?

It might throw her off long enough to let her forget whatever made her hate me in the first place.

She shudders visibly, then says, "I will not be rewarding you, *cabrón.* And if you need to be praised for a job well done, call your mother," she says right before she starts running around the length of the court to warm up.

Charlie and Papá are snickering, but my father tilts his head in Cata's direction to get me to move my ass. With a groan, I start running, picking up my pace to catch up with her.

Cata and I jog in silence. Warming up our muscles by rotating our arms in circles. Running with our knees high, stretching after. Then, we start hitting balls back and forth, slowly and consistently.

Well, until I "accidentally" hit a ball too fast and too far placed in the corner of the court for her to reach.

Competition follows after that.

We're playing as if it's a game with points, both of us probably counting in our heads so we know the score and can remember it later.

"Alright, you two, enough! You're supposed to be partners, not rivals. You're acting like children, and I'm sick of it. We're doing drills until you pass out. Let's go," Papá says, but Charlie just stands next to him with their arms crossed in front of their chest and a smile on their face. They will let us continue this until either Cata or I give up.

Which won't happen until one of us drops dead.

Papá makes us run.

*A lot.*

He drills our backhands and forehands until every muscle in my body hurts. Cata is breathing heavily by the time he tells us to practice our serves. She bends over at the waist, taking several deep breaths. I sip my water before holding out my bottle for her. She emptied hers about ten minutes ago, and Charlie hasn't returned with Cata's refill.

"Here," I offer, making my hitting partner and fake girlfriend look up before she eyes the bottle with distrust. "You saw me drink out of it. It's not poisoned," I say with a laugh, so she snatches the bottle out of my grasp and downs the entire thing. "*Bruja,*" I curse when she hands me the empty bottle.

"*Pendejo.*" She sinks into a squat, still breathing heavily. My heart is also still racing, my lungs burning, so I can't even make fun of her.

"Now we only have to practice our serves and then we can go our separate ways for today," I promise her, holding out a hand to help her up. We've been training for two hours without a single break longer than two minutes.

"Give me a second. Your father is ruthless," she says, waving my hand away.

Even after two hours of training, Cata looks good. Her long hair is still firmly wrapped in a bun, but her baby hairs are sticking to her forehead. Her cheeks are perfectly pink and her lips, too.

Not that I'm looking at her lips.

"While we're taking a break, I'd like to discuss our first date," I say, hating myself for forgetting to raise my fingers to put quotation marks around the word.

"God, I hate that word. 'Date.' It used to mean excitement, anticipation, thrill. Now it means obligation, torture, and misery," she replies, but I'm not entirely sure if she meant to say that out loud to me. I mean, logically I know she must have. People don't just talk without being aware they said something, but it's so vulnerable, I can't quite believe she'd admit how she feels to me.

"It's not ideal for me either," I reply, but Cata laughs at that.

"You have no idea what it means to go on a date, Santi. You don't go out with people to date them. You go out with them to fuck them. I *love* going on dates. I love planning dates to take beautiful people on. I love kissing them at the end of the night with the promise that we'll go on another date. And another after that until we're falling into something consuming and full of emotion. I date to fall in love, not to fuck around. You don't understand that because you've never felt anything like it."

Catalina is right. I've never been on a date like the ones she's describing. I've never wanted to be with someone for longer than a night, but I have no idea why. I always thought it was easier because of my job. But when I look at Cata and she looks up at me with her breathtakingly pretty scowl, I get a feeling it's not that simple.

I've never been in love before.

*Have I?*

"You're right, but I have an idea for our first public date that you will also enjoy. Do you want to hear it or not?" Cata gives me a skeptical look but also a small nod, so I sit down next to where she's squatting and pull out my phone to show her.

"Isabella Ada has a concert in France?" she asks, her eyes lighting up with happiness. Isabella Ada is Cata's favorite artist. The Colombian makes music that the entire world is obsessed with, including Cata and me.

"Yes, and I got us front row tickets," I say with a proud, smug smile.

Catalina stares at me, dumbfounded, mouth hanging open for several seconds before dropping her gaze back down to my phone screen. Then back up to my eyes. Down to the screen. Up to my eyes.

"Is this a trick?" she asks.

"Yes, it's a trick. I'll bring you there and then right before we go inside, I'll laugh and say, 'just kidding!'" I say, but instead of laughing, she looks at me like that's a real possibility. "Do you really not trust me at all?"

"Have you given me a reason to?" That shuts me up. "If this is real, then thank you. If it isn't, I'll gut you."

"Sounds good." She shoves my phone back into my hands and stands up to grab her racket.

Catalina always plays with rackets made by *Spin*, her biggest sponsor. She also usually has a rainbow incorporated into the design. If I wasn't sponsored by *New Light*, I'd switch to *Spin* so I could have those rackets, too. Instead, I only get all black ones with no meaningful message.

With her back to me, Cata starts serving, the words on her shirt shifting with every move. I have to hand it to her, she's funny and creative. I know it was most likely supposed to bother me, but I can't stop smiling at the thought of Catalina sitting in front of her laptop and making this shirt. Choosing the right font and style. Maybe even smiling to herself like an evil villain.

*Mi pequeña villana.*

I watch her for a few more serves, noticing her stance is slightly off. She's leaning a bit too far back, which causes her to lose momentum and use more energy than necessary. It's something I struggled with for a long time, too, until Papá made me serve and serve and serve until I did it the right way.

Charlie is too preoccupied talking to him to notice, so I step up behind Cata, stopping her a moment before she serves again.

"Do you mind?" she asks, looking over her shoulder at me.

"Let me help you and your shoulder," I offer, my hands hovering over her arms.

"My shoulder is fine, Santi," she replies, taking a ball out of the pocket of her pants.

"Then your back. Whatever made you flinch a few times the other night. Don't lean so far back. Your weight shouldn't drag you backward. Instead, throw the ball a bit more straight and forward," I explain, my hands still not touching her even though my fingers are itching to wrap around her arms.

"I've been serving like this for years. I'm consistent, able to place the ball well, and have decent speed," she argues, but when she moves her arm again to bounce the ball on the ground, she flinches visibly. "Fuck. Okay, show me how to improve it."

If there is one thing I've always adored about Cata, it's the way she handles feedback or suggestions. Even though she hates me, she's going to listen. She's going to take my advice into consideration and learn from it.

"May I put my hands on you?" I ask, my chest rising and falling a little too quickly for my liking.

"You don't have to touch me. Do it yourself and show me that way," she says, and I almost sigh. We're never going to allow her to build trust with me if she shuts down all my attempts at intimacy.

"Just... let me," I whisper, my mouth suddenly closer to her ear than I intended for it to be. Cata stiffens momentarily, but then her shoulders untense as she lets out a deep breath.

"Okay." Her voice is equally quiet and soft.

My hands finally make contact with the soft skin on her arms, my fingers wrapping around them to lift them into position. One of my arms snakes around her, my hand splaying across her middle. She sucks in a sharp breath and lowers my touch to her stomach.

"Not up there. I'm sore," she says, not giving me any other information, but I also don't press.

This is too intimate a moment, and I don't want to ruin it.

"Down here it is," I reply softly.

Everywhere her body touches mine suddenly comes to life. My heart starts fluttering. My skin lights on fire. My muscles tense with anticipation. I've never touched Cata this way, she's never allowed me, and my entire being seems only too happy that she and I are finally this close. Even if it's only for a moment.

"Alright, lift your arms like you're doing your serve," I instruct, and, to my surprise, she puts her racket to the side before doing as I've asked. I'd have expected she would hit me with it the first chance she got.

Instead, she lifts her arms and fixes her stance, about to serve with neither a ball nor a racket. Only me holding onto her. We go through the motion and right as she leans back, I press my chest to her back to stop her, using the hand on her stomach to steady her.

"See, right here. This is where you lose so much of your speed and put everything on your back. Let your arms do more work," I say and guide her into the proper stance. "Try it again."

We do the same movement for the serve once more, this time with me giving her space, watching her do it from a distance. I adjust her stance twice more, and then she picks up her racket to try it with a ball this time. She does wonderfully, her serve fast and precise.

"That's it, *mariquita*, good girl," I praise her, watching her cheeks turn pink from the words.

"That's enough for today," she says, picking up the balls closest to her and then rushing over to her bag.

"Dammit," I mumble to myself, letting my head fall backward.

I really don't know how to talk to Cata without saying something that ruins the moment.

# CHAPTER 9
## CATALINA

Having Santiago Castillo's hands on me yesterday had me feeling things I never, ever want to feel for him again.

And yet, I can't stop thinking about the way he felt pressed against me. The feeling of his quick heartbeat against my back. His hot breath ghosting the sensitive skin on my ear. His hand on my stomach, steadying me, guiding me. The words falling from his lips, the way he praised me.

I hate him so much.

For our past and what he's doing to me now.

For how good it felt to have his strong arms around me.

"Catalina, are you still listening?" my sister, Ori, says.

She's the eldest out of all our siblings and the smartest Sanchez to ever walk the Earth. She's studying environmental science, trying to further research in renewable energies and, to summarize, save the fucking planet.

"Yes, sorry. You were telling me about the presentation you can't finish because..." I trail off, hoping she'll jump in and finish the sentence because I definitely zoned out.

Whenever Ori starts talking about science, my brain wanders. Not voluntarily, I know it's important, but I don't understand half the terms she uses. I studied business and economics in my three-year university program, not science.

"Never mind. Let's just talk about the fact that Hernanda got her third golfing trophy of the year," Ori says with a proud smile, one I feel lighting up my face too.

"She won the junior tournament?" I ask, adjusting on my bed where I've been lying in only a towel for the past thirty minutes video calling with Ori.

"Yes. She did so well they even gave her the award for best sportswoman at the tournament." I fight back the tears of pride for my little sister that threaten to spill from the corners of my eyes.

Ori and I were already teenagers when Mamá passed away, but Hernanda and our little brother Samuel were only four and two. They don't remember Mamá as well as Ori and I do, so when they were growing up, they came to us when they needed something. Dad was always working to support us, so Ori and I became parents to our younger siblings.

Their achievements mean more to me than my own.

"Is she home? Can I talk to her?" I manage to croak out, emotion making my tongue as heavy as a brick and my vocal cords feel like steel.

"No, she's out with friends," Ori replies, offering me a comforting smile.

"What about Sami?"

"He went to work with Dad." I breathe past another wave of tears. "But he loves his new wheelchair. He sent you a letter saying thank you for buying it for him." Tears shoot into my eyes.

"I hope I'll get some time off soon so I can visit all of you," I say instead of focusing on the homesick feeling camping out in my chest.

It won't get me anywhere. I'll only make Ori feel bad too, and that's the last thing I want. My older sister has enough on her plate as is. Even if I want to cry to her about this whole Santi situation. Even if I want to ask her to fly to Monaco to be with me. I need my big sister to hold my hand while the entire world hates me for something that didn't even happen.

"Talk to me. Are they still spreading that rumor?" Ori asks, dragging me out of my thoughts.

"Yeah, and I have to go on my first date with Santi in about two hours. He's picking me up and driving us to Nice where Isabella Ada is performing so we can pretend we're a happy couple," I say, scrunching my nose up in disgust.

"I know all of this is difficult, especially so close to the start of the season, but I want you to know I'm proud of you. You're carrying so much on those shoulders, no wonder you have such back problems," she teases, and I burst into laughter, but all my sister offers me is a small grin.

Then, she turns serious again, so I do, too.

"They gave you an image you've been trying to break since the day you got it. You came out as pan and broke it a little, but now you shattered it in a way you didn't mean to. I know Santi is your way of not letting these rumors cost you your sponsorships, but don't lose who you are in the process. Don't attempt to fit that box they've been trying to put you back into since you came out publicly. Don't let them warp you into someone else. It's one thing to fix a scandal and another to pretend you're someone you're not."

Ori's words sit with me long after our call ended. It's why I put on a shirt with a pride flag printed across the chest area, the words "love is love" written underneath it. Santi and I will be seen and photographed today, and I want to wear something that makes me feel a little bit more like myself and less like the person the media wants me to be.

Just because I'm dating a man doesn't mean I'm not queer, which is something the media always accuses me of when I'm with a man. It's like I have to constantly prove I'm not straight for them, so they stop saying things like, "Oh, she's with a man now, she must have outgrown *that phase*." It's not a fucking phase, but people like to throw that at my head to take away from who I am.

I hate it.

It makes me feel bad about myself, almost like I don't feel right in my own skin. Society has expectations. They expect women to date men, and men to date women. While things are significantly better nowadays, as a public figure, expectations on top of expectations rest on me. Either I'm the "fake" queer woman dating a man, or I'm the "real" queer woman they don't know what to do with in the world of tennis.

I know all of my friends deal with the same thing. Everyone I know is part of the LGBTQIA+ community in one way or another. Since I decided to be out in the world of tennis—a scandal according to the media—my friends also started dating men, women, and non gender conforming people openly. Santiago has never announced it publicly, but I know he's queer, too. He told me when we were young.

It's my belief that gender identity should never determine why two people should or shouldn't be together in our society, but in the world of sports, that is a very difficult message to make stick.

So, I have to do what makes me feel good. And I do when I'm in a shirt that makes me feel more like myself.

I like expressing who I am through my clothing, I always have. It's one of many things I got from my dad. I remember when I was growing up, he'd always wear shirts with messages written on them. Most days, he wore shirts that said he was happy. Some days, that he was tired. On rare occasions, he wore shirts that had special messages for my siblings and me.

*"Dream it into reality."*

*"Love whoever you want."*

*"You're perfect just the way you are."*

There were more, and new ones follow every year. So, I picked up a similar habit. *Spin* also encourages my passion. The first year they sponsored me, they had the words "Equality For Women In Sports" written on my chest area. It was small to ensure that while we pissed people off, we started slowly to prepare them for what came after. Bigger letters. Flags. Pride everywhere.

I almost smile at the thought of how many homophobic people I probably pissed off, how many *men*, over the years.

A text lights up my phone.

Santi: I'm here. The concert starts soon. We don't have time for you to make me wait just to annoy me.

Me: But I love annoying you. It gives me great pleasure.

I finally smile as I pick up my purse, but it's an evil smile. Definitely not an "I enjoy talking to Santi smile."

Santi: How about I give you a different form of pleasure in exchange for not making me wait?

Me: I'd rather get a full-body wax after getting sunburned.

Santiago is smiling brilliantly as I make my way toward his brand-new car. He told me he picked it up yesterday, but he didn't tell me it'd be a Spark Lightning Bolt in a muddy gray that shouldn't look as good as it does. It's a sports car, similar to my Velocità Rossa, but it's sleeker. Sexier.

When his eyes catch me, they soften, and his attention lingers on the rainbow painted across my shirt, along with the words written underneath it.

"I love that shirt," he says as I slip into the passenger seat. "Much better than the one you wore yesterday at training." I almost snort at the reminder.

For our training session yesterday, I wore a shirt that said, "Eyes off my tits" on the front and "Eyes off my ass" on my lower back.

"You mean the shirt you completely ignored while doing both of the things it told you not to do?" I ask, raising both brows in challenge. Santi gives me a cocky smile.

"You've got a body to die for, Cata. I try to keep my eyes off you, but they always drift back anyway," he says, making my heart tumble all over itself.

"Shut up, Santi," I say, my cheeks heating. Turning my head away, I break eye contact and focus on slowing my nervous heartbeat.

"Sure, but then you're in charge of the music because I can't sit in silence."

He told me it's because he starts overthinking in silence, so he'd rather distract his brain. It's a habit he's had since he was diagnosed with depression as a kid. From what he's told me, he's found coping mechanisms so his symptoms have become more manageable over time—we may hate each other, but I do care about his mental well-being.

"What do you want to listen to?" I ask as I pick up his phone, studying the picture of his parents that he made his background.

My chest warms at the sight.

"Whatever you want."

I'll use any excuse not to talk to Santi before I risk feeling things I shouldn't.

Things I've been suppressing since we were kids.

# CHAPTER 10
## SANTIAGO

I'm nervous. This is the first time Cata and I are going out, and the fact it's for a fake date makes me want to run and hide forever. Usually, I'd be excited to go out and find a nice, beautiful person to lose myself in.

I won't be losing myself in Cata tonight or... ever.

"Let's get this torturous night over with," Cata says, forcing reality back into my thoughts.

"With that pessimistic attitude, of course it's going to be torture. But if you allow for the possibility of tonight to be fun, it could be!" I say, packing as much cheer into my tone as I can. Cata, my little rain cloud, frowns at me. "Fine, it's going to be hell, but at least we'll get to see Isabella Ada."

That almost makes her smile.

"Thanks for making this our first date, *cabrón*," she says and punches my shoulder. It's too hard to be considered playful, but it doesn't hurt either, so I'm too busy hyperfixating on the fact that she chose to put her hand on me. No matter how briefly.

"You can't call me that tonight," I remind her.

"Then let me get them all out now. *cabrón*, *cabrón*, *cabrón*. Okay, I'm good." I burst into laughter, but Catalina opens her door and gets out of the car, leaving me to stare after her for a moment.

We make our way through security without anyone recognizing us, or, if they do, they don't approach us. I got us VIP tickets, so we get to go through first. Crowds make me uncomfortable, so I always make sure there are no lines I have to stand in.

Cata heads for the merchandise table without waiting for me to put my wallet and phone back into my pocket. I catch up to her with a groan, grabbing her hand once I'm beside her again.

"What the hell are you doing?" she asks, attempting to snatch her hand back, but I hold on as I smile down at her.

"What do you mean, *cariño*?" I ask, still faking a smile at her. She rolls her eyes at me.

"Just because we're *dating*—" She breaks off to shudder visibly. "—doesn't mean we have to touch all the time." Her blue eyes give me a challenging look.

"You're supposed to be in love with me. Do you remember how you treated your ex-girlfriend when you were in love?" They couldn't stop touching. Everywhere they went, cameras caught their adorable PDA moments.

And I definitely wasn't jealous.

"Fine, you've got a point."

Cata drags me toward the merchandise table, her brown hair perfectly bouncing because of the sway in her step. As soon as we're in front of the person selling the shirts, hats, tote bags, and posters, Cata leans into me. I instinctively place my hand on the small of her back to bring her closer while she studies the merch and gasps loudly.

"You want to buy me one of each because Isabella Ada is one of my favorite artists? You're the best, *mi corazón*," Cata announces to everyone at the stand, pressing a soft kiss to my jaw a moment later.

I grind my molars together, both because I can't believe what she pulled but also because she kissed me and it's muddling my brain.

"Of course, my ray of sunshine. It's my pleasure," I say through gritted teeth, faking a smile at the salesperson. "One of everything in a medium size, please."

Cata's hand pulses on my shirt as she attempts to step away, but I push her toward me by the small of her back, cupping her chin with my other hand. Her breath hitches as I grin down at her, loving the way her skin flushes pink at our proximity.

"I'm a millionaire, Cata. This may annoy me, but if your intention was to hurt my bank account, you're going to have to try harder than that." A defiant glimmer enters her eye, and it only makes me smirk harder.

"I didn't want to hurt your bank account. I wanted to annoy you, so I'm glad it worked." Both of us are keeping our voices low, speaking so close together, to any outsider it would look like an intimate conversation.

If only they knew.

"*Bruja*," I whisper, leaning in so our mouths almost touch. Cata doesn't lean away, even though the grip I have on her chin is as light as a feather.

"*Cabrón.*" Her lips almost touch mine as they form the word, and I get a little weak in the knees thinking about what it would feel like to kiss her. "Santi," Cata breathes out, making a shiver of pleasure run down my spine.

"Yeah?" I croak out, still watching her mouth.

"What are you doing?" She's still not moving away, and I almost give in. But it wouldn't be right, not while she doesn't want my lips on hers.

"Might change my mind about the no-kissing rule," I admit, caressing the small of her back until she melts into my touch.

"Why?"

"I want to know if it would make you hate me less." Kind of. Mostly, I want to know what Catalina tastes like. I always have.

"Then kiss me and find out," she challenges, knowing full well I would never.

Not while she looks at me like she wants to kill me.

"Here you go, one of everything in a medium as well as the tote bag and cap," the salesperson says, interrupting our moment.

Cata smirks as she steps away, grabbing the bags handed to her while I pay the outrageous sum. I refrain from rolling my eyes as we make our way to our front row seats.

There's a little skip in her step when she sees how close we are, and I smile at her happiness.

Ever since her mom passed away about ten years ago, Catalina has lost a bit of the joy she used to carry around like a second skin. It broke something inside of me when I first noticed the change in her, something that hasn't been repaired since. But, right now, as she spins on the spot because one of her favorite songs is playing over the speakers, I feel that part of me getting its first stitch in years.

All because I brought her here.

"Come on, Santi," she says, and I realize I've been standing in the same spot, watching her, for longer than I should.

But how could I not?

Cata enchants me.

"We're so close," Catalina mumbles as we sit down, wiggling in her seat a little. Excitement wafts off her, and I can't help but smile as she moves to the edge of her seat, staring straight ahead at the stage.

Along with having a general admission area, Isabella Ada's concert venue also has seating near the stage. They're separated, making sure we won't be crowded in later while also getting to be in the front row. If this option hadn't existed when I was getting the tickets, I'd have had to seat us somewhere in the back, away from everyone else.

"Your claustrophobia really came through with these seats," Cata says, surprising a laugh out of me.

"What?" I ask, my hands starting to sweat.

"Your claustrophobia. It's why we're so far in front and away from the people, isn't it?" she asks, finally turning to me again. Her eyes drop to my mouth before she catches herself, and I temporarily forget about what we were talking about.

"I never told you about that," I point out, catching the way she leans forward a little and takes a deep breath.

Is she... smelling me?

Fuck, my heart stumbles at the very possibility.

"You didn't have to, Santi. We've known each other for over a decade," she replies, turning her head to face the stage again.

We don't speak for a while after that. I simply place an arm around the back of her seat in casual affection, mulling over her words.

I wonder what else she knows about me that she's found out by watching me.

"You ask for a picture," I hear someone whisper from a little way behind us.

Cata's shoulders shake as she covers her mouth, and I realize she heard the same thing I did. I play with one of the strands of her hair, but she doesn't seem to notice because she's too busy snickering into her hand. It's such a wonderful sight, I can't do anything but stay as still as possible so I don't interrupt her.

Only once she lowers her hand and rolls her lips to hide her amusement do I say, "I think we've found ourselves some fans, *mariquita*." Catalina's hair flies a little as she moves her whole body to face me once more. "Should we kiss? Demonstrate that we're together?" I ask even though I was the one who said no kissing.

It was me.

She asked me if we should, but I said no. Maybe if I remind myself of that, I'll stop asking her to put her mouth on me.

"Be my guest, but I should warn you, my lip gloss may or may not have poison in it." She's so full of shit, but I love the way she smirks, challenging me.

I dip my head without thinking. My lips are so close to hers, my nose brushing over hers in a playful sort of way that has her breathing hitching. The thought of her not moving away because she has to be here, because this is the image we have to uphold, has me placing a kiss on her cheek instead of her lips. She doesn't trust me yet, and Cata needs trust to be touched intimately, even if it's something as simple as a kiss.

Then again, I doubt kissing Catalina is anything but simple.

"Catalina Sanchez? We're so sorry to bother you, but would you mind taking a picture with us? We're huge fans," the person, whose voice I heard only minutes ago, asks, their breathing fast and uneven. They're obviously nervous, but my fake girlfriend has this energy about her that puts people at ease.

"Of course. Santiago will take it," she assures both fans before standing up to get in the middle of them, smirking in a way that lets me know she's enjoying the fact that they recognized her but not me.

"Well, I think they probably took enough video evidence for us to be covered by every news outlet in the world," Cata says after the fans leave and she sits back down beside me. "Then we can finally make it social media official, too, and Charlie and Carlos will be happy." I place my arm around the back of her chair again, continuing to play with her hair.

"Yeah," I reply, not sure what else to say.

My eyes stay on the side of her face, realizing for the millionth time since meeting her all those years ago that Catalina is physically flawless.

At least to me.

The slope of her nose, the fullness of her lips, her slightly bigger-than-average forehead... she's flawless. I know she would never agree. She was bullied for most of her school life because of her broad shoulders and strong body, but I find it just as stunning as the rest of her. My ladybug has the kind of body that will win her the big trophies.

"Santi?" she says, not looking at me.

"Yes, Cata?"

"Stop staring at me. I'm getting hives." That makes me burst into laughter.

"Sorry," I say, forcing my gaze to the stage.

Luckily, we're distracted by the opening act. Neither Cata nor I know them, so we stay seated, clapping whenever they finish a song and showing respect to their performance even if it's not our style.

However, as soon as Isabella Ada makes her way onto the stage, we're on our feet. Cata is screaming at the top of her lungs, clapping as enthusiastically as I am. The first few songs are fast-paced, and Cata sways her hips to the music in a way that has me watching her with a smile instead of focusing on Isabella almost the whole time.

When one of her slower songs streams through the speakers, I slip my fingers through Cata's and twist her until she's pressed against me.

"*Baila conmigo, cariño.*"

The words are out of my mouth before I can stop them, the desire to voice them too strong to resist. She rolls her eyes but places her arms around my nape, allowing me to put my hands on her hips. Her fresh, senses-consuming scent fills my nose as I place my cheek on the crown of her head, swaying to the music.

It's so very difficult to remember that this is fake when nothing has ever felt this right to me before.

# CHAPTER 11
## SANTIAGO

Manuela is sitting across from me, smirking like she's having the time of her life. Growing up as a twin, I've become used to seeing my face reflected back at me whenever I look at my sister. We may not be identical, but we might as well be, considering how much alike we look. We share the same nose, brown hair, amber eyes, and sharp facial structure. But as my sister continues smirking, I finally realize why Cata hates it so much when I wear that expression.

It's irritating.

"So, how was the concert?" my sister asks, crossing her legs and playing with the hem of her shirt.

"That was two weeks ago," I remind her, but she shrugs.

"Well, I only came back today. I need to be filled in on everything," she says, crossing her arms in front of her chest and showing off her trained forearms.

"Alright, so, the media has been posting us everywhere. Clips of the concert have gone viral. Cata and I made our relationship official on social media. We have been training together almost every single day for the past three weeks, and while we are getting better as hitting partners instead of acting like rivals, we've refrained from going on any more public dates." I take a deep breath before continuing, my eyes trained on the chaos on the table in front of me. "We've had two more mandatory dinners, but we hardly spoke during those." Tornado jumps on the couch beside me before hopping onto my lap and making himself comfortable while I keep scrapbooking. I swear, sometimes he's more like a cat than a bunny in all of his mannerisms, and I know it's because he grew up with them in his previous home, but it never fails to amaze me.

Even though I've finished my rant and have piled on a lot of information, Manu stays silent, still smirking.

"Okay, would you fucking stop that?" I ask, my little outburst making Tornado look up at me with annoyance in his copper eyes. I stroke his tri-color—brown, black, and white—fur.

"Stop what?" Manu asks, feigning confusion.

"That look. Stop it. I know what you're thinking," I reply, but she bursts into laughter.

"Oh, Santi, I doubt that." Manuela's vagueness is nothing new to me, but when it comes to talking about Cata, I can't stand it. I know so little about my own feelings. The least she could do is share hers with me. "You have no other plans to be seen with her in public?"

"I do. We're going out for New Year's Eve tomorrow night. Matteo is throwing his annual party, which has gotten out of hand with all the people he has invited, but I'm not surprised. Matteo's parties always turn into chaos."

I shudder at the thought of his Halloween party three years ago.

"A party? Papá approved this?" she asks, standing up to cross the space between us, lift Tornado into her arms, and flop back onto her couch with my son while I scowl because she took him from me.

"Yeah, I discussed it with him, but since I'm taking my *girlfriend*, he was only too happy about it." I clear my throat before saying, "*I think that's a great idea*, mijo. *One last chance to make a statement before we leave for the Australian Open a week later.*"

My imitation of our father has Manu laughing so hard, tears collect at the corners of her eyes. I can't help but join her until I'm face first on the couch. I don't know how long it takes until both of us sober up, but eventually, silence fills the space between us.

It's comfortable.

It always is with Manu.

I go back to scrapbooking, all of my tools on the coffee table in front of me. I pick up the scissors and cut out a piece of paper from a magazine Manu brought me from when she was traveling.

"How's Madalena?" I ask, the mention of her girlfriend's name making her face fall from amused to irritated. "Oh no. What happened?"

"Nothing, Santi. We're having problems, but I'm not ready to talk about them yet. Once I know how I feel, understand how she feels, I'll let you know," Manu says, locking her feelings away from me.

Papá thinks she's so perfect, that there is nothing she would ever need to improve on, but I disagree. Manu never asks for help. She always has to figure out how to deal with her feelings on her own. Meanwhile, I go to her for everything. When I first started feeling the symptoms of my depression, I went to her. I asked her what was wrong with me, why I was having all of those intrusive thoughts. Why my energy levels had dropped so drastically.

When I was first diagnosed with depression, Manuela and I started looking into coping mechanisms for me. One thing I personally gravitated toward, one thing that allowed me to silence my intrusive thoughts, was scrapbooking while listening to music. It was both picking up a new hobby and allowing me to set realistic goals I could accomplish. Half a page. One page if I was feeling energized enough to set that goal.

I didn't go to therapy or on medication. It was Manu and I who found things that helped me. Plant-based treatments. Going on new adventures. Talking. A lot of talking. And while that may not help other people, it did wonders for me. I still have periods when my symptoms make getting out of bed nearly impossible, but they're a lot more manageable than they used to be.

"You know you can always talk to me, Manu. I'm here for you," I promise her, but she gives me a sad smile.

"I love you, Santiago, but you have to focus on more important things than my relationship. While Cata is fighting for her number one spot this season, you are defending yours. And all of that while faking a relationship. You need all your energy not to crack under the pressure. Maybe some of mine, too."

Catalina is wearing a golden dress. It's sparkly and tight and…

*Fuck me.*

She painted her eyelids in a glittery gold, too. Her lips are painted red, and she added some blush to the apples of her cheeks, making her glow.

My plan was to get out of the car and open the door for her, be a true gentleman, but I can't feel my legs. The sight of her in that dress, which was somehow made to fit all of her curves perfectly, has me feeling lightheaded. And when she turns around to make sure the door of her apartment complex closes properly, revealing that the dress is backless, I feel even more so. Sucking in a sharp breath doesn't help the tension building everywhere inside of me.

I wish someone would dump a bucket of ice-cold water on my overheating body.

"You know, it wouldn't kill you to actually get out and open the door for me," she says as she gets into the car. She reaches for my door, which opens upward instead of sideways, shutting it once more.

"I tried," is the only answer I muster. She gives me a confused look but doesn't ask me to elaborate.

"Try harder next time, *cabrón*. Would you let me open my doors if I was your real girlfriend?" I open my mouth to answer, but Cata keeps talking before I get a chance to. "The answer better not be 'yes.' I opened every single door for my ex-girlfriend because that's how it's done."

"So why don't you open my doors?" I challenge, but instead of smiling at my teasing, Cata rolls her eyes.

"Because I hate you far more than you dislike me."

My heart sinks in defeat as I pull out of her apartment complex and onto the main road.

Silence lingers between us until I can no longer stand it. Until the question I've been meaning to ask for weeks finally bursts out of me.

"Why do you?" It's long overdue to ask that question, and Charlie's words continue to haunt me.

*"I'm assuming you don't know because that only makes you slightly stupid. If you know and are pretending it wasn't your fault, then you're not just an asshole but also the most emotionally incompetent person I've ever met."*

What the fuck did I do?

"Hate you?" she asks to clarify, and I nod as my fingers wrap more tightly around the steering wheel. "Do you truly want to get into this before a party where we have to play people who are in love with each other?"

"I want to know why you don't trust me to touch you. I want to know why the mere sight of me is enough to ruin your day. Most of all, I want to know how to fix that," I rant, pointing at the street in front of us like it will give me all of the answers.

She waits until we're all the way at the party venue, staring down at her hands as she answers my questions.

"You left me."

Cata's hate for me vanishes to reveal how deeply she's hurting because of what I did.

"We were in the doubles finals, our school having made it to the top in the country because of us, and you left me to play a singles game," she explains, making realization set in.

She's right. I did do that. I had the chance to qualify for one of the biggest junior tournaments in Spain, and it was on the same day as our game. After I qualified, I didn't really think about Cata or missing our match. I was too busy being selfish to remember, and then I blamed her for the tension that was suddenly between us. I was mad at her for not being happy for me, and she was disappointed in me.

Angry because I left her.

Catalina accused me of prioritizing my career over any goals we had as partners, and for the first time since I chose myself, I realize she's right. I didn't remember, didn't even think twice about it, and I was so mad at her. So upset because she wasn't happy for me.

Now I know.

My fake girlfriend's hate for me is justified while mine for her is completely and utterly not.

I hate myself a little bit right now.

"We lost the match, we lost our standing, and we lost our reputation for being the best there is. I looked like an ass, waiting there for you for forty-seven minutes until they called it." She lifts her gaze, revealing that she's shut down her emotions. "You can't fix that, Santi. You can't magically take away the resentment I've built toward you," she explains, shaking her head as she lets out a sad laugh.

My hand reaches out to grab her chin between my fingers, keeping her attention on me as I say, "Don't underestimate my determination, Cata. I'll earn your forgiveness, and I'll prove to you that my career isn't more important than our goals."

Cata gives me an unimpressed look I wish I could wipe off her face.

"Sure, Santi, and tomorrow, pigs will fly," she says, leaning away to break skin contact and get out of the car.

Determination fills me as I follow her.

If there is a way to make Catalina forgive me, I'll find it.

I'll earn it.

Because, if I'm being honest with myself, all this time, I've been looking for a reason to stop pretending. I tell myself I don't like spending time with her, but a mere moment in her presence has me smiling almost excessively. And I'm not irritated with her. I'm always irritated because I don't know how to talk to her without making her angry.

I'll do whatever it takes to make her hate me less. I'll beg. I'll get on my knees, whatever she needs, because Catalina deserves it.

After what I've done, she deserves the world laid at her feet.

Now I only have to figure out what that means for her.

# CHAPTER 12
## CATALINA

THE PARTY IS AS full of people as I was expecting. Santi stayed glued to my side for most of the first hour, watching me drink and chat with some people while he sipped on his water and kept his hand casually placed on my hip.

It didn't even irritate me as much as I wish it had, which is why I used the first chance of him getting distracted by an acquaintance to leave and move around the room on my own.

And that's when I spotted one of my favorite people in the world and the host of this party.

Matteo Ricci.

We met several years ago on the tennis court when we were paired up to play doubles for a charity event and have spent countless evenings together since. I'm not as close to him as I am to Sage, Ness, and Charlie, but spending time with him brightens up my days. He's fun, easy-going, and always finds ways to make me laugh.

After my conversation with Santi in the car, I really don't feel like doing anything other than glaring at every single person around me, but Matteo doesn't give me that choice.

"Catalina Sanchez, you are far more beautiful than anyone has a right to be," he says as he approaches me, placing two kisses on my cheeks. "Will you dance with me, *dolcezza*?" he asks, and I find myself blushing at the muscular Italian with deep brown eyes, dark brown skin, and short, curly hair. The three glasses of champagne I've downed also have made me tipsy and my chest all warm.

"Absolutely," I reply, placing my hand in his when he holds it out for me.

I'm well aware I should be spending all my time with Santiago, selling this fake relationship of ours, but we were already photographed together outside of the venue. I think I get one minute to enjoy with someone I actually like, especially because Matteo vetted every single person here, making them sign something that said no video and photography is allowed.

Whatever happens at his parties will not be shared on the internet.

"Uh oh, Lina. Your boyfriend isn't happy that I'm touching you," Matteo says right after he grabs my hips to spin me around, his body behind mine as we keep dancing. He tilts my chin in Santi's direction so that I look at him, and when his usually happy mouth is downturned into the most irritated scowl, I bite my lip to keep him from seeing my smile.

"First of all, he isn't my actual boyfriend. Secondly, good. Let him be pissed." I spin back around in Matteo's arms, swaying my hips to the music.

Matteo is a very attractive man, and when he touches my lower back, I get butterflies in my stomach. He seems to notice because he's smiling down at me knowingly, bringing his hand even lower. I trust Matteo, I always have, so I don't stop him when he looks at me for permission. If anything, I sway my hips more, inviting his hand to brush against me.

Right before he slips it onto my ass, I feel someone grab Matteo's wrist, and then I'm pulled against a very hard chest that's vibrating with anger.

"Hi, Santiago," Matteo says, a challenging sparkle in his eyes.

"Hi, Matteo," he replies, the words making his chest brush against my back, and I realize he's not even holding me against him anymore. I simply haven't moved away. "Do you like your hands attached to your arms?" Santi asks next, making Matteo cock a brow.

"Sure do." He's finding this all awfully amusing, even as his best friend threatens him.

"Then keep them off Catalina."

Santi's words are followed by his hands grabbing my hips before he throws me over his shoulder, storming away from the dance floor with me draped across it.

"Santiago Javier Castillo, if you don't put me down, I'm going to cut your dick off in your sleep," I say, pushing myself off his back in an attempt to make him understand me better with our loud surroundings.

"Cata, my patience has run out. Don't test me," he says, still carrying me away from the party.

"Or what?" I bite back.

"Wanna find out, *cariño*?"

The dangerous edge he put in his voice, a promise of things my body is very on board with, has me shutting up until we reach a private room. It looks like the sort of place where people put their jackets, but there is nothing in here but a singular table and empty racks. Santiago places my ass on the table, stepping away from me to run his hands through his hair.

I watch him trying to collect himself, crossing my legs and leaning back on my hands. He spins abruptly and stalks toward me, stopping a meter away from me. His chest is rising and falling so very quickly, and I can't help but smile at the sight.

It may be the alcohol, but jealous Santi is incredibly sexy.

"You can't possibly be upset that someone else was touching me, Santi. We're not actually together," I remind him, dangling my feet to appear bored.

"Of course I'm upset, Catalina. We have to uphold appearances. You can't be seen with my best friend's hands all over your ass, grinding against you," he says, crossing his arms in front of his chest to refrain from throwing his hands around in frustration like he usually does. "If I can't fuck anyone else, you sure as shit can't either," he blurts out, and I almost laugh.

No part of me intends to risk exposing our fake relationship by sleeping with someone else, but Santi doesn't have to know that.

"But it felt so good having Matteo's hand on my body." For someone who is the very embodiment of sunshine, Santi looks ready to kill someone.

"If you want another's hands on your body, you will have to ask for mine, *mariquita*. For the next however many months, if you want pleasure, you'll have to use me to get it."

Never mind having butterflies. I barely stop my entire body from shaking at the very thought of *using Santi for pleasure*. I press my legs more firmly together, and he tracks the movement with his eyes. He takes another step toward me, but I lift my heel to press against his chest and keep him back. His eyes drop to where the sharp heel pushes against his stomach, a smile curling the corners of his mouth.

"If I want pleasure, Santi, I will fuck myself to get it. I don't need you," I say and push off the table, attempting to walk out of the room when his fingers wrap around my wrist in a gentle but firm grip.

His eyes soften as he takes me in, but there is still a fire burning inside of him that he hasn't quite managed to extinguish.

A fire fueled by his desire for... me.

"It's one thing to hate me for our past, Cata, and another to risk everything we could possibly build now because of it. I will earn your forgiveness, but I need you to work with me until I do."

This time, I do laugh.

"Don't bother, Santi. Your apologies will be as meaningless to me as any other moment we spend together. If I have to, I'll stop dancing with other people, but I won't ask you to dance with me instead. This relationship isn't real, and I won't pretend it is."

He releases me, and I walk out of the room, trying to ignore the stinging in my eyes.

There was a time when I thought I was falling in love with Santiago Castillo, but I was a child and he was my rival. There is no way that was what I was feeling.

And yet, no other reason is strong enough to explain the way my heart breaks a little every time I'm reminded I *can't* trust him. Not again. Not after he broke my heart in a way it had never been broken before.

I've been running around, aimlessly searching for grapes for the last twenty minutes.

There are many Spanish traditions my family continues to do, even after my mother's passing. Eating twelve grapes when the clock strikes midnight, ringing in the new year, is one of them.

But there are no grapes anywhere.

Panic has my chest in a deathly grip, making it nearly impossible to breathe as I ask yet another waitress if there are any grapes in the kitchen. She gives me the same answer as all the others.

No.

A familiar wave of grief hits me until the tears return to my eyes. I got them under control after my confrontation with Santi half an hour ago, but they return tenfold now.

*"Twelve grapes,* mija. *You have to eat twelve at midnight."*

The sound of my mother's voice fills my ears, making tears drop down my cheeks. I cover my mouth, feeling a sense of hopelessness.

"Cata, take a deep breath for me."

I don't want his voice to soothe me. It's not fair that I feel less overwhelmed simply because he appears in front of me, grabbing my arms to steady me.

I hate that his love language is physical touch. I hate it because it feels so good to be touched and comforted by him, by his strong grip.

"Tell me what's wrong, and I will fix it. I promise." When he said it earlier, I wanted to punch him in the face. Now? I kind of want to hug him.

It's easy to get lost in my grief. It's easy to forget I'm not alone when I feel this way, stuck in darkness. Having Santi here, steadying me is everything I need to feel tethered to reality again.

"Santi, I don't have grapes. My mother said I always have to eat grapes," I explain, taking a deep breath to slow my breathing. He runs a gentle hand over my arm, staring directly into my eyes.

"I brought grapes, *cariño*. I remember your tradition, and I didn't know if they would have some here, so I brought them. Come with me," he says, taking my hand to lead me to where he had given his bag to be checked earlier. The man behind the counter takes Santi's ticket before disappearing to grab his black backpack.

As soon as it's in Santi's hand, he guides me to the terrace of the venue, sitting down with me at one of the empty tables right as someone shouts that it's one minute to midnight.

"Here," he says, handing me green grapes—because I don't like red ones—that he packed in a tupperware.

I stare at the container, dumbfounded, then at him.

"Santiago—" I start but cut off because I'm not entirely sure what to say.

"Come on, *mariquita*. Open them so we can eat them."

Someone starts counting down from ten seconds to midnight, and I keep my eyes on Santiago's the entire time as we count aloud with everyone else.

The clock strikes twelve, both of us saying "Happy New Year."

Never in a million years did I think I'd ever share such a personal tradition with Santi, but as we eat the grapes in silence, him counting out loud to make sure we don't miss one, I let my shoulders untense for the first time in years.

I don't have to be on edge right now. He has no intention to have another fight, and I'm too relieved to yell at him when he made sure I didn't have to feel disconnected from Mamá tonight.

"Thank you, Santi," I hear myself saying once we've eaten the grapes. He reaches out to wipe under the left corner of my mouth, probably cleaning up my lipstick.

"You're welcome, Cata."

I hate my heart for stumbling because of the way he looks at me, because of the soft touch of his thumb on my face.

If this is how we start the new year, we might be able to make it to the end of the season without killing each other, after all.

Or, more accurately, me killing him.

# CHAPTER 13
## SANTIAGO

It's our first Grand Slam tournament of the season.

The Australian Open is most often held during the second week of January until the end of the month. Twenty days of tournament. Mine starts a day before Cata's, so she and I are currently playing rallies to warm me up for my match later.

The first match she will be in my box as my girlfriend.

Fake girlfriend.

I've got to remember that.

Today, Catalina is wearing a dark blue tennis skirt in a dark blue as well as a matching shirt with the words, "Consistency is key" written across her chest. An obvious jab at my inconsistent way of playing, but I haven't done more than grin at it. My favorite shirt so far has been the one she wore when we were practicing three days ago.

"Santiago Castillo's Best Quality: Having Catalina Sanchez as a Hitting Partner."

There was nothing else written on it, and I was laughing the whole time.

"Focus, Santi. You don't want to be kicked out of the tournament during the first match, do you?" she asks after I've missed another ball by hitting it too wide. It went in the doubles alley instead of staying within the singles lines.

She storms toward the net, a scolding look taking over her face. I stay at the baseline, keeping my distance from her. It's what I've been doing since New Year's. It's what I need to do while she's still mad at me.

Otherwise, I'll end up begging to touch her, and that isn't a good look if Cata says no. If she doesn't want me to.

"You make me nervous," I reply, staring directly into her blue eyes from across the court. She leans a little against the net as she crosses her arms over her magnificent chest.

"What part of me makes you nervous, Santi? My tennis skills or my tits?" she challenges, clearly not having my ogling. I drag my gaze back to her face, feeling my features turning into a frown.

"All of you makes me nervous, Cata. I feel like you're aiming for me with every hit, trying to hit me in the face or balls."

This makes her crack a smile as she slowly backs away.

"I am."

It's her only reply before she serves the ball, an underhand serve she places perfectly in front of me. I hit it back to her, doing my best to listen to her feedback in the same way she listens to mine. I have this habit of being stubborn when it comes to my tennis. It's not a very flattering personality trait, thinking I know my tennis best and there is nothing I need to improve on because I am winning matches and I'm number one in the world.

I listen to Papá, but only because he's my coach and he's been in the world of tennis a lot longer than I have. He knows things I'll never learn without his help.

But Cata?

I don't *have to* take her criticisms under consideration. She's my hitting partner, not my trainer. We're stuck together because we've been forced to be this way.

That doesn't mean that I don't admire her tennis and want her to teach me, too.

I just have a harder time with it.

"Santi, stop aiming for the fucking line. If you aim for the line every time, you're going to have your ball go straight back into the doubles alley," Cata calls out from the other side of the court, waving her hands around in frustration.

"But if I don't take risks, I won't make points."

I won't entertain.

I'll disappoint my fans.

I'll disappoint everyone attending the match.

Cata studies me for a second before making her way back to the net. This time, she doesn't stop there. She jumps over it, more gracefully than anyone has a right to, and storms toward me. Part of me thinks about running away as she stalks toward me like a predator, but another is so mesmerized by *her*, all I manage to do is observe every little movement of hers. The way her long, brown hair sways with every step she takes. The way her clothes shift against her skin. The way her eyes burn with irritation.

"What is it with you?" she asks, poking my left shoulder.

"I don't know what you mean," I reply, attempting to take a step away from her but my legs aren't moving. One look at her, one inhale of her fresh and sweet scent, and I'm cemented in place, unable to escape Cata's pull on me.

Her blue eyes study my face, as if she could find the answer to her question written in my features.

And perhaps she does, because what she says next is so accurate, it sends a chill down my spine.

"You're scared."

I try to play it off with a *pffft* sound that I drag out, but she pokes me again to bring my attention back to her face.

"You are. You're scared of failure. You're scared of not being the golden boy of tennis anymore. You're scared you won't be good enough."

This finally breaks her curse of enchantment—it has to be a curse because if I had it my way, I would not be attracted to her. I stumble backward ever so slightly, attempting to swallow the panic rising in my chest.

"You don't know me. Don't pretend you do," I croak out, but it's useless. Tears shoot into my eyes at the very thought of being exactly what she claimed I was scared of becoming.

A failure.

For the first time in years, Cata's eyes soften in a way that gives me hope for our future.

"Santi, you don't have to be perfect. I know everyone expects it of you, even your own parents, but being the golden boy is a ridiculous concept. You should be whoever you'd like to be. Play however you want to play. If that means taking risks, fine. But if taking risks puts more pressure on you, there's no shame in playing it safe." Instead of poking me, Cata places her hand on my left pec, patting it gently once.

The gesture is so sweet, it has my stomach in such knots, I close the distance between us to place my forehead against hers.

I could lash out. I could tell her I'm number one and she's number two, so what the hell would she know, but I don't want to. It would be bullshit, and I want her comfort. I want her touch. I want her to calm me because, despite pretending I'm so put together, I'm actually terrified of getting kicked out in the first round.

I'd never live down the shame the media would put on me.

*Santiago Castillo doesn't even make it through the first round of the first major tournament of the season.*

"Santi, there is no one watching us. You can stop with the act," she says, but I don't back away.

"Someone is always watching," is my lame excuse. "Can I put my hands on your hips, *mariquita*? Can I touch you?" Her hand hasn't fallen from my chest, and I want to place mine on her throat to feel her quick heartbeat beneath my fingertips.

"No, Santi, you can't. You need to stop touching me when people aren't watching," she says and moves away, my forehead no longer touching hers, her hand nowhere near me anymore.

"Why?" Defeat takes over my voice, but she doesn't seem to notice, or if she does, she doesn't comment on it.

"Because I can't do this. Not again," Cata says, lifting her hands as she backs further away. She shakes her head and sprints toward her bag, placing her racket inside.

I don't try to stop her, and she doesn't look back to see if I am. This confusing woman is not running to be chased, she's running to be left alone and figure out her feelings, and I will not pressure her to do so on the spot.

Hell, I haven't even figured mine out entirely.

This constant need to touch her and see her and... I shudder as the list continues on and on in my thoughts.

There is no point looking at any of those things too closely.

What Catalina and I have isn't real.

We're playing the happy couple for the world, but once the season is over and my deal with Papá is done, that's it.

She'll never want to see me again, and there is no way I can change her mind unless she allows me to.

Unless she offers me the piece of her that used to belong to me before I fucked everything up.

Pre-match jitters are a pain in the ass.

Once I've warmed up and the match starts, I'm fine. Beforehand? It feels like my organs are twisting to make knots.

When I was diagnosed with depression, I was also diagnosed with mild anxiety. And while I've found coping methods for my depression, it's not that easy with my anxiety. It has a habit of only showing up before matches, so I haven't figured out how to stop my heart from racing, my hands from tingling, or my breathing from turning shallow.

Music helps. Moving around helps. Doing breathing exercises helps.

But it's still always there, always bothering me in one way or another.

This is only the first round, and I've been matched up with a player who doesn't have a high ranking. He qualified to be in the Australian Open, which means he has a lot less experience.

That also means if I lose, it'll look even worse on me.

*Stop thinking like that, Santiago,* I scold myself, something I have to do a lot before the match begins to keep my anxiety from sending me into a full-blown attack.

My opponent, Harry Jackson, is announced first. Then, my name is called, and I step out of the little area where we were told to wait. With my tennis bag slung over my shoulder, I wave to the crowd, the entire stadium packed with fans. They are screaming for me, and I am smiling as brightly as I can, soaking in their enthusiasm. They'll be here cheering me on, fueling me.

I take a deep breath that finally settles some of my nerves, but what has my anxiety levels dropping all the way is seeing Catalina with sunglasses pushed up the bridge of her nose as she sits in my box. She's scowling, looking ready to rip someone's head off, and I can't help but grin.

She really is my little rain cloud.

The pre-match rituals are as they always are. Flip a coin to find out who will start serving, shake hands, take some pictures, do a bunch of sportsmanship things like saying "good game," and then warm up.

I win the coin flip, which means I get to start serving. Harry chooses a side of the court, which is fine by me. There is no side that has more sun to blind us at the moment.

The warm-up calms me even more. We're playing on a hard court, meaning the ball bounces higher and faster than on others. It's always a challenge to figure out how to adjust your hits to match the conditions you're playing on, but after all my training sessions with Papá and Catalina, I feel confident.

I feel ready.

Before we start, I take one sip of water and wink at Cata. She remains in the same position, with her trained arms crossed in front of her chest, sunglasses covering her eyes, and a scowl on her lips.

She's so divine, it hurts to look at her.

But what's a little pain for a bit longer when my reward is looking at Catalina Sanchez as she plays my girlfriend.

# CHAPTER 14
## CATALINA

WATCHING SANTIAGO PLAY TENNIS is, for lack of a better word, a pleasure.

The way that man moves is glorious.

He's quick on his feet, powerful in his shots, and he really is entertaining to watch. When he misses a point in a long rally, he laughs at himself. When he wins a good point, he riles up the crowd until they're screaming his name.

For some reason, he keeps looking my way as well.

In the first set, I didn't move. He played so well, he won it six games to two. But the second set has me on the edge of my seat.

He's currently down four games to two, and Harry looks determined to take this one from him. Santi has been making so many unforced errors this set, I can tell he's out of the game a little.

Which means we have to bring him back into it.

"Santiago, get your head out of your ass and back in the game," I say in Spanish as soon as he steps under his box to wipe sweat off his brow with his towel. Carlos chuckles beside me, for the first time today, looking less stoic.

"I'm trying. I lost my rhythm," he replies in our mother tongue, looking all shades of overwhelmed. He's usually more confident than this, has a better handle on his emotions. I'm the one who gets nervous when I'm down a few points.

Not him.

"If it's because I'm sitting here, making you nervous, then I'm leaving." It better not be. We're both professionals. Santi should be able to separate his personal life from the match.

"If you go anywhere, I'll throw you over my shoulder and carry you back to your seat, *mariquita*," he says, throwing his towel back to where it was resting before, taking his racket.

"Get his service game," I call out before he walks back to the baseline.

He needs a break, to win Harry's service game, and he needs it desperately to get his confidence back.

I'm at the edge of my seat again, my leg bouncing up and down as I watch Santi squat, positioning himself to return Harry's serve. He's standing farther behind the baseline for the first serve, but when his opponent goes too wide, Santiago moves up, anticipating the second serve being slower.

Santiago returns it beautifully, placing it right in the corner where Harry can't get the ball.

"*Vamos!*" I call out and clap, just like the rest of the fans. Santi throws me a small smile, clearly enjoying how invested I am.

Santiago wins the second point as well, making it love-thirty for him. I momentarily get distracted by his thick, trained thighs as the muscles in his legs flex. Then, I get distracted by his round ass again before finally shaking my head and refocusing on the match.

This is why I don't watch Santi play anymore.

He looks mouth-wateringly good.

Especially in that dark blue outfit his sponsor, *New Light,* put him in.

No sleeves for his shirt, naturally, because it shows off his massive arms.

I think Santi may be allergic to sleeves.

"How's he doing?" Charlie asks as they join me in Santi's box, handing me a bottle of water. I told them I forgot one earlier, and they nearly ripped my head off over the phone.

*A day before your first match is not the time to be dehydrated*, they scolded me.

"Better now that Catalina yelled at him to get his head out of his ass," Carlos chimes in, but then we all fall silent when they start playing the next point.

Santiago's return is slower, positioned right at Harry's feet, so his opponent hits it back to him, taking control of the rally. My breath catches in my throat as I watch them hit the ball back and forth. Santi attacks the ball and approaches the net, volleying it in a way that the ball goes deep into the court. Harry barely catches it, hitting it high so that Santiago overhead smashes it, winning himself the point.

Love-forty.

He has three break points.

Good.

There is a bar on the edge of the balcony of the box where I'm sitting with Carlos, his mother Alana, and the rest of Santi's team, and I grab hold of it. It steadies me a little.

"Come on, Santiago," I mumble as I watch him get into position once more.

Harry places his serve in the left corner of the service box, and Santiago barely manages to return it. It goes short, so Harry attacks it, sending it to the other side of the court. I'm watching my fake boyfriend run for his life, somehow getting to the ball. He hits it back, but Harry is at the net, which means he's quick about positioning the ball on the other side of the court again.

Santi already anticipated that though, and gets to the ball once more. This time, he sends it straight down the court, away from Harry. It lands on the singles line, earning him the point and getting him that break he desperately needed.

I'm out of my seat, cheering and clapping for him as pride consumes me.

I blame my love for tennis for this visceral reaction.

Santiago won his match in three sets yesterday. After he got the break, he took every game in the second set, and then he won the third six games to one. It was impressive, to say the least.

Today is my turn.

I'm playing against Maria Timmons, number twenty-seven in the world in the women's singles ranking. I've played her several times already in the past.

I've won every match so far.

Charlie told me Maria has been struggling on the hard court from what they saw when they were sneakily watching her train this morning. I almost burst out laughing at my coach's face when they were telling me how they put on a cap and jacket to hide. I assured them I wasn't too worried about Maria. I'm worried about my biggest rival—besides Santi. Layla Adel is number one in the world, and she's an incredible tennis player. She's also one of the nicest people I've ever met, but I still want to take that number one spot for myself.

I'm *going to* take it this season.

My back bothers me a little as I warm up with Maria, getting ready for my first match. Usually, I would have started with the Brisbane International tennis tournament, but Charlie and I agreed that with everything happening with my reputation, and Santiago becoming my hitting partner and fake boyfriend, it would be best to skip it.

It isn't required for tennis players to partake in every single tournament. There are specific ones we have to do—like all of the Grand Slams, eight specific tournaments of the ATP or WTA, and so on—and with everything going on in my life, I have decided to focus on the required tournaments for this season.

And fuck, it's a busy season.

I have sixteen tournaments lined up, while Santi has eighteen because, of course, he does.

*Overachiever.*

The coin toss determines Maria will start serving, so after we've warmed up, I take one last sip of water, wipe the sweat off my forehead with my towel, and smooth a hand down the front of my dress. Vanessa outdid herself with this design. Unlike so many other tennis dresses, the shorts underneath are actually much longer and have pockets to slip my second ball into when I serve. It's just the right amount of tight to keep everything in place while also being airy enough to let me move with ease.

This dress wasn't designed to simply look good, which of course it does as well. It was made for comfort and practicality.

Another reason to love *Spin* and Ness.

My eyes drift to my box where Charlie, Santiago, and the rest of my team are sitting. Usually, my family would sit beside my physio, agent, Charlie, and now Santi, I guess, but Hernanda and Samuel have school, and Ori is too busy with work to join. Dad has to take care of them, so there is no way he could be here either.

It shouldn't hurt as much as it does, but it's hard not to miss them.

It's hard not to miss my mother every single time I think about her not being here. She never got to see me participate in these tournaments. She never got to see me play on the courts that she won her grand slam titles on. She never got to see me make a name for myself.

Santiago throws me a smile I can only describe as soft and gentle, as if he can sense my sadness and is trying to comfort me with that expression alone. I give him a tight nod, swallowing down every little piece of my hurt to focus on winning this match.

Returning is one of my stronger areas. I often preferred it to serving because there was always something that felt off during my serve. My back would ache for a split second after I hit the ball, but a split second is a long time when I have to prepare for my opponent to return the ball to me.

It doesn't happen as much anymore.

My serve has been feeling a lot better since Santi's tips, and, as much as I still hate him, I'm so grateful I don't have to dread my serve as much anymore.

That doesn't mean I'm not still a fantastic returner.

Maria's serve isn't necessarily fast, but she places it in the corners of the serving box, making it more difficult for me to recover quickly. Her first one goes into the net, so I move up the court, getting closer to the baseline. My eyes are trained on her until the moment the ball flies toward me. I jump a little for my split step, positioning myself to attack the ball slightly more than I would be able to on a first serve.

I send it down the line, away from where Maria is, earning me the first point of the match. Without celebrating, I move on to the second, walking toward the other side of the court to receive the serve.

The first set flies by, and I win it six games to three. Maria is getting frustrated with me continuing to take service games from her, and she's started groaning in frustration when she misses a ball. It's not uncommon for tennis players to be very vocal during a match. Men and women have been grunting and screaming for decades, but unless I use *a lot* of force or am very tired, not a sound comes from me. Not even when I win a particularly good point.

I think it irritates my opponents even more, and it's definitely one of the reasons the crowds never know what to do with me. They love it when Santiago screams *"VAMOS!"* from the top of his lungs. They love it when he places a finger to his ear and waves his other hand around to get the crowd to scream louder for him.

I'm more stoic. Controlled. Unwilling to give them any reason to criticize me or doubt my sportswomanship.

"More footwork, Lina," Charlie says as I place my towel in its designated spot at the back of the court after the break between sets is called to an end. "You're not getting to enough balls. You're watching after them instead of running, and I need you to try a little harder, okay?" they go on, and I throw them a look I hope reveals what I think of their instructions.

"You need to pay closer attention, Charlie. I'm on every ball," I complain, the exhaustion making me a bit grumpy.

Technically, it's not forbidden anymore to listen to your coaches when you're on the side of the court where they are, but there is a time limit until we have to start playing again, and mine is running out. I don't look at Charlie or Santi as I twist my racket and prepare for Maria to serve again.

Her serve has been getting worse and worse with every game that she gets more frustrated, and I use that opportunity to attack her second serve more, running to the net to win my point there. It's what I do in the first point of the set, sprinting to the net to volley the ball back. She goes cross-court, and I backhand volley the ball, making my way to the center line. Maria goes down the line, but I forehand volley it, a short hit that lands right in the corner of the service box.

She doesn't manage to get it.

"Come on!" Maria screams, raising her racket as if to smash it on the ground, but she stops herself a second before she makes contact.

I simply move on to the next point.

My eyes catch sight of Santiago's smug smile as I grab my towel.

"Stop that," I call out in Spanish, not looking at him.

"Can't. The way you play, Cata... It's fucking magnificent."

The compliment has the corners of my mouth curling, but I hide the expression by wiping my face until it's gone.

The rest of the match is easy. Because Maria is so rattled, she doesn't even try to go for my balls anymore when I hit drop shots or go wide in the corners. She lets it happen, almost like she's already given up.

Which is a damn shame because when I win, I don't feel accomplished.

It's easy to win against someone who gives up.

It's infinitely harder to win against someone who will throw everything they have at you, even when they're losing.

# CHAPTER 15
## SANTIAGO

C ATALINA AND I HAVE both made it to the semi-finals of the Australian Open. Matteo lost against Blake Hauser yesterday and Cata's friend Sage lost against Layla. Cata has been on edge since. If she makes it to the final against Layla, she isn't sure she will be able to win.

And if she doesn't believe in herself, she *won't*.

In a sport where you are competing for yourself, if you are not sure of your abilities and skills, you won't get anywhere.

Catalina and I are meant to go on a public date to celebrate her twenty-fourth birthday today, trying to sell our fake relationship during the first tournament of the season. She's expecting us to simply go to a restaurant, a place Charlie and Mamá tipped the paparazzi off that we were going to, but I have a different plan in mind.

Something grander.

Something that will make my little rain cloud very happy with me.

When she was a kid, her mother would organize scavenger hunts for Catalina. Usually, they would take place on her birthday, and she'd have to figure out all these clues to find the location that held all of her presents.

So, that is exactly what we're doing today.

It's convenient that neither Cata nor I have a match today, and while it's important to train, a recovery day is equally as important. It allows us to rest, to fully hydrate ourselves, and to get some much-needed pain relief through massages and stretching.

It also gives us time to mentally recover.

And as emotional as she might be initially when I reveal what we'll be doing, I hope the fun of it all will overpower everything else.

"Well, well, happy birthday to me," she says, pulling me out of my thoughts.

I'm mid stretch, my legs straddling the ground as I thrust my hips forward in a slightly inappropriate motion that is also very good at stretching out my hips. A smirk covers my lips as I keep going, not the least bit ashamed. This is part of my routine, and while I've never had anyone but Papá in the room while I did it, I can't say I hate the way Cata watches me with lust in her eyes.

Normally, she's very good at shutting down her desire for me since her contempt overpowers it, but she's not so successful now.

"Want to join me?" I ask, still watching her as I keep going. Ten more seconds, and I'd be done, but I don't want to stop while *mi mariquita* watches me like that.

"I'd rather never have sex again," she replies, crossing those trained arms of hers over her chest and glaring at me.

"Come on, be honest with me for once, *cariño*. You've thought about fucking me, haven't you?" I ask, watching her roll her eyes. I stop stretching, kneeling as I wait for her response, which is as I expected it to be.

It's so very Catalina.

"I've also thought about sticking my hand in boiling hot oil, but the goal is not to let intrusive thoughts win, Santiago."

A snort slips free, making pride glimmer in her eyes.

"I think you should let all your intrusive thoughts about me win," I reply, standing up and closing the distance between us.

Cata doesn't move away, even as I lift a hand to her cheek. I wait for her permission before touching her, and she turns her head to put her cheek in my hand with a frown.

"Fine, but you should know, I always fight my intrusive thoughts of stabbing you with my fork when we have dinner. Considering you're taking me out today, you might want to reconsider that statement." I notice her staring at my bare arms before she catches herself and shifts her attention back to me.

"Don't worry. Forks are going to be the last thing on your mind today."

She gives me a confused look, but I simply grin at her and hold out my hand, waiting for her to put hers in mine. Cata rolls her eyes one last time before taking my hand and allowing me to pull her out of the gym.

Today is going to be fun.

It's summertime in Australia, so Catalina is wearing a flowy white dress with a burst of colors from several different flowers all over it. Her skin appears to be glowing in the light of the afternoon sun, and her blue eyes are complemented by the dark eyeshadow she's wearing. She braided her long, brown hair into two dutch braids, a few strands framing her face.

Her scowl is firmly set in place, but when she sees me, clad in a white dress shirt that matches her outfit, and dark blue jeans with a bouquet of daffodils—her favorites—in my hand, her gaze softens.

"Happy Birthday, *mariquita*," I say and step toward her, handing her the flowers. She takes them from me, and I lean down to place a kiss on her cheek. Her eyes flutter shut before I make contact, which is all the reassurance I need.

My lips press to the soft skin on her left cheek, and I linger because I can't help myself. She smells fresh and sweet, so I inhale subtly, trying to get my fill of her scent for the millionth time since we've met. It's been over a decade, but Catalina has always smelled this way.

And even though I linger, she doesn't push me away. She doesn't tell me she'll gut me like I would have expected. Cata simply places her free hand on my chest and gently presses to break the skin contact.

"I think the paparazzi got their picture," she says, her eyes drifting over my shoulder.

We're in front of her hotel, and I know for certain Charlie and Mamá did *not* tip them off that we'd meet here. It's too dangerous for Cata for anyone to know where she's staying.

"Relax, they've known where I'm staying since I arrived. It's fine," she says, but I'm not happy about this at all.

"You're coming to stay with me at my hotel," I blurt out, attempting to storm past her and up the stairs to the entrance of her hotel when she wraps her fingers around my wrist to stop me.

"I most certainly am not, Santi. It's enough that we are forced to spend so much time together. I am not voluntarily going to be around you more," she says, walking toward where I parked my rental car to pick her up.

I bite down my frustrated rant about her not taking her safety seriously enough. There is no point. If she doesn't want to come with me, she won't.

But that doesn't stop me from texting Charlie and telling them to get some security for Catalina for the last week that we're going to be here in Melbourne. It's a wonder people have known about her staying here for a week already without any incidents.

"Santiago, let it go. I'm fine," she says, and I wonder for the millionth time *why* I care. Why her safety is so important to me. Why I'm trying to find ways to make her forgive me and even despise me less.

It's not because I want a lasting relationship with her that isn't fake. Of course it's not. That would not only be extremely out of character for me since I've never been in a relationship before, it would also be plain stupid.

But this season is going to be long, so it only makes sense that I'm trying to find ways to bond with her. To bicker less. To... well, fuck me, but I want to kiss her, even if we're faking it, while she isn't so damn angry with me all the time.

"Get a move on, *cabrón*. I'm going to get my first grey hair waiting for you," she says right before slipping into the passenger seat.

A sigh of utter frustration slips past my lips, but I do as she wants and get into the car.

"Would it kill you to be a bit more positive about spending time with me?" I ask once I drive onto the highway and toward our first location. Catalina looks thoughtful for a moment as she seems to consider my words.

The key-word being "seems."

"I'm not sure, but I'd rather not find out," she replies, which has me smiling despite how much I want to shake her.

"Let's make another deal. If by the end of the day you hate me a little less, I want you to give me a hug. Not a fake one. A real one. The kind of hugs you give Charlie," I say, still grinning because Cata throws a disgusted look my way.

"It'd take a miracle, so sure, Santi. And if I don't hate you less?"

"I'll buy you whatever you want."

"Sounds good. I've always wanted my own private jet that flies me to my own private island."

I burst into laughter, and finally, she joins me, her melodic voice filling the rental car until there is nothing left for me in the world but the extraordinary woman beside me.

# CHAPTER 16
## CATALINA

"What are we doing here?" I ask Santiago as he leads me to a restaurant/café called Higher Ground. He went so far as to reserve a table for us, and as nice as it is, I don't see any paparazzi to photograph us anywhere.

"We're here because this is our first stop of the day. And because when you get hungry, you get even angrier with me, and I'm trying to avoid that," he says right as a waitress places our cups of cappuccino in front of us, as well as the food we ordered.

"How thoughtful. Is our next stop a session of kickboxing so I refrain from kicking you, too?" His mouth stretches into one of his easy-going smiles, but he doesn't respond as he takes a bite of his Eggs Benedict.

"Eat, *mariquita*. We've got a long day ahead of us," he says, gesturing toward my matching eggs benedict.

I ordered first, and the jerk copied me.

"Of course, *mi corazón*," I reply through gritted teeth and a fake smile. That only makes him chuckle.

Santiago doesn't stop talking the whole time we're eating. He tells me about his matches and his strategy, and I listen even when I tell myself not to. What he's saying is interesting, and it's giving me ideas for my own strategy for my match the day after tomorrow. I curse him as I ask more questions, keeping the conversation going. I don't want to enjoy talking to Santiago. The silence that usually sat between us was much more comfortable than this awful feeling in my chest every time I realize how... *nice* this feels.

"Are you finished eating?" he eventually asks, leaning back in his seat.

I really do hate him for how effortlessly gorgeous he is. His brown hair is perfectly fluffy and styled, his amber eyes are practically sparkling with happiness, and his chiseled features and full, plump lips have me even more drawn to his face.

"Yes," I finally manage to reply when I remember he asked me a question. My face heats in embarrassment, but for once, Santi is kind enough not to point it out and make me even more aware of how painfully attracted I've always been to him.

"I have an exciting day planned, but if at any point, it gets too much for you, we can stop and do something else," he promises, leaning forward again to rummage around in the backpack he brought.

"You're scaring me, Santiago," I say with a breathless laugh because, while I'm not scared, I *am* nervous.

He doesn't say anything else, merely slides an envelope toward me.

On the back of it, it says, "Catalina's 24th Birthday Scavenger Hunt."

I deflate in my seat, sinking into it as tears shoot into my eyes. Every single birthday with my mother replays itself in my head, until my heart is crying, forcing more tears into my eyes. It isn't necessarily in a bad way. It's nostalgic, and while that is a bittersweet feeling in itself, I don't hate it. It makes me feel a little closer to the woman I loved with my whole heart and have been missing for so long.

"Hate it?" Santi asks softly, and I notice one of his hands has reached across the table in an offering. If I want his comfort, he will give it to me. If I don't want it, at least it'll be there in case I change my mind.

"Not even a little," I admit, placing the letter on my chest and taking a deep breath to fight back the tears.

"It's probably not as good as Doralis' scavenger hunts used to be, but I did my best."

His hand is still there, between us, and maybe it's because I miss Mamá so much. Maybe it's because he did something so wonderful for me, something I've been missing since she passed away. But I reach out and lace my fingers through his, letting his rough, callused hand spread warmth through my very system. Playing as much tennis as we do, it's difficult not to have rough hands. To have calluses at the top of our palms. I used to be so insecure about it, but Santi makes me feel a little less alone that way.

He makes me feel less alone in many ways.

"Thank you for this, Santiago," I manage to croak out, and he gives me a comforting smile.

"You're welcome, Catalina."

He urges me to open the letter for my first clue, and I can't help but smile as I do. He chose a paper with sea turtles painted along the borders, and I feel my stomach tumble all over again because he remembers.

He met my mamá once, but he remembers what she used to say because I told him one time when we were still kids.

On the paper inside, he wrote:

I'M COLORFUL AND COME IN VARIOUS SHAPES, SIZES, AND FORMS. I'M HAPPIEST WHEN THE SUN FINDS ME AND WHEN I GET TO DRINK LOTS OF WATER. YOU CAN FIND ME IN A SPECIAL PLACE WHERE PEOPLE STROLL PAST ME ALL DAY, ADMIRING ME.

It's an easy enough clue, but I don't mind. I like that the first one is easy because I know the next ones might get harder.

"Give me your keys. I'm driving," I say and hold out my hand. Santi doesn't waste a second to place it in the palm of my hand, smiling when he realizes I've already figured out where we have to go for the first clue.

We drive to the Royal Botanic Gardens Victoria here in Melbourne, and I jump giddily in my spot when Santiago tells me to find the second clue, we will have to go explore the gardens. I've always loved being in nature, and this is a perfect way to spend my birthday.

I find myself inching just a little closer to Santi without meaning to, simply because it feels right. When he notices, he takes my hand without commenting, and I tell myself it's because we might be surrounded by people who will recognize us or photograph us.

Not because he wants to hold my hand.

The best way I can describe parts of the botanical gardens is as a jungle you can easily walk through, with paths made by people for people. I admire all of the different types of plants and trees, studying the flowers even more closely.

Santiago and I walk and talk the whole way, and I find myself smiling so much, my cheeks burn. His amber eyes land on me the entire time, and when I see the pure joy in his eyes, I can't help but return it because this gift is so thoughtful.

"A clue hides in this section, so look even more closely," he says, and I see him staring at one tree about a hundred meters from where we are right now.

"You're horrible at this, Santi!" I scream before running to the tree, only to find nothing there.

"Am I?" he challenges once he's taken his sweet time walking toward me. I place my fists on my hips, staring at him as if that would tell me where the clue is. The smug smirk on his face tells me he didn't hide the clue anywhere here.

He must still have it on him, somewhere.

"Is it on you?" I ask, but he merely shrugs.

"Put your hands on me and find out," he offers, lifting his arms as if to invite me to inspect him.

"*Eres un cabrón*," I mumble with a suppressed smile as I stalk toward him, raising my hands to his chest. Santi continues to watch me with amusement, but lust creeps into his gaze too, making my heart race.

I slide my hands over his arms and back, but I find nothing. He waits patiently, but I hesitate when I reach his chest and stomach. My hands hover over him, my body almost shaking from what I'm doing.

What I'm about to do once he gives me the permission I'm seeking.

"Please touch me, *cariño*. I'm dying for you to," he begs, and I shiver visibly, something that doesn't go past Santi. He snakes two fingers around my wrist, pressing down on my pulse point. "Does this excite you as much as it does me?" he asks, using his free hand to lift his shirt and then guide my hand beneath it.

"No," I lie, but when I finally make contact with his abs, when I feel the hardness of them underneath my fingertips, I shiver all over again. My other hand slips under his shirt too, and Santiago tenses, his muscles pulling even tighter.

I barely bite back a surprised gasp, but I don't have time to celebrate keeping it inside when Santi shifts, making my fingers drop to the V-line that disappears into his pants. My stomach tumbles, and I feel a pulsing very... very low in my body.

I swallow hard.

"Santi, the clue isn't on you, is it?" He takes another step toward me, his eyes glazed over with desire.

"You haven't explored my mouth yet. Maybe it's hiding in there," he says, his voice hoarse. He leans down, his nose pressing against mine. "If I beg you to kiss me, will you?" God, would I? I do love it when men beg, preferably while they're on their knees, but everything with Santi is so complicated.

I need to slow things down.

Before I make a mistake.

"For someone who didn't want to kiss at the start of this, you sure have been taking every opportunity to try and get my mouth on yours," I say, his breath ghosting my lips, but he doesn't get closer. He never does. He always leaves it up to me if this is something we're going to do or not.

"I've wanted to kiss you for years, Catalina. Put me out of my misery." His words make the breath in my lungs turn to sand.

"I think you miss having sex, Santi. I don't think you want this."

"Two things can be true at the same time," he replies with a shiver, making me notice my hands are still under his shirt, my fingers mindlessly tracing his abs. "Do you want this?" he asks as I inhale, taking in his enchanting scent.

I blame that on finding him so irresistible right now.

"I don't know what I want." It's the honest answer, but if I'd known he'd pull away from me a little, I wouldn't have said it.

Which means I do know what I want.

And that turns my whole world upside down.

"One day, when you know, I'll ask again, and I hope you will kiss me then." He presses his lips against my cheek, then pulls back entirely, causing my hands to drop from his stomach. "Alright, well, the clue isn't on me," he admits with a laugh, but my head is still spinning, and I'm having a hard time getting over the fact that I'm… disappointed.

"Then where is it?" I ask once I find the ground under my feet again.

"Keep looking. It's in an obvious spot a little further ahead," he promises and walks past me, still smiling. There's a new tension to his body, but I have a feeling it isn't from anger. Maybe our moment had the same effect on him as it had on me. "*Vamos*, Catalina," he says when all I do is stare at his magnificent, round ass.

"*Ya voy*," I call back, blushing again.

The note ends up being taped under the table we pass, and I only notice it because Santi nudges me in the right direction.

This one reads:

I HOLD A THOUSAND STORIES. A THOUSAND LIFETIMES CAN BE LIVED IN HERE. I HOLD SECRETS FROM PEOPLE WHO HAVE NEVER LIVED IN OUR WORLD. I HOLD THE KIND OF LOVE AND MAGIC THE REAL WORLD WILL NEVER OFFER.

This one doesn't take me any time at all to figure out either, because he picked another favorite place of mine.

A bookstore.

"Which bookstore is it?" I ask, my gaze meeting his.

"I may have made these too easy. You keep finding out what they mean in three seconds," he says with a laugh, rubbing the back of his neck nervously. "I'm sorry."

"No, Santi, they are perfect. I love them so much," I say because I think of my mother's notes and how difficult it always was to figure out what she meant. I love Santi's because I don't think I could handle it if every detail was the same.

This is Santi's version.

Just his.

The Paperback Bookshop clue led us to the National Gallery of Victoria. From there, we went to the State Library Victoria, where we are right now. We can't speak loudly here, but Santiago keeps making me laugh anyway. We walk through the romantasy section, my favorite one, and I hate him for knowing that about me as well. I hate that he put the last note of the day in here.

"You pay way too much attention to me," I say as I pull it out from between not only one of my favorite books, but two of them.

"I disagree," he replies, tugging a loose strand of hair behind my ear.

His thumb briefly caresses the shell of it, but I stare down at the note to ignore how the tips of my ears are now burning.

IF YOU HADN'T BECOME A TENNIS PLAYER, THIS IS WHERE YOU WOULD HAVE SPENT ONE OUT OF TWENTY—SOMETHING IMPORTANT WEEKENDS OF THE YEAR.

I furrow my brows for a moment, not knowing what it means.

"I think I'm going to need another clue," I say, so he takes a step toward me, handing me another envelope.

I giggle at the two words written on this one.

## Vroom vroom.

When I was a kid, I used to go karting with my friend Lucian. For a while, I even thought about getting into racing, but tennis has always had my heart. And suddenly, his note makes complete sense.

"Please tell me this means we get to go to the Albert Park Grand Prix Circuit." Santi just holds out his hand, gesturing for me to go back to the exit and into the car.

I'm sprinting. Then, I'm almost speeding down the road to get there. It's seven in the evening now, but I'm too overfilled with adrenaline to feel tired. Santi is still grinning beside me, my happiness making him happy.

Because the race isn't for another couple of months, the track looks very different from how it does during the race weekend. But I still take it all in, joy ebbing and flowing through me in waves.

"This is the best gift anyone has given me in a long, long time, Santi," I say, covering my mouth with my hand as it forms an O-shape from pure amazement.

"Actually, I think this might be even better than the scavenger hunt," he replies, grabbing my free hand to twist me his way, all the way against his chest. He's holding another envelope, and I take it out of his hand, feeling extra greedy.

Inside hide two paddock passes to the Monaco Grand Prix and a note from Santi saying I will be able to get the hot lap experience with none other than my favorite Formula One driver.

Valentina Romana.

"The Monaco Grand Prix is at the same time we both have a little bit of a break. I thought we could attend it together, but you can take Charlie or—" I cut him off by wrapping my arms around him in a fierce hug.

I know he'll figure out my feelings for him are changing. It was our bet, after all, but I can't help it. The tears I was doing my best to hold back all day finally drop down my face, but at least I'm getting my revenge on Santi by soaking his nice shirt with them.

"I really thought you'd be the worst fake boyfriend, but you're actually pretty decent," I say, my palms flat against his muscular back.

"I'll take pretty decent," he says with a chuckle, and I feel his lips pressing against the crown of my head.

"Thank you for everything, Santi. I'm so happy right now," I add, because I know tomorrow I can go back to being irritated with him.

For now, he's done something so sweet, it feels wrong to let our past taint the moment.

"Happy birthday, *mi mariquita*."

# CHAPTER 17
## SANTIAGO

Catalina hugged me.

For several minutes.

I smile every time I think about it.

Yes, she touched me before. She couldn't stop touching my body in the park, but there is a difference between touching someone out of desire and touching them because you're so overcome by emotion, the only thing you can do is hold onto them. To let them hold you in return and steady you while you work through the truckload of emotions hitting your chest.

That's what that hug was yesterday, and fuck, I know it was *just a hug*, but it was one from Catalina. They're as rare as seeing a shooting star in the night sky, and they feel as good as a warm bath after a physically exhausting day.

"Semi-finals, Santiago. I'm going to need you to stop thinking about Catalina long enough to win this match," Papá says, dragging me out of my thoughts.

"I'm not thinking about her," I lie, still stretching to warm up.

"And I don't think about your mother twenty-three hours a day. We can lie to each other, but it won't get us anywhere," he replies, making me grin. God, that man is so wrapped around Mamá's finger. It's adorable.

"You think about her in your sleep?" I challenge, but he crosses his muscular arms over his chest and smirks at me.

"Naturally. She is the star of all my dreams. Isn't Cata the star of yours?" I throw my towel at his head, but he catches it with a chuckle.

Manuela appears in my warm-up room, the dark circles underneath her eyes making my heart drop. She told me she was going to be here before my match, but she sounded okay over the phone. She didn't sound like she looks.

Devastated.

"Manu, *que pasó?*" I ask, standing up and taking three quick strides toward her. My hands find her arms, and she lets me hold onto her as she tells me something that shatters my heart for her.

"She broke up with me," she says, tears filling her already reddened eyes. Manu must have been crying a lot since it happened, and I feel even worse for not having been there for her.

"I'm so sorry," I say and pull her into a hug. She lets it happen for several seconds before stepping back and letting out a breath.

"It doesn't matter now. Go win your match. We can talk after." I'm not happy with that at all, but Papá pulls Manu into a bear hug, offering her comfort. She starts sobbing into his chest, and I realize she doesn't need me.

My sister needs her parents.

I shove all of that aside, no matter how much I don't want to.

There is a match I have to win. Cata will be watching, too, which means I have to be even more impressive. We already practiced early this morning, when she wore a shirt that read, "Women should rule the world."

She seemed very content with my consistency. In turn, I was impressed with the drop shots, volleys, and overhead smashes she was hitting my way.

Her listening to my feedback and adjusting her game to take more risks, try out more things, is hopefully going to help her win her first Grand Slam this week.

She's so close. Yet again, she's only two matches from winning a title, and I want that for her. I want her to know what it feels like to soak in the glory of winning a tournament like this. Plus, it would help her immensely in getting closer to overtaking Layla as the number one female tennis player in the world.

My competition of the day is Winston Finnick. He's number four in the world, and I'm a little more nervous this time than I was last time. My anxiety has my hands shaking and my heart racing, but I take several deep breaths, holding them for a few seconds, before releasing them again. The sight of Cata eases the feeling of panic even more, and I wish I knew why all it takes to settle me is that grumpy look on her face. She's locked down her feelings once more, even after how much we bonded yesterday, but I don't mind.

I know what happened between us.

She knows.

Nothing can take that away from us.

My thoughts are interrupted by the umpire urging me to meet Winston at the net so we can flip the coin, like it's done before every match. We take pictures, we shake hands with the umpire, and then it's time to warm up. I'm allowed to start serving once more, which is a nice change from the three-in-a-row matches I was not allowed to begin.

"Remember, his backhand is his strongest shot. Go for his forehand," Cata says as I drop my towel in its proper place. I nod but don't look at her again because I'm trying to focus.

We're in the Rod Laver Arena, which is the main court during this tournament. As the number one player, they always put me on the main one. It's how it's done in tennis.

I notice several people staring intensely at my arms, which are covered by nothing. There is a reason the designer of *New Light* never puts sleeves on my shirts. Well, except during Wimbledon, but only because they have certain rules there that need to be abided.

The umpire says what she needs to and then we're finally allowed to start the game. My nerves settle even more as I position myself at the baseline, near the center of it. The toe of my shoe points to the outer pole of the net, my left hand holding the ball to serve and my right holding my racket in the proper grip. I take one more deep breath as I bounce the ball, drowning out the rest of the world.

People who don't play tennis wouldn't understand how much this simple bouncing motion helps center a player. How it prepares them for the rally that could win them or cost them a point.

For me, it's vital.

As a fast server, I welcome the opportunity to set the tone of my match. And today, I set it by serving an ace right down the center line at two hundred and twenty kilometers per hour—which is fucking fast—and leaving Winston standing in the same spot, frustration already seeping in.

No part of me is planning to take it easy on him. That is not who tennis players are. Any athlete, really. We come to win, and we will fight with everything we've got.

The first game goes to me, and it takes mere minutes. The second game also goes to me, which is not good for him but fantastic for me. The third game is mine as well. I don't celebrate the shots he doesn't get in, only the ones I place well in the corners or the drop shots I manage to surprise him with, so he doesn't reach them in time.

The first set flies by, and he only manages to win two of his service games. We sit down for the set break, and I take a sip of my electrolytes, water, and even bite off a piece of my banana to keep up my energy. While I'm playing well so far, I have to ensure I continue to do so until I have secured three sets.

The afternoon sun is blinding on one side of the court now, the one I'm occupying at the moment. Catalina, Papá, Mamá, Manu, and the rest of my team are on the opposite side, and I have to squint my eyes a little in order to see them. Catalina is wearing her sunglasses, like always, and Papá is talking to her about something that makes her nod over and over. Manu has her expression shut down, and I do my best to breathe past the worry in my chest.

Winston pulls my attention to him as he positions himself across the court from me, and I get ready to serve again. I win the first game of the second set without much of a threat from him. But when we get to his service game, he steps it up so much, I'm struggling to get to his balls. He's in full control of most rallies, and I have no idea what the fuck happened to make him come back so strong after the set break.

*"Joder,"* I mumble to myself after he wins his game in four points, which means I made no points.

I wipe my face with my towel, then my hands. My eyes drift to Cata without meaning to, and I notice she's lifted her sunglasses to let me see the determination in her blue eyes. She shifts them to where Winston is wiping his face, too. I love that my little rain cloud glares at him like she wants me to rip his head off, and I love it even more when I remember that she used to look at me that way, but now her expression softens when she glances my way once more.

The message is clear, no words needing to be spoken.

Determination sets in stronger than ever before.

My next service game is another easy win because he's still struggling to get my fast and well-placed serve, so I focus on his service game.

I want to steal it.

Winston gets ready to serve, his body turned the other way than mine would be because he's left-handed.

He usually places the ball wide in the service box, so I stand a bit nearer to the edge of the court, anticipating where he's going to go. If he were me, he'd go down the center line, but he isn't. He goes wide, as I expected, and I send the ball straight down the court. Winston somehow makes it to it, but I'm already running to the net to volley it to the other side of the court. With a beautifully placed backhand volley, I win the point.

The crowd roars my name, and I smirk to myself as I take it all in. They love me. I'm their golden boy. They want me to win, so I'm going to win for them. I'm going to give them the final they're hoping for, now that my biggest rival and number two player in the world RenjunChoi got kicked out in the quarter final. Playing against him is a challenge because he's basically a wall, every shot gets back to you if you don't switch things up.

Winston places the serve near the center line this time, but since it's his second serve, it comes slower, and I have enough time to react. I return the ball, and it lands right in front of him. He takes control of the rally, making me run left to right to left, then forward toward the net. I'm sprinting to get every ball, and when one of his shots hits the net but drops down my side close to the front, I practically stumble to get it. I don't know how the fuck it lands on the opposite side of him, making it impossible for him to catch it, but my heart almost explodes from happiness.

"*Vamos!*" I scream, hearing Catalina yell the same word. I lift my hand and rile up the crowd, my eyes finding my fake girlfriend. She's standing and clapping, punching the air with her fist proudly.

It's in that moment when I realize I've always loved celebrating with my team, but I was missing her up there all along. I was missing my ex-doubles partner and rival, turned enemy, turned fake girlfriend, sending more victory through my veins, even if it's just for one point. Granted, it was a difficult, nearly impossible point to get, but it's just a point.

I have yet to win the match.

For the last time today, I serve my ball fast and wide, an ace that wins me the match and sends me into the finals. A victorious sound leaves my lips, and I face my team directly as I let it out. Cata is standing again, clapping and nodding because she's still so proud of me, and Papá, Mamá, and Manu mimic her stance.

The adrenaline has my heart racing as I walk toward my bag. I take my time removing my shirt and putting on the hoodie *New Light* made me. I add the watch from my other sponsor and then drink some more water.

After every match, except the final, the person who lost leaves the court while the person who won stays to get interviewed. Today, I'm getting interviewed by tennis legend Nicholas Gonzales. He's got a warm smile on his face, his brown eyes sparkling with the kind of pride I wouldn't have expected him to feel for me. I've only ever met this man twice, but perhaps he's proud of me because I play for Spain, just like he did.

"Well done, Santiago. What a match you played," he starts, and I smile at him as I stand behind the microphone they put on the court for me. It's in a stand, so I don't even have to hold it. I can simply talk into it, which helps with all of my pent-up nervous energy.

"Thank you," I reply, my attention drifting behind him where Cata is sitting, watching me. "Honestly, the crowd is amazing, and having my girlfriend here to support me for the first tournament has spurred me on even more," I say, and the people go wild in their seats, whistling and screaming. My cheeks heat a little, but Cata just covers her eyes, which have widened ever so slightly, with her sunglasses and crosses her arms in front of her chest.

I didn't have to do that. After our date yesterday, pictures of us have circulated everywhere. Ever since the beginning of the tournament, people in the tennis world have not stopped discussing our relationship. How we sit in each other's boxes. How I look at her. How we seem perfect for one another.

So, I didn't have to lay it on so thick, but it isn't a lie.

I love having her here.

And I don't have to fake a thing when I tell the world that.

# CHAPTER 18
## CATALINA

"We wish we could be there," Ori says, and I offer her, Hernanda, and Samuel a sad smile. They're all video calling me before the final game of the Australian Open. A couple of days ago, I won my semi-final match and made it into the final.

To play against Layla.

My hands have been shaking all day, but I try to ignore them as much as I can, especially in front of my siblings. Hernanda and Samuel expect me to always stay put together. I'm their older sister who has been like a parent figure for them most of their life. I cannot fall apart from nerves and self-doubts. They wouldn't know what to do, especially because they're still so young. I cannot burden them with any of my problems.

"I wish you were here, too, but hey, at least Hernanda didn't have to miss the golf tournament where she won *another* trophy," I say with the biggest grin on my face. Hernanda's pale skin turns a dark pink shade around the apples of her cheeks as she blushes. Her dark brown eyes sparkle with pride she's trying to hide.

"It was nothing," she mumbles, moving out of the frame so the attention is no longer on her. She's the shyest out of all of us Sanchez's, even with her family.

"How about me winning the Science Fair trophy?" Samuel chimes in, but he doesn't bother to hide his smile. His whole face lights up with it, and I welcome his happy expression. My little brother is the most confident of us all. He's smarter than anyone his age has a right to be, and he's also extremely popular with all of his classmates.

"You did? Congratulations, Sam, I am so proud," I say, tears shooting into my eyes. I keep stretching to warm up, taking several deep breaths to get rid of the emotion weighing heavily on my chest.

"Thank you! And thank you for my new wheelchair. My last one kept stalling randomly," he explains, but I already knew that.

Ori had spoken to me about his need for a new wheelchair. He has spina bifida, which caused him to be born without the ability to walk. Before I became a professional tennis player who earned a lot of money, I vowed I would earn enough to buy my brother a wheelchair that worked better than what he had to struggle with before. I bought him one a while ago, a good one, but a wheelchair can only last so long until there are some issues with it. And even if they can be fixed, I have the means to continue to buy my brother the top-of-the-line ones for his comfort.

"Anything for you, Sami," I reply, and he throws me a kiss before putting his hands on the sides of his wheelchair and rolling out of the frame, leaving Ori and me alone.

"I know you're very nervous. I know this feels like an impossible task, but no matter what happens today, I am so proud of you. Mamá would be so proud of you, *hermanita*. You have accomplished so much in your twenty-four years. You will achieve so much more."

I appreciate what she's trying to do, but it's not helping.

Not today.

"I have achieved nothing that Mamá had achieved at my age. I have not won a title. I have not been number one at any point. If I don't win today, I have a horrible feeling hopelessness is going to take over, and I won't be able to find a way out."

Layla has taken the first set.

Nothing I'm doing is working. It's as if she's prepared for any type of strategy I attempt to use to get a point. She is in control of every single rally. I hardly got any points in the first set. The crowd is mostly silent because they are so shocked at how horribly I am playing.

Okay, maybe that isn't why they're not cheering as much. Perhaps they're so quiet because they came for an epic match, but all I've given them so far is disappointment. My face falls as I think about that, but my heart is racing too quickly for me to try to fight for a neutral expression to take over again. When I'm losing, I get incredibly nervous. Panic always wraps itself around me like vines around trees.

Tears sometimes fill my eyes too, like right now. The possibility of more failure, another Grand Slam lost, has my pain pooling in my eyes. I grab my towel and cover my face, taking deep breaths to fight back the urge to cry.

I used to do that as a child. When I was playing matches and was losing, I'd throw tantrums. I'd scream. I'd be so afraid of failing, I'd run off the court.

I'm not a child anymore, so I don't run. I don't scream. I certainly don't throw tantrums, but I can't help the way my body responds when I feel cornered. When nothing I do is working against Layla.

"*Inhala y exhala*, Cata," I tell myself, taking one deep breath and then releasing it again.

Things are far from over, and I won't give up yet.

Once my tears are under control, I lower my towel again, grabbing my electrolytes. I take a big swig, then another sip of my water, still avoiding eye contact with anyone in my box. Santiago has been standing since the set break started, trying to get my attention.

I've been ignoring him.

I know what he'll tell me.

*Take risks, Catalina.*

*Get out of your comfort zone and try something new.*

*You won't win if you don't change things up.*

And while he would be right about all of it, I *have* tried other things. I have taken risks, but Layla is too strong a tennis player.

It's my turn to serve when the second set starts, and I hate that I have to put my towel where Santi, Charlie, and the rest of my team are sitting.

"*Cariño*, get out of your head. You won't win if you keep overthinking everything. You have to feel the game." Santiago's words are nothing more than background noise I drown out.

*Feeling* the game is a bullshit concept I can't do anything with. I need a strategy that works. I need to find a rhythm for myself that knocks Layla off balance.

I need, I need, I need.

The ball kid on my side of the court throws me several balls, and I inspect three of them before handing one back, sliding another into the pocket of the shorts that are under my dress, and bouncing the last one up and down. I take a few deep breaths, doing my best to focus on the game.

She will need two sets to win, and I won't make this easy on her.

Mamá used to tell me five words to think about when I was losing. Five words that would give me back balance and help me win the game, even if it seemed hopeless.

Breathe.

Analyze.

Adjust.

Focus.

Win.

It's almost as if she was giving me steps to follow. Breathe to slow my nervous heart. Analyze the game. Adjust according to my analysis. Focus on going through with my new plan. And win.

Simple enough when one looks at it from such a two-dimensional view.

Things are never so easy, though.

"*Vamos, mariquita,*" Santi calls out before the whole crowd in the Rod Laver Arena goes silent as I prepare to serve.

My first serve goes too far, which doesn't help with my whole "recentering" thing because it only makes me feel even less confident. My hands start shaking as I bounce the ball to get ready for my second serve.

It goes out, too.

A double fault is not fucking great at this point in the game. I swallow another wave of tears as I wipe my face with my towel. Love-fifteen.

What a way to start the set.

"Come on, Catalina," I mumble to myself as I place the towel down again, letting one of the ball kids hand me three more balls. I repeat the same process as earlier, only this time, I don't care which ball I choose. I pretend like I do for the crowd, but I'm not actually looking.

I don't know how not to get rattled. It's always been like this. Sometimes I wonder how I even got the second-place spot in the world rankings, considering how horribly I react once I'm under pressure. Tennis players are taught to deal with these feelings, to ignore the score and go one point at a time.

Seems like I didn't get the fucking memo.

The second point of the game goes to Layla too, making it love-thirty.

More nerves continue to make my hands shake, and I barely keep my whole body from trembling.

"Thank you," I hear the umpire say, and I realize the crowd has started chanting.

For... me.

They keep going, even as the umpire repeatedly tells them to quiet down, and I don't miss that Santiago is the one screaming the loudest. Spurring me on. Encouraging me. Showing me he believes in me.

Crowds do this when their favorite players are losing, to try and build them up and give them new energy.

A new wave of emotion hits my chest at the realization of how many people support me, want me to win. I thought most of the people here are Layla's fans, and while they are, the rest that are mine are using their voice to the fullest extent.

There are rows upon rows screaming my name, urging me on in this tennis battle that I'm losing at the moment.

But when I serve again, and though it's a fantastic serve, Layla's return is too good for me to catch.

The next point, a break point for her, I lose, too.

She takes my first service game of the set, and all she has to do is bring home her service games until she reaches six games.

Which she does.

Layla wins the match in two sets, and I leave all of my fans, my family, my team, everyone disappointed once more as the Grand Slam title slips through my fingers and right into my biggest rival's hands.

I fucked up.

This is entirely my fault.

And I want to scream at the top of my lungs because Mamá isn't even here to hold me and tell me everything will be alright, that I'll get another chance.

Tears fall and I don't stop them this time.

I'm in too much pain to do so.

# CHAPTER 19
## SANTIAGO

Catalina has been hiding from me for hours since she lost the match against Layla. I tried to go to her after the match to comfort her, but she disappeared. Charlie left to go with her, but they wouldn't tell me where they were going.

Up until twenty minutes ago, when they texted me, telling me Catalina needed me.

*Me.*

Granted, I'm convinced she didn't ask for me and Charlie is simply lost trying to help my *mariquita*, but I'm more than happy to have Cata scream at me for an hour if it makes her feel better about the result today. If she needs to let out her anger, if she needs me to be her punching bag, I'll be the recipient of her frustration.

It's become abundantly clear to me that I'd be just about anything for Catalina if it means she lets me be around her a little longer.

Some might call me pathetic—with some I mean Matteo—but I can't help it.

I crave her presence like water during a particularly humid match.

My knuckles brush against her hotel room door, but Cata doesn't open it for me. Instead, Charlie reveals their worried expression as they unlock it.

"Where is she?" I ask, even more concern filling my chest.

"On the floor, in front of her bed, staring blankly at the television," they reply, grabbing their bag and jacket before moving back toward the door. "I'll go grab her some *patatas bravas* and a bit of *leche frita* to cheer her up. She likes to feel close to her mamá when she loses a tournament like this, and food and music are a big way for her to do so," Charlie explains and then leaves, shutting the door behind them.

I waste no time getting to Catalina.

As Charlie said, she's sitting on the floor, tears streaming down her face as she stares at the television that isn't turned on. It's a black screen, but I'm almost glad she isn't torturing herself by watching replays of her match.

"Hey, *cariño*," I say softly, but Cata doesn't even lift her head to look at me. "Can I sit with you?" Nothing. No response. She simply continues staring at the TV, not moving except for the steady stream of tears flowing down her cheeks.

This is exactly how I get during a depressive episode. I don't talk much. Darkness consumes every part of me, so I often don't have the energy to do anything at all. Manu usually helps me open up, to talk about it until I feel better, but everyone responds to depression, anxiety, or any other mental illness differently.

But I only know one way to deal with it from experience, so I go with what I know best.

"I'm absolutely terrified about the match tomorrow. Blake is a really good player, and although I've won every match against him so far, I don't feel as confident as I normally do," I rant, trying to get any kind of reaction out of her.

Cata doesn't even look at me.

"Have you eaten yet? I'm starving. Charlie said they're getting some food, so I'm very excited. Papá never lets me eat whatever I want the night before matches because—" Catalina carefully places a hand over my mouth, shutting me up mid-sentence.

"*Yo sé que a ti te encanta el sonido de tu voz, pero no necesito tus palabras. Necesito silencio,*" she says, keeping her hand on my mouth. I kiss the palm of her hand, surprising her so much, she removes it, giving me the chance to speak. I don't. Not yet.

Words won't help her. The fact that she hasn't yelled at me yet for being here, for being so annoying, shows how detached she feels from reality as she wallows in her pain.

I lift my hand to wipe away a tear that drips down her face, and Cata leans into the touch as soon as I cup her face. My heart flutters at the sight, my stomach tumbling. One wrong move, and I will ruin the moment, so I stay as still as possible.

A habit I've adopted since I promised myself I'd make it up to Catalina.

She stares directly into my eyes, and I feel myself holding my breath, hoping she will never look away. Hoping she might want to stay in this moment for as long as I do.

"You have such beautiful eyes," she says seconds later, my thumb finding courage in her words to start rubbing along the apple of her cheek.

"I do?" I ask, my voice breaking a little.

Catalina is the romantic one of the two of us. It's not surprising she'd say something so sweet. It simply surprises me that she would say that to *me*.

"I've always thought so, but I never said it out loud. I was too angry," she replies, raising her hand to run her fingers over my left brow. I drop my hand to the side of her neck, letting her study me as much as she wants.

"Are you not angry with me anymore?" The only thing keeping me from begging for her forgiveness is me biting down on my tongue.

"I still am. You fucked up and didn't even apologize for it. You got angry with me in return, and that isn't something I can simply let go of. Not after a decade of building resentment."

Although her words have my heart beating a little more heavily, she continues to trace my features. She even uses her second hand to place her thumb on my bottom lip, running it along its length.

"Which is a shame because you have a wonderful soul, Santi. You are kind and so special. You used to be one of my favorite people, and it makes me sad whenever I think about how far apart we've drifted."

"Catalina—" She presses her finger down where it rests on my mouth, shutting me up before I can respond to everything she's said.

"I'm emotional because of the loss today and saying things I'll probably regret having voiced tomorrow. There is nothing you can say to magically fix anything right now, so maybe it's best if you say nothing at all," she goes on, and I can't even argue with her because I'm not about to tell her how to feel.

Cata has gone through a lot today, and while I thought she might scream at me, call me every terrible name in the English and Spanish languages, she hasn't.

Perhaps letting her anger out on me isn't what she needs after all.

"I am sorry, though. For everything, Catalina. I had no right to my anger. You didn't deserve my prioritizing my career over our goals. You didn't deserve many of the things I did." She runs her index finger over my other eyebrow now, studying its thick shape.

"You deserved a lot of the things I did and said." She smiles a little, but it falls soon after. Her eyes drop to my lips, stopping my breathing once more.

"I did," I whisper, trying not to tremble when she leans forward, still studying my mouth.

"Santi?" she asks, and I press down on the side of her neck, trying to feel if her heart is racing as quickly as mine is.

It is.

"Yes, *cariño*?"

"I kind of want to do something else I'll regret tomorrow." I swallow hard, attempting to speak, but I can't find words when she drops her hand from my brow to my bicep and squeezes it gently.

Her thumb stays on my bottom lip.

"And what is that?" I don't sound like myself, but that might be because of the hope and excitement in my chest taking over as she moves even closer to me.

"I want to put my lips here," she says, her thumb pressing down on my bottom lip before she drops it.

I lean toward her without hesitation, desperate for exactly what she's describing.

But then the door flies open as Charlie walks back into the hotel suite, sending me flying backwards.

Catalina slowly leans away, dragging her knees to her chest and closing herself off from me once more.

Fuck.

"I'll see you tomorrow, Santi."

It's a clear dismissal, and I hate the way I want to run, too. I have to get out of here. I have to go find Matteo and talk to him because only my best friend is going to be able to talk to me about what the fuck is happening.

I kiss the top of Catalina's head, squeeze Charlie's arm as I walk past them, and then sprint all the way to Matteo's room door as panic consumes me.

My fist connects with his door aggressively, over and over, until he opens it, revealing he's in nothing but boxers and his hair is all over the place.

I've never been more glad that he's staying at the same hotel as Cata, even when he looks ready to kill me.

"Santiago, what the fuck do you want? I was trying to sleep," he says, but I storm past him and into his room, unable to breathe properly.

This is usually how I feel before my anxiety attacks, but for some reason, it also feels entirely different. It's more panic than anxiety, which is bad enough in its own way.

"Okay, you're scaring me. What's wrong?" Matteo asks as I sink down on his couch, wrapping the blanket he put there around myself. I cover my head and body until all he can see is my face.

"I'm in so much trouble," I state, holding the blanket around me more firmly.

"Why? Did you rob a bank?" I shake my head. "Did your nudes get leaked?" Again, I shake my head. "Then what can be so bad?"

"I think you were right. I think I... I have feelings for my fake girlfriend."

Rocking back and forth on my best friend's hotel room couch, I keep the blanket clutched in my hands and wrapped around myself. I've been in this exact same position for a while now, but Matteo left five minutes ago, after unsuccessfully trying to snap me out of my panicked state.

I've never had falling-in-love type of *feelings* for someone before. I've been amazing at avoiding them, mostly because a relationship has never been appealing to me. The overthinking, being absolutely naked emotionally, the commitment, it all terrified me.

And most of all, I have always been too scared of dragging someone down into the depths of my depression and anxiety to truly let them in.

And I was so fucking unsuccessful. I didn't want anything more than a night with a person for so long, but I should have known the reason for that wasn't because I was trying to spare myself and the other person.

The reason was and has always been Catalina.

"How long has he been like this?" I hear my sister ask as she walks through the door.

"Twenty minutes, more or less," Matteo replies, and if I could, I'd refocus my gaze enough to look at both of them. Then again, if I could, I'd tell them I'm fine. Even if it would be a bold lie they'd be able to see through.

"Santi, talk to me. Is this an anxiety attack?" Manu asks, but I shake my head.

We saw each other mere hours ago, talking about how she was feeling about the breakup, but when I left she looked worse than she does right now. I think worrying about me is allowing her to forget about her own pain, which is at least something.

"No? Then what's wrong? Why have you cocooned yourself?" she asks, waving her hands around to gesture at my current appearance.

"I... have feelings for Cata," I say, hiding even more in the blanket to shield me from whatever expression that is going to take over my sister's face.

"This is a rather dramatic response, don't you think? We all knew you had feelings for her, Santi. How you didn't is beyond me." I lower the blanket just enough to peek at her, still attempting to hide because this conversation terrifies me.

"How did you know?" I ask, my words muffled through the blanket.

"Hmm, let me think. You constantly talk about her. You have done so ever since you met her. You are incapable of committing to a relationship, but ever since you started 'dating' Lina, you have not looked at anyone else. You claim to be a playboy, fucking your way through all of Monaco, but you've done that as a way to ignore the fact that it's always been Catalina. From the moment you met over ten years ago, it has been her, and that hasn't changed. If anything, since finding out you were the jerk to ruin your relationship with her, you've done everything in your power to fight for her forgiveness."

I swallow hard, trying to form words and tell her how ridiculous that is, but the argument dies on my tongue seconds before I can bring it to life.

"You can lie and pretend all you'd like, but you're not fooling anyone. You want to be with Catalina. Not because you're forced to be together. You want to be with her because you care for her, and you want her to desire you in the same way."

"Manu, the more you talk, the less I can breathe," I admit, placing a hand on my chest to settle my racing heart back into a normal rhythm.

It's a hopeless attempt.

"I won't say anything more except that you need to get some rest. Tomorrow is an important day. You can freak out about this realization after winning another Slam, okay?"

Tennis is good. Tennis is a safe topic.

I'd much rather focus on that, on all of the pressure that will be on my shoulders tomorrow, than on the one currently pressing down on my chest.

Catalina Sanchez will not distract me from my career.

I might have feelings for her, but they mean nothing. They *can't* mean anything.

I don't want the first and only person I've had feelings for to be the one who hates me most in the world.

But with my fucking luck, of course she is.

# CHAPTER 20
## CATALINA

Two regrets gnaw at me today.

One, I could have played better yesterday and won my first title.

Two, I almost kissed Santiago, and if Charlie hadn't walked in, I would have.

It wasn't because I was sad either. It wasn't because he was the only one who was there and comforting me. It was because he's been doing everything in his power to allow us to grow closer, and no matter how much I'm fighting it, fighting this draw he has on me, it's impossible. Santi has always been irresistible to me because of his smile, the way physical touch is his love language, and the way he cares for people. His good looks and charisma are the cherries on top, and with his maximum effort put into getting me to like him, I have found myself inching closer and closer, blurring the line I drew between us after what happened years ago.

But it can't happen again. When this season is over, Santi and I will go our separate ways. We will "break up" for the whole world to witness, and then we will never see each other again.

It's what I told him I wanted only a few weeks ago.

So why does the thought of not constantly being around him make me feel so... sad?

"He's got this. You don't have to look so scared," Carlos says, dragging me out of my thoughts. I look up at Santi's dad, a man who looks identical to him, from his dark brown hair to his tan skin and amber eyes.

"I know he does. I'm not worried," I reply.

I'm not worried Santi will lose today. I'm worried about the feelings I'm developing for him again. Because this isn't the first time I've felt something for Santiago Javier Castillo.

In a way, I wish it was because then I wouldn't have the regret from last time reminding me what a horrible decision it is to feel anything but contempt for the man with the tree trunks as thighs and the sunshine smile.

Charlie settles down in the seat beside me, placing a comforting arm around my shoulders as we watch Santi warm up for his match with his rival of the day, world number four, Blake Houser. Normally, this box is for Santi's team and friends. It isn't for Charlie, but he allows them to be here, with me, every single match. He knows that their company brings me a lot of comfort, and the jerk seems to be obsessed with my happiness these days.

"How are you feeling?" Charlie asks for the third time today, and I lean into their embrace.

"Like ass. But I have to put on a show. For Santi. For our fake relationship." And if I'm being honest, being here distracts me from my failure and all the dark thoughts it comes with.

Wondering if I'll ever be good enough to win a title.

Wondering if I'll ever be good enough to become number one.

Wondering if I've wasted my life in a sport that I will never be as good at as my mother.

Wondering if she'd be disappointed in me if she could see how often I've failed at something she excelled at.

"Fuck the pretense, Catalina. If you're not feeling up for it, we will leave."

There are no words for how much I love Charlie. They are my best friend, without a shadow of doubt, and they're always in my corner when I need them. It shouldn't be possible to be so close to someone who manages my career and kicks my ass in training more often than not, but somehow, we make it work.

"That's not very managery of you," I say with a small smile, and they squeeze my shoulder.

"Your mental health will always come first."

Their lips find the side of my head before they let go of me entirely, clapping along with the rest of the people present here in the Rod Laver Arena for the final match of the Australian Open.

I clap too, watching Santiago and Blake get ready to start their first set.

My fake boyfriend has this habit of looking at me before, during, and after his matches, and he does the same now. His eyes meet mine, and I give him a single nod, my scowl firmly set in place even as he smiles at me.

The first half hour of the match is uneventful. Blake started serving, and there have been no break points for either of them. It's three games to three, both of them so evenly matched that not even I have any clue how Santi could adjust his game to be more aggressive and fight for a break point. He already plays a lot more aggressively than most, but Blake has been in the world of tennis for a lot longer than Santi. He's more experienced, and he has this way of anticipating what Santi is about to do before he even raises his racket.

"He needs to approach the net more," I tell Carlos after three more games, the score now five games to four for Blake.

"It's risky. Blake is too good at placing his shots wherever he needs them to go with consistency," he replies, our voices quiet as we wait for both players to finish their water breaks.

They only have ninety seconds between games, two minutes between sets, but those can feel like an eternity for me. I don't like sitting still at any point in my matches. I know it's important, Charlie always tells me it is, but I have this irrational fear that if I sit down during a match I'm doing well in, I'll lose my rhythm.

"Yeah, but if he keeps going like this, I can assure you, they'll be fighting out every set in tiebreaks, and Santi isn't the best at those."

As if he heard my words, Santi looks up at me, smiling in amusement.

Since he's already looking at me, I lean forward in my seat, placing my hands on the railing in front of me like I did last time. I mouth the words, "Approach the net more," in Spanish for him, and he tilts his head, confused. I mouth them again, and this time, his eyes widen in understanding. His eyes drift to the net as he seems to consider my words, then he slowly starts nodding repeatedly.

"I hope it won't come back to bite him in the ass," Carlos says, but I shake my head.

"No, Santi is fantastic at the net. He has to start approaching it," I say, hearing Carlos chuckle beside me. "What?"

"You two were so set on being against this relationship, against becoming hitting partners, but both of you are absolutely amazing at it. Down to pretending you care even when no one is watching."

My lips seal shut, but if I didn't respect him so much, I would shoot Carlos a disgusted look. Unfortunately, I think he's a great coach, a good father, a kind human being, and an amazing tennis player.

Plus, he's not wrong.

I care. No one is watching me right now, they're too busy focusing on the match, and yet, I care so much I try to find ways to help Santi win. I could blame my love for tennis, but if that were the case, I might as well give Blake tips on how to beat Santi. Except only thinking about that makes me sick to my stomach.

Santiago moves to the baseline on his side of the court, waiting for the ball kid to hand him three balls. He inspects them carefully before giving the ball back, sliding one of them into his pockets and bouncing the other on the court.

"*Vamos*, Santi." I clap after the words have left my mouth, encouraging him.

His eyes are trained on the ball, but he smiles like he's very happy I'm so invested. He should only be focusing on his match, but this man apparently has time to be distracted by me anyway.

If I didn't know better, I'd think Santi is obsessed with me.

His first serve of the game is aggressive, sending Blake to the side far enough, that Santi has a chance to run to the net and volley his return to the other side of the court.

A bright smile covers his face as he spins to point his racket my way. He uses his left hand and the face of the racket to clap, clearly applauding my advice. I blush instantly, sliding down in my seat to avoid the way several hundreds of eyes move in my direction. It's pointless, but trying makes me feel a bit better.

The second point he wins is an ace. The third one is an unforced error from Blake, and the fourth is a forehand winner from Santi, a powerful shot that has me standing up and clapping.

It's now five games to five.

"Get that break, Santi," Carlos calls out from beside me as his son wipes his face with his towel. He doesn't look at his father, but he nods, acknowledging the words.

Blake is still composed despite how badly he lost the previous game, but he's not known for being quick to anger on the tennis court. I think in his entire fifteen-year career as a professional tennis player, he's slammed his racket against the ground once. Even Santi has done so more frequently out of frustration, but he has never broken a racket.

In general, it's against the rules to break your rackets or be so angry you behave unsportsmanly. You either get warnings or, if it happens often enough, you get disqualified. Tennis is very strict when it comes to respecting your equipment, opponent, and all the people who make a match happen.

It's unlike many other sports.

Santiago battles for every point in this next game. He approaches the net twice, winning one more point and losing another to a mistake he makes. All in all, I think approaching the net more is helping him in the way I hoped it would, and he even starts becoming more creative. More like his usual playing. He switches between forehand and backhand winners, dropshots, and volleys. He's doing so well, minutes later, he finally has a break point. The first of the match.

I hold my breath as Blake positions himself at the baseline, bouncing his ball as he prepares to serve. His first one goes too long, and his second one is slow enough for Santi to hit it hard and place it in the corner, another forehand winner.

"Let's go!" I call out as the crowd cheers, roaring in the way they tend to do for their favorite players.

Santi points at me again, then places his index finger on his temple. I throw him a kiss because everyone is watching us, and it feels like the girlfriend thing to do. He blushes so violently, I can't help feeling one creep up my neck too.

Carlos chuckles, but this time, I nudge him in the side, trying not to feel as embarrassed as I do. Not because I'm embarrassed Santi and I had a moment. We've been having those for weeks. I'm embarrassed that it felt real and the whole world watched.

Santiago brings his service game home, securing him the first set of the game.

One out of three.

The way he's playing right now, there is nothing standing in his way of winning this title.

# CHAPTER 21
## SANTIAGO



It's two sets to two.

It all comes down to this last set, and I'm fucking exhausted. I started off so well, winning the first set, but then everything went downhill for the following two sets. Blake has been so consistent and crafty, not even I could reach his shots for those two sets. I doubt anyone could have.

In the fourth set, I finally managed to get my act together, and I won it six games to four, so it's all going to come down to this set. Whether I have it in me to win or if I'm going to be too distracted and out of it to do so. Which is fucking ridiculous because I want this. I want this so much, it feels like I won't be able to breathe properly until I have that win. But seeing Catalina, one of the most amazing tennis players and the person who deserves to win her first title, lose another chance yesterday showed me that no matter how deserving you are, it all comes down to you.

I get to start serving in this set, which is a huge advantage. It offers me a confidence boost by being the one to lead the set if I manage to bring my service game through and not lose it to Blake.

He looks more and more tired with every game, and I'm hoping my stamina will get me this win. We've been playing for three and a half hours, and that's a long fucking time in tennis matches. Three and a half hours, and we still have a set left.

My body is exhausted, but there's no letting up yet.

I have to win this.

Because every time I look at Cata, I realize she needs me to win this for both of us.

My first service game of the set is a battle. We go from deuce—forty all—to advantage me to back to deuce. It terrifies me when he's the one who has the advantage, but I manage to bring us back to deuce.

Sweat drips down the side of my face, down my back, and arms. It's so hot, and I'm so exhausted, all I can do is wipe the sweat off my brow with the wrist sweatband I wear on my left arm. I serve again, the score still deuce. It's a well-placed shot down the center line, but Blake returns it as if it's the easiest shot I've played all match long. He aims for my backhand, so I hit the ball back to him, going for *his* backhand. It's not his strongest shot, so I do my best to keep this cross-court thing going, from my backhand to his.

He goes down the line, and I get to the ball, but it's a reaching sort of shot. My eyes catch him running to the net at the same time, so I do exactly what he did, placing my shot down the line. He doesn't reach it.

Advantage me.

I take a deep breath, not letting a sense of victory course through me yet.

It's only when I serve again, another ace, and secure my service game, that I scream victoriously because, fuck, this was too close. It shouldn't have been so close. If I want to win, I have to be in control of my service games *and* take his from him at the same time.

After another brief water break, we switch sides of the court again, and I'm finally back on Catalina's side.

I mean, on my team's side.

But my eyes do tend to drift to her more. I blame her shirt, which says, "Team Santiago" today, and I've never been so happy. Especially, because of the little ladybug resting on the O of my name.

"I know you're tired, Santi, but you're so close. You can do it," Catalina calls to me as I place my towel down, clapping a little for encouragement.

"With my beautiful girl cheering for me, how could I lose?" The words slip free, but I wish I could catch them mid-air and throw them back in my mouth because *what the fuck was that?*

"Shut up, Santi," she mumbles, leaning back in her chair. I notice a smile slipping onto her lips, but she covers her mouth to keep me from seeing it.

And suddenly, I don't regret the words at all.

Not when my little rain cloud seems so positively impacted by them and any smile from her is a reward in itself.

Blake takes a long time to serve. There is a time limit between points, and he already got a time violation earlier, but this is all part of his strategy. He's trying to derail me, make me wait long enough to unsteady me and take me out of the game mentally. He's trying to irritate me so I make mistakes more easily.

It does irritate me, but he's risking another time violation, which works in my favor.

"Time violation number two. Love-fifteen," the umpire says, and the crowd cheers because they were also getting irritated with it.

Blake shakes his head and calls out something to the umpire, but she simply shakes her head, unimpressed with his arguments.

It's an easy point handed to me, a major mistake on his part. If I can get three more points now, I will be able to snatch his service game, and then all I'll have left is winning all of mine to win the match.

I can do this.

I make a mistake, an unforced error, on the next point, and I curse myself out for being such an idiot.

"*Enfócate*, Santi!" I hear Papá call out to me. I turn to him and frown.

"*Ya sé*," I mumble to myself, squatting a little again as I get in position to return the serve.

It's a tedious battle, much like the first service game of the set, but when it's advantage me, I take a deep breath, waiting for him to serve. I hear Cata's words ring in my ears when Blake misses his first serve. I step forward, toward the baseline, and attack his second, slower serve. My legs bring me to the net, jumping for my split step as I get ready to volley, but Blake lobs me, sending the ball flying too high for me to reach. A gasp escapes me as I run back toward the baseline, but the only way I get the ball is by going between the legs.

A tweener I place right in the corner of the left side of his court side, opposite of where he's standing.

"*Vamos!*" I scream, taking his service game for myself.

The crowd goes back to cheering my name because they know how much this break point means to me. To the potential ending of this game.

I take my next service game easily, and to everyone's surprise, Blake's next service game goes to me as well. It's four games to zero. I only need two more for another title.

Two more.

My next service game is another battle that has sweat dripping down my back and arms. I blow on my fingers where they grip my racket, because my hands are sweating too. The heat is weighing heavily on me, but I'm so close. I'm almost there. I serve over and over, winning a point, then losing another. Our rallies have shortened significantly from what they used to be, but that's mostly because we're both exhausted.

We've been playing for over four hours.

I finally win my service game, which leaves his.

But I lose his game, dragging out the match even more.

My limbs hurt so badly, not even the adrenaline rush of playing is helping the way I feel. Taking a sip of my electrolytes, I draw on the very last strings of my strength, rolling out my neck and shoulders.

It's five games to one.

All I have to do is win my service game to win the match, and I've been saving some of my energy in my serve for this very point in the match.

I ace my first serve.

I ace my second.

My third is a short rally because Blake hardly gets to my ball, and I run to the net to volley it to the opposite side of the court from him.

Forty-love.

I need one more point.

It's me who risks a time violation now, but I need the extra seconds to prepare myself for this serve. I've been sending all of my other ones wide in the last three points, and I attempt the same now, but it goes out.

Fuck.

There are two ways I can play this now. I could risk it and serve my second serve at the same speed I did my first, surprising Blake. Or I could play it safe and hit it slower, as one usually would.

But I've never been one to play it safe, especially not when I have such a lead.

This time, I aim for the center line, and with the speed of it and the placement, Blake is too surprised to reach it.

I win with a fucking ace.

Dropping to my knees, a sound of victory, utter exhaustion, and relief bursts out of me, echoing through the arena before the rest of the people explode into cheers. My gaze flies across the court, right back to Catalina, where she is punching the air with her fist, screaming for me.

I don't hesitate. I run to the net, jumping over it and briefly shaking Blake's hand—we have to do this before we do anything else for sportsmanship—before moving to the umpire as well. I drop my racket, only half paying attention while throwing my wrist sweatbands and the balls I had in my pocket to the crowd because I'm fixated on getting to my team.

To Catalina.

It takes me too long. I'm climbing over seats, a new burst of adrenaline giving me energy I didn't have before. Security tries to keep the people away from me, but I'm too fast for the crowd anyway.

I need to get to her.

A sigh of relief escapes me as I reach my box, and arms immediately wrap around me from my physio and doctor, then follow Mamá's and Papá's. I hug them back, even though my goal is still to reach Cata. I squeeze my parents once more, then Manu, before finally stepping back and moving around them to step in front of her.

I expect it to be awkward, for us to stand together and stare at each other, but Catalina surprises me as she flings her arms around me, hugging me.

"I'm so sweaty," I say, tears stinging my eyes because Cata is hugging me again right after I've won a grand slam, and there is hardly anything sweeter.

"I don't care," she replies, her fingers sliding onto the top of my nape to grip the hair there. "I'm so proud of you."

"So proud you could finally kiss me?" I ask, making her snort into my ear. She tries to step back, but I'm not ready yet. I hold onto the back of her shirt, then push her closer by the small of her back. Her chest flush against mine.

"Santi," Catalina says, and I realize she probably wants me to back away, so I attempt to step away when she suddenly reaches for my wrist, pulling me back toward her. "Fuck it," she mumbles right before stealing my breath.

Cata's hands find my cheeks, pulling my face down to hers and then she's kissing me.

Catalina is kissing me.

Oh my God, *my Catalina is kissing me.*

Her mouth finds mine and the crowd explodes into even more cheers, but they slowly fade away in my head as I taste my fake girlfriend for the first time. Well, as much as I can taste her with only her lips on mine. I push my tongue a little against her lips, looking for permission, and if I had the strength to pull away, I'd beg for it.

But I don't have to because Cata's lips part as soon as she feels my tongue. It's a slow kiss, the kind I hope gives her as many butterflies as it gives me. My hands move to her back, holding her as I kiss her longer, deeper.

This is the kind of kiss that sends someone to another dimension.

The kind of kiss you dream about but never think you will actually have.

This kiss is life-altering, and I know if I let this go on for another second, I will become addicted to Catalina Sanchez.

Who am I kidding?

I'm already addicted to her.

Catalina's hands drop to my abs as I gently explore her mouth before she pulls back and buries her face in my chest.

The crowd is waiting for me, but this kiss couldn't have been longer than fifteen seconds. I know because it wasn't enough.

It wasn't *nearly* enough.

"Go, Santi," she urges and pushes me softly toward the steps to go back down to the court.

Happiness has taken over every part of me, so I kiss her cheek before practically skipping all the way back to the court.

Winning the Australian Open *and* Catalina finally kissing me?

I don't think I'm going to stop smiling any time soon.

LIGHT
LIGHT
NL

# CHAPTER 22
## CATALINA



"You kissed Santiago."

It's the fifth time Charlie has said this to me today, but I'm not even annoyed because it's clear they're trying to process that fact as much as I am.

It still doesn't feel real to me.

"I kissed Santiago," I echo, staring at my hands.

"Why?" Ness chimes in, and I look up, into her dark brown eyes, trying to look for an explanation.

"I don't know. He asked if I would, and I didn't think I would, but when he started walking away, I realized I *did* want to kiss him. *Joder.* Why did I want to kiss him?" My rant comes to an end, and I cover my mouth, trying to keep any more words from slipping free.

"Maybe because you've always had feelings for him and he's slowly pulling you in again?" Sage chimes in, and I throw her a dirty look.

"I would much rather shave off my eyebrows and never wear clothes again than have feelings for Santiago Javier Castillo." I visibly shudder, making the three people around me grin.

"Feelings are as uncontrollable as the weather, sweetheart. Sometimes, you've got a beautiful outfit on and you're in a fantastic mood, but then rain pours down and ruins everything. Feelings are like that. You can be in a fantastic mood, feeling like the ruler of the world, and then they can ruin everything."

"What a pep talk, Ness. Fuck, you should become a therapist," I say sarcastically, but she frowns at me, clearly not having finished speaking.

"But they can also be warm and comfortable, a source of vitamins you need for a good quality of life. So even if they're unpredictable, sometimes they're vital for our happiness," she goes on, and Charlie flings an arm around her shoulders, hugging her from the side.

"Ah my sweet, naive friend. Feelings are shit. They are the beginning of all drama and the end of many relationships. They are the incentives of impulsive behaviors, and the reason people cry themselves to sleep. If Cata doesn't want to address her feelings, then leave her be. She has enough on her plate as is."

Charlie's words have me throwing a kiss their way, and they wink at me before squeezing Ness again and stepping away to help me with my stretches.

It's been a week since Santi won the Australian Open, since I kissed him for the first time, and I have been avoiding him for the entire seven days. He hasn't pressured me into meeting for our weekly dinner, but he's been sending me texts, asking me how I'm doing mentally since losing.

He seems very concerned about my mental well-being, and I know it comes from his own experience with anxiety and depression, so I always text him back. I return the question. And then we move on until he checks in again the next day. He doesn't push, but part of me wishes he did so I could be angry with him.

This way, he's only making me want to kiss him again.

"We have another two weeks until you are partaking in the Dubai Tennis Championships. Eventually, you're going to have to take two days rest. You know my rules. Training is important, but your body can only handle so much," Charlie says, lifting my leg and stretching it out in a way that has my back crying in complaint.

"Fuck, whatever you just did, please don't do it again," I say, fighting back the tears that shot into my eyes in response to the pain.

"Your back?" Charlie asks, and I let out a strained breath.

"Yeah," I reply, noticing Ness and Sage walking toward where I am on the floor with worry on their faces.

"Okay, that is it. You are taking a three-day break from training. Go lie by the pool and do absolutely nothing today before our flight tomorrow," Charlie announces.

"Preferably go into the sauna too, get some heat on your body. Sweat everything out," they go on, helping me finish up my stretches.

"I can't. There is too much to do. I have to go to Argentina for Santi's next tournament, *train for my next tournament*, figure out a way to be around Santi, and, and, and," I say, hopefully making my point that there is no time to rest.

"I don't care if the whole world explodes if you lie down. You need rest, or your back is only going to get worse," Charlie says, earning several nods from Sage and Vanessa.

"Fine, I'll take the rest of the day and tomorrow off. It's a long flight to Argentina anyway." Twenty hours, give or take.

Usually, if I'm sitting for that long, I make it my mission to do some sort of workout before, to tire myself out, but Charlie is right. I need to rest if I want to win my next tournament. Plus, I want my back to get better.

"Good girl. Now go," Charlie says, and I hate them for smirking at me when a blush takes over my entire face.

I throw my sweaty towel at their face and leave the room.

### *Santiago*

I've been giving Catalina space, but when Charlie texted me, telling me to figure my shit out with her before the next tournament—to make sure there will be no tension between us after that amazing kiss that went on the front pages of every news outlet—I ran at the chance to see my *mariquita*.

It was out of respect for her that I've stayed away, that I didn't ask her to tell me why she kissed me after all. Why she chose one of the best moments in my life and made it even better. I want to ask her if she might have feelings for me too, or if it's all one-sided. But the last question is never going to come out of my mouth, at least not if I can help it.

Then again, I also told myself I'd never have feelings for another person, and here I fucking am, speedwalking to get to Cata.

Charlie told me she'd be at the pool area, but Cata still takes my breath away. She's spread out on a lounge chair by the pool, nothing but a bikini and hat covering her. It's an indoor pool area you need access to with a keycard—Charlie gave me theirs—so I understand why she's not on guard right now, why she looks so relaxed and peaceful. No one who isn't also a guest here could walk in, but there is no one here.

She's all by herself in that tiny bikini, and I feel heat consuming my whole body.

I didn't know she had a tattoo, let alone several. I'm too far away to study any of them, but I like the fact that she has them. It's something we can potentially bond over, our love for the ink on our skin. There are several on my chest and back, a few hidden near my ankle where I can always cover them with socks. My favorites are the two vines running along where my V-line is, Tornado's face tattooed near my ribcage, and the tennis racket incorporated into a heartbeat line to show I live and breathe for the sport I love.

My feet move long before I manage to catch my jaw off the floor, but I don't care. I'm too busy studying her curves, the thickness of her thighs, the swoop of her breasts, the width of her shoulders, the sharpness of her facial features. I study all of her. Her pale skin tone, her long hair, and the way she scowls at whatever book she's reading on her ereader at the moment.

"Catalina," I say, her name full of the tension I feel all over my body because of her. Because I have never, ever seen her in a bikini before, so much of her exposed to me, and it's fucking with my head.

All of that fades away, though, as she panics and reaches for her towel, covering her chest.

"I'm sorry, I didn't mean to—" She cuts me off before I can finish my apology.

"It's fine." Cata puts her ereader away, grabbing her shirt and slipping it over her head to hide from me. "What are you doing here?" she asks, studying me, her eyes getting stuck on my naked chest.

"I thought we could talk," I start, settling down in the lounge chair beside hers.

"About?"

"Don't play dumb, Cata. You're far too smart for me to believe that shit," I reply, blushing a little when she studies the lines of my tattoos on my upper body. "I want to talk about that kiss." Cata snorts before looking me dead in the eye.

"It was the heat of the moment. It meant nothing," she says, her voice firm.

"To you," I clarify, making her look at me with confusion.

"What?" Her blue eyes are full of all the feelings that terrify her. The same ones that terrify me, but in very different ways. She's scared I'll hurt her again. I'm scared because she's the only one I've ever felt this way about.

"It meant nothing to you. You don't get to decide what it meant to me." Her features soften, but she shakes her head like this is a conversation we shouldn't even have in the first place.

"It can't have meant anything, Santi. It can't happen again." My next words practically fly out of my mouth.

"But I want it to. I want to kiss you. As a matter of fact, I want to do all sorts of things with you."

Cata's breath hitches as I lean forward, lifting my index finger to wrap around the chain of her necklace. I don't tug on it because I know how valuable it is to her, but the mere proximity of my finger to her skin is enough to make goosebumps spread over her arms.

"Aren't you curious, *cariño*? Don't you want to know what it would feel like to have me on my knees for you, doing everything you demand of me?" She shivers, and I let my gaze drop to her mouth as she pulls half her bottom lip between her teeth.

I want to bite her lip.

I want her to bite mine.

"Santi, if we cross that line, there will be no going back. We have months of faking left ahead of us. Adding sex to the mix will make things incredibly messy," she says, but the distance between us is still closing, and *I* haven't moved a centimeter.

"But what if we start and never want to stop? We could just keep going until—" I cut off, not entirely certain where the fuck I'm going with this.

Cata leans back, breaking the contact between us as she lets out a dry laugh.

"Until what, Santiago? Until we get married, have babies, grow old together? Don't be absurd. You don't do relationships, and I don't do men who have hurt me once already. The second time would be on me for giving you another chance, and like you said, I'm too smart to make such a foolish decision."

She stands up, grabbing her ereader and towel before staring down at me. I'm too dumbfounded, too lost in how desperately I want what she was describing, to form any words.

Panic slips back around my throat, squeezing and further preventing me from speaking.

I don't understand why all of a sudden I want a relationship. No, I don't want *a* relationship. I want a relationship with Catalina.

Maybe it's because I had never taken anyone on a date, but every time I take her, it feels wholeheartedly and unquestionably right.

Maybe it's because I don't care if people frown at me, but I'd pay a million euros just to have Catalina smile my way.

Maybe it's because when I spend time with her, I don't miss the way my life used to be and instead feel at peace.

Our history sits tall between us, separating us like a valley separates mountains. It's something I'm working on making up to her, but if I think about only meeting her later in life, I shudder. No matter what, every moment with Catalina, from the beginning to now, is important to me, and I wouldn't give them up for anything.

"Tell me this isn't one-sided. Tell me you feel something for me. Tell me I'm not imagining things."

*Didn't I just promise myself not to say anything remotely like this?*

But it's a desperate attempt to get hope back into my chest.

I need to know.

"I can't tell you that, but I can show you something I've never shown anyone but Charlie, Sage, and Vanessa before. A sign of the trust I'm putting in you."

"I'll take it. I'll take anything you want to give me."

*Oh my God, Santiago, shut the fuck up.*

Catalina gives me an unsure look before putting everything down again. I stand up to be in front of her, and she lets out a nervous breath before lifting her shirt over her head. My whole body goes stiff at the sight of her breasts only covered by her small bikini top. Her nipples are pebbled and press against the fabric, showing the outlines of her piercings.

Fuck.

Me.

"I know you love my tits, Santi, but I wanted to show you the tattoo." I lick my lips as a bright smile covers my face.

"Do I get to see the piercings after?" I ask, meeting her gaze with a smug look. She smacks my arm playfully, but I chuckle when I notice the smirk on her face.

"Can you be serious for a second?" she asks, her expression falling a little when she presses a single finger to the tattoo on her chest. My smile disappears immediately, all of my attention shifting to the sad, nostalgic look covering her features.

This is about her mom.

I've known Catalina long enough to know that look by heart.

Mostly because my heart usually cries for her at the sight of it.

"I got this for my mamá." She says the words as she picks up my hand to bring it to her tattoo, inviting me to trace it. Cata lets go of my wrist before I make contact, allowing me to make the decision whether to touch her.

Of course I do.

There is a sea turtle painted onto her skin from the top of her cleavage all the way under her breasts where its body extends. It's shaded in some areas, lines in others, and completely black in the rest. The words, "*La vida de una tortuga marina es una vida libre*" are written beneath it, to the left of her chest, and I trail my fingers over the words too, remembering Cata telling me her mom used to say this.

"I feel closer to her again through this, which may be silly, but—" I have to cut her off, have to reassure her.

"It's not silly. This is beautiful. I think your mamá would have loved this intricate design," I say, still studying it. "Why would you share this with me if you haven't shared it with anyone else?" I can't quite make myself drop my hand, so I run it down her stomach, toward the three butterflies she got tattooed above her hip bone.

"One for each of my siblings," she explains before adding, "I told you because we have to start somewhere. Don't make me regret this, okay?" she says, and I look back up into her blue eyes.

"I won't. This will stay between us." It's a promise I'm going to use everything I have to keep. "Can I kiss you? Not on the lips, somewhere else," I explain, and when she seems to hold her breath, I hold mine.

"Where?" she asks, but she isn't pulling back.

She stays in place as I lower myself until my mouth hovers over her tattoo. I bring my gaze back to hers, tilting my head to look up at her.

"Here," I whisper, my voice soft enough to almost get lost in the sounds around us.

A single nod is all the permission I need before pressing a soft kiss to the middle of the sea turtle.

It takes all of my willpower to stop there, not to keep going, kissing every single centimeter of her body.

"I won't tell a soul." Cata steps back, finally bringing a smile to her lips.

"We'll see. But if you manage to keep your mouth shut, maybe I'll let you kiss me somewhere even lower next time."

I always knew Cata would kill me, but I didn't think it would be this way.

Dying because of how much I want her.

# CHAPTER 23
## SANTIAGO

A DAY BEFORE MY final in the Argentinian Open, Catalina left for her tournament in Dubai. She won it a few days after I lost the Argentinian Open, but I couldn't be with her because directly after that tournament, I flew to Rio for the next one. She came afterward to join me, sitting in my box, as promised, for the final.

Perhaps it's superstition—I'm an athlete after all, it's practically part of the job description to have some superstitions—but whenever she's around, I seem to win tournaments. When she's not, I lose them. It's pure coincidence, rationally I know that, but I'd much rather believe Catalina truly is my lucky charm.

*Mi mariquita.*

We haven't spent any alone time together because we've been apart for the past couple of weeks, but for the next two tournaments, the *Indian Wells Open* and *Miami Open*, Cata and I will be together the whole time. We're both taking part in them, which means I can finally take her on another date either before or in between the tournaments.

Depends on when she's available and if she wants to see me.

Fuck, I hope she wants to see me.

"I swear, this whole relationship thing is a fucking joke," Manu says, pulling me out of my thoughts.

"What happened?" I ask, surprised by her willingness to speak to me at the moment something is frustrating her instead of keeping it all down until she's figured out what's wrong and how she's feeling exactly.

"I don't know. Ever since we broke up, Madalena has been texting me, sending me all of these sad videos. I don't even understand why she's still texting me. She's the one who broke up with *me*, not the other way around," she explains, flopping down on the bed in her hotel room. She's also in California for the tournament, playing doubles with her partner Alessandra.

"Maybe she regrets it?" I ask, but in truth, I have no fucking clue why people do what they do in relationships. I don't even know why I'm acting the way I am at the moment, and my relationship is fake.

"Whatever. It's time I finally block her anyway. She doesn't deserve another second of my time."

My sister's determination is followed by some angry tapping on her screen before she throws the phone at the head of the bed and falls backward until she's lying down. Grabbing a pillow, she places it over her head and screams into it, all of her frustration coming out with the sound.

"Do you want me to stay with you?" I ask, nudging her knee with mine where it's hanging over the edge of her bed.

"No, go train with Catalina." Manuela sits up and wipes her face. "And do me a favor, Santiago. Don't fuck it up again. She may forgive you once, somewhen down the line, but Lina is not the type of person to forgive an idiot twice," she says, making a wave of panic and dread shoot through me at the thought of Catalina never forgiving me, never letting me in again.

"If she even forgives me once."

It's the last thing I say before kissing the top of her head and walking out her room, the urge to see Cata and make her smile today taking over.

With every day we spend together, I know we're getting closer. I know her anger fades more. It irritates her that it's fading, I know that, but I have no intention of making another stupid mistake like last time.

Today, my breathtaking girl is wearing a shirt that says, "Member of Santiago Castillo's Ass' Fan Club."

"Catalina Sanchez, are you flirting with me?" I ask when I read it, the brightest of smiles taking over my face. This is the first shirt she's ever worn around me that has anything remotely flirty on it, and I'm having a hard time keeping back a very excited laugh.

"Charlie had this made for me, and I thought it was too funny not to wear," she explains, but a smile tugs up the right corner of her mouth.

"You wore it because it's true. You don't wear shirts with messages on them if you don't agree with them or if they don't apply to you," I point out, and Cata rolls her lips, obviously trying to hold back a full-faced smile.

"What can I say, Santi? You have a phenomenal ass." She picks up her racket, spinning it once in her hand. The smirk on my face makes her blush. "Stop looking at me like that," she says and swats my forearm, but it's a gentle touch despite her irritation with me.

"You are free to touch it any time you'd like. How's right now?" I ask and take a step toward her, so giddy from this playful conversation.

It feels like she's taken a hundred steps toward me emotionally, and I'm so pleasantly surprised, I can't stop grinning. I truly thought being apart for weeks would make her drift away from me.

The opposite has happened.

"You're impossible, Santi," she says and shakes her head, still blushing.

Cata stares at the toe of her shoe, suddenly a bit shy, and I can't help but tilt her head up to make her look at me again.

"Did you miss me, *cariño*?" Her gaze drops to my lips, and she swallows hard as she forcefully drags it back to my eyes.

"Like a sunburnt person misses the sun," she replies, making me chuckle.

"Come on, tell me the truth. Did you? Just a little?" I caress her jaw, loving the way her eyes fall shut a little instead of the way she used to avoid my touch at all costs.

"A little," she admits.

Hope blooms in my chest.

"Yeah?" I ask, my voice dropping an octave because of how much she affects me.

"Yeah."

"I've missed you too, Catalina."

My thumb runs over her bottom lip, tracing its shape because I can't kiss her again. Not until she tells me she wants it too. Not until she makes the first move.

"Let's train," she says and pokes at my stomach, trying to get me to move away. My hand drops from her face. Her body language and words are enough to tell me she wants distance now. I take a step back, grabbing my racket.

"Alright, but take it easy on me. I still haven't recovered from the knowledge of you loving my ass." She uses her racket head to poke me in the side, making me burst into laughter.

Catalina doesn't respond, but I don't speak again either. I simply watch her walk away, my eyes trailing down her muscular back, the curve of her ass, and finally her thick, trained thighs.

It's a vicious cycle that I'm putting myself through whenever I'm around her.

Admire her.

Remember I can't have her in any other way than as a fake girlfriend.

Realize how beautiful she is.

Recalling the pain in her face when she told me why she doesn't like me anymore.

Over and over, like a merry-go-round, my thoughts repeat themselves, but I also *can't* tear my eyes off her. I can't stop thinking about ways to make it up to her. I'm planning dates to take her on in my head, and while, for now, I can justify it as part of our fake relationship, what the fuck am I going to do by the end of this season?

When she'll walk away and leave me in her rearview mirror?

Catalina and I train in silence for an hour. Papá and Charlie join eventually, watching us train and adjusting our stances and swings every now and then. We listen to our coaches the whole time, but even though Cata has adjusted, has taken my feedback into consideration, one of the worst things in the world happens.

Cata screams in pain.

Right as she twists to hit her forehand, her strongest shot, she cries out, dropping her racket and sinking to her knees.

"Fuck!" she calls out, but I'm already sprinting toward her, jumping over the net and dropping my racket to get to her. Charlie is by my side as I bend down to take Cata's hand in mine, my heart dropping when I see the tears run down her face.

She's choking for breath, which only causes more panic to slice through me.

"Charlie, what do we do?" I ask, my body shaking in fear.

"Catalina, you need to breathe through it," Charlie replies, ignoring me.

"Can't," she cries, arching her back as if she's looking for any position that will make her feel less pain.

"She's had this before. Her back is in spasm from her overusing it. We have to roll her onto her stomach so I can gently massage the area," they explain, and I shift until my ass is flat on the court, position myself so Catalina can put her head on my legs.

"I'm fine," she mumbles, but she's breathing heavily, obviously still in immense pain.

"Put your head in my lap, *cariño*. We will make you feel better," I promise her, wiping a few strands of hair off her sweaty forehead.

"Santi, I'm so scared," she admits, her fingers fisting my pants once she's positioned in my lap.

"It'll be okay. Everything will be fine," I promise her, running a single hand over her hair.

"Deep breath, Lina," Charlie says right before they start massaging Cata, making her cry in my lap. Her hand finds one of mine, squeezing so hard, I fight back a grunt of pain. "Breathe." Their voice is firmer now, less asking and more demanding, and it makes the beautiful woman in my lap finally take a deep breath.

"That's it, Cata," I say, and her grip on me tightens as she curses me out several times.

It takes minutes until her back stops spasming, but she remains in my lap, letting me massage her head as Charlie runs to get a heating pack and an ice pack as well as painkillers and some sort of salve. They also tell me they're going to get Cata's physiotherapist, who should be here at all times anyway. It's only because she trusts Charlie more than anyone and is so used to only having them around that she doesn't ask her physio to be with her all the time.

I take her hair out of the ponytail it's in to sift my fingers through it more easily, going back to massaging her scalp. Catalina doesn't move, and I think she's enjoying the way I'm touching her. I, on the other hand, am still too full of panic to appreciate the way she melts against me.

"How often does this happen, *mariquita*?" I ask, running a hand over her forehead. I can only see the side of her face, but it's enough for me to know she doesn't want to tell me.

"Not often, only when I really overdo it. I think this was the fourth time now," she says, and I reach down to run a single hand up and down her spine.

It's a soft touch because I don't want to hurt her and am also not remotely qualified enough to massage her properly. Charlie has some training in physiotherapy, but they also only did as much as they could given the information they probably had from the first three times this happened.

"I went to three different doctors, but they couldn't help me. They told me to take things slow and deal with it with painkillers."

I want to strangle all of those doctors.

"Catalina, I know you don't want me to say it, but I think you have to take a break. You have to slow down." As soon as the words have left my mouth, she sits up. She presses her lips together, probably to keep from screaming in pain. I try to help her, but she swats my hands away.

"I can't. You know my goals for the season. How can I achieve them if I take a break?" When she tries to get up, I place a hand on her arm, stopping her.

"You don't have to take a break. Maybe slowing down will be enough," I say softly. She looks irritated, but not with me.

I think she's frustrated with her body.

"What do you suggest?"

The answer lies on the tip of my tongue.

And it practically flies out of my mouth because this is what I want more than anything else at the moment.

I want to take the pressure and load off her shoulders.

I want to give her a way to keep playing, keep partaking in tournaments, while also allowing her to slow down a little.

And most of all, I want to prove to her that my career does *not* mean more to me than hers.

This is finally the way I can prove it to her.

"Play doubles with me in the next two tournaments."

# CHAPTER 24
## CATALINA

My mouth is so wide open, there is no way I will be able to close it unless I use the palm of my hand to press it shut again.

My back is still aching and uncomfortable, but at least the spasming has stopped.

Santiago is right.

I need to slow things down. I have to think about the big tournaments, the grand slams, if I want to win them, and if I played doubles, it would be less on my back because I could perhaps rely on Santi more. I wouldn't have to serve as much as I do during singles matches.

Damn him for giving me an option I'm actually considering.

Well, at least before I remember a very important detail.

"Very funny, Santi. You can't possibly play singles and doubles at the same time. It's too much," I say, shaking my head at him.

"I wouldn't. I'd only play doubles with you." I snort, but the sound dies out when I see how serious he looks.

He's still got his hand on my arm, and that single touch is enough to keep me in place. Sat on this tennis court where I just fell to my knees in pain. Staring at Santi as if I've never seen him before.

"I don't know what you're trying to achieve by giving me this 'option' when we both know you wouldn't go through with it."

"Yes, I would. Let me prove it to you. Let me show you what your career means to me."

His amber eyes are full of determination and hope, as if he's begging me with a single gaze to play doubles with him. To allow him to do exactly what he said he wants to: prove that my career means a lot to him, too. That he wants me to succeed.

"Why would you do this?" I ask, leaning away from him because I'm too shocked to jump at the opportunity.

It won't count toward my points in the singles rankings, but I could still play in tournaments. I wouldn't have to feel like a huge failure, not like I would if I didn't play in the tournaments. I could still win prize money to support my family.

"Because I care about you, Catalina. I thought that was obvious," he replies, making me snort.

"You are extremely good at faking this relationship, I will give you that, but I don't believe it has gotten to the point where you would prioritize me over you," I say, and Santi frowns instantly, his sunshine smile nowhere to be found.

"I know you're angry with me, and you have every right to be, but you can't possibly still believe this is fake." His words would have me stumbling back if I was standing. "Cata, I have no idea what the fuck I'm feeling, but it's real. Yes, I'm taking you on dates to keep up the image, but I'm also taking you on dates because spending time with you makes me happy. Not the superficial type of happiness that leaves minutes after you're finished with whatever you were doing. It's the type of joy that lingers and every time you recall the event, it makes you giddy all over."

My heart retreats to the deepest part of my body to keep from getting affected by his words.

"I don't constantly look at you when you sit in my box during my matches because we're supposed to be fake dating. I do it because the mere sight of you calms my anxiety. It's so rare for me to find anything that can comfort me when I deal with my anxiety, and I don't know why you, out of all people, have this strong effect on me, but that isn't a question I need to find an answer to. It's enough for me to take things for what they are instead."

All I can do is stare and blink at him because it takes all of my strength not to let tears fill my eyes.

"I don't seek you out when no one is looking in secret hopes we get caught. I seek you out because I'm hoping to have a moment just between the two of us. I want the intimate and private moments even more than the grand and spectacular ones. Because it's during the quiet ones, where it's just us, that you open up to me, and that's one of the most beautiful things in the world."

Ignoring my aching back, I pull my knees to my chest and wrap my arms around my legs, never looking away from Santi because he hasn't looked away from me since he started this conversation. I'd understand if he had. Sharing your feelings, especially when you have no idea what exactly they are, is terrifying. On top of that, he still thinks I hate him with every fiber of my being, and while I'm still a bit angry, I don't hate Santiago anymore.

I did.

For a long time, I hated him so much, but I've made a grave mistake after he took me on our first date. I went off the path of hate. Now I'm lost in the land between love and hate, and I know I'm not walking back toward the latter one. I don't want to. I might be scared of what it would mean to develop positive feelings for Santi again, but I'm not stubborn enough to disregard what is happening between us.

What has been happening since Carlos and Charlie made us become hitting partners who have regular dinners, go on dates, sit in each other's boxes, and more.

So much more.

"Will you say something, Cata? I feel like I'm standing here naked and all you're doing is staring at me like you can't quite decide if you like what you see," he says with a nervous laugh, but he's right, isn't he? Isn't that exactly what is happening, even if it's only metaphorically speaking?

"For someone as unromantic as you, you certainly know how to use words to make another person speechless," I reply, stretching out my legs again because I don't know what to do with myself.

"I don't know what it is about you, *cariño*, but I don't think I'd be saying any of this if I was talking to someone else," he admits, rubbing the back of his neck as he stares down at the ground. "I know you're not where I am. I don't expect you to be, but it feels wrong to offer you to play doubles, to put your trust in me, if you didn't know how deeply I care for you," Santi adds, his attention shifting back to my face.

The intensity of his gaze has me sucking in a sharp breath, making me stare down at my hands because what I'm about to say isn't what he will want to hear.

"Words can be so pretty, Santi. Remember when you told me it was you and me, that nothing and no one could stop us as long as we fought them together?" I ask, and he brings his fingers to my chin to nudge my head up, forcing my eyes back to his.

"I was so stupid, Cata, and if I could do it all over again, I'd choose you. I'd choose us."

I open my mouth to respond, but no words come out, no matter how hard I try to make them leave my lips.

"You need actions, not words. I understand that. So let me prove it. Play doubles with me for the next two tournaments or for however long you need to until your back feels better so you can keep playing tournaments on your own," he says, caressing my jaw with his thumb in a way that makes me visibly shiver.

"Renjun Choi could close the distance between you and him in the singles ranking standings," I remind him, because I don't think he has thought this through.

"I don't care."

An expression of suspicion and disbelief covers my face because there is no way he means that. I know Santi. He's as competitive as I am.

Sensing that I'm not buying his act, he leans forward closing the distance between us until his lips almost brush mine.

"One chance, Cata, give me one. Please. I'll prove it to you," he says, and I find myself leaning closer when his fresh scent fills my nose.

"And then what?" I whisper, almost against his lips because of how close we are, and I notice Santi tensing.

"Then, maybe, you'll let me take you on a real date where I can kiss you properly while no one is watching," he says, and I hate how much I want that too.

"No one is watching right now," I blurt out, but I hear footsteps approaching the court.

It's right before I pull back that Santi's grip on me tightens a little, keeping me in place before his lips find mine for a slow, soft kiss that makes my stomach tumble. It's too quick, too little contact, but a tiny whimper escapes me when his tongue briefly slips into my mouth again.

There is nothing quite like kissing Santiago Javier Castillo, especially after he's shared his feelings with me.

After he bared himself to me and offered me something so sweet.

And if Charlie and Winn, my physio, weren't approaching, I'd pull his mouth back to mine to demand more.

More, more, more of the dangerous drug that is him.

# CHAPTER 25
## SANTIAGO

"Santiago, you can't be serious right now," Mamá says with irritation, but it's Papá's smile that makes me grin.

"I am," I reply, feeling oddly confident and comfortable with my decision.

No part of me is scared I will regret this.

"You are a lovestruck fool," Papá chimes in, but he finds this all so amusing, he's having a hard time hiding that fact. "You gave me so much shit three and a half months ago about pairing you up with her, and now you'd risk your ranking for her."

They make it sound so dramatic when I have a good buffer between myself and Renjun. Missing two small tournaments, not a Grand Slam, isn't as big a deal as everyone thinks it is. Or perhaps for me, it doesn't feel that way because I'll be playing mixed doubles with Catalina. She can slow down. There are so many upsides to this decision that the downsides have faded into nothingness for me.

"What can I say? I'm a changed man."

Changed or perhaps I've simply stopped lying to myself about how much she means to me. Matteo and Thomas would kick my ass and tell me they were saying I had feelings for her for over a decade, which is most likely why I haven't discussed Cata with the crown prince of Monaco for months. Not that he has any time for me with his royal duties at the moment anyway.

I cross my arms in front of my chest, incapable of keeping the smile off my face. It's hard not to smile every time I think of Cata now. She kissed me back yesterday on the court. She's giving me a chance, and I'll be damned if I don't prove to her that I'll do whatever it takes to earn her forgiveness.

"Go fuck someone else. I'm giving you permission. It'll screw your head back on properly so you stop making decisions with your sex-deprived dick. Catalina is nothing more to you than a means to have sex, the only means at the moment if you think about it," Papá says, and I'm on my feet and in his face a second later.

"I fucking dare you to call Catalina that again. You might be my father and coach, but I'll knock you on your ass without a second thought."

The child in me screams because I'm threatening Papá, but my heart is in charge, and it's not having any disrespect directed toward Catalina.

My father studies me for a long time, but I don't back down from his stare. His amber eyes, the ones he gave me, show no remorse for what he said.

Then, he places a hand on my shoulder and smiles.

"Good, I just wanted to make sure you were serious about Catalina if you're already making decisions based on your feelings for her."

He lets go of me and drops down on the seat beside Mamá, wrapping an arm around her shoulders and kissing her cheek. Her shoulders untense immediately.

"Winning is important. Your ranking is important. But there is more to life than work, even if you're living your dream. Love is a wonderful thing which I was lucky enough to find. If you've found it for the first time in Catalina, I suggest you hold onto it. It may never come again for someone as anti-love as you," Papá adds, causing the smile to drop off my face.

"I'm not anti-love. I—" I don't know what I am, if I'm being honest.

"You what, Santiago?" Mamá asks softly, genuine concern in her eyes for me.

"I have never wanted anything with anyone except for Cata. I think I've always wanted more than friendship with her, ever since we were playing doubles." I sink into the chair opposite Mamá and Papá. "Fuck, what does that even mean? More than ten years of pining after the same person, never wanting another like I want her?"

My parents both smile, and I'm glad they do because that means they have an answer. I'm their kid. I don't know everything they do about love and life. I don't know so many things they haven't taught me yet, and I'm so grateful they're both here to teach me.

I'm very lucky.

"I think it means you're in love with her, that she is your person," Mamá says, but it's Papá's words that make my heart stop.

"Catalina Sanchez is your soulmate, *mijo*, so you better make damn well sure you don't fuck up and lose her."

Catalina and I have officially signed up to play doubles in the *Indian Wells Open* and because they love how much publicity we are going to give them—playing doubles as a couple for the first time in a tournament—they didn't have any problems with our withdrawals from the singles tournament.

All they have asked us to do is a photoshoot that has Catalina nervous. She assured me her back feels much better today, but I see how stiff it must be from the way she walks. Or perhaps it's her nerves.

"Talk to me, *mariquita*. Does your back hurt or are you nervous?" I ask because she has been staring at the same spot on the wall in front of her for a few minutes with her shoulders slightly raised and a frown on her face.

"I don't like photoshoots. I loathe taking pictures and seeing them afterward," she replies and I love the way she turns to me and puts her forehead against my shoulder as she groans.

"Really? Someone as beautiful as you should love seeing themself in photos. I certainly love seeing myself," I tease to take her mind off it, and the way she snorts has me grinning from ear to ear.

"You're an arrogant asshole," she mumbles, her words muffled because she's still resting her forehead on my shoulder. "I hope you know I'm seeking comfort from you because of how uncomfortable I am with this situation. For no other reason, *cabrón*," she says, and I take that as an invitation to give her even more comfort.

My arms wrap around her, pressing her more firmly against me. She twists her head so her face is nuzzled in the area between my neck and collarbone, her arms flying around me too. She lets out a sigh I feel deep in my bones as a smile covers my entire face.

I love hugging Catalina. It feels like my body was molded to wrap around hers, and every time she hugs me, we connect like two pieces of broken glass that were separated by hate for far too long.

"For no other reason?" I ask, rubbing her back until she relaxes even more against me.

"For no other reason," she repeats, but I don't miss the way she takes a deep breath, inhaling my scent.

"You're so full of shit," I say, calling her out on her lie.

"Let me lie, Santi. It makes me feel better." I chuckle again, kissing the top of her head.

"For today. Tomorrow, I won't let you lie anymore," I reply, still rubbing her back, too.

"Well, tomorrow I won't let you touch me, so I won't have to lie."

"That's too bad. I do love touching you."

I can't see her face, but I know my Catalina. She's blushing right now, which is why she buries her face in my neck even more, hiding from the rest of the world.

"Alright, Santiago, you can go get dressed and get your makeup done. Catalina, you as well."

Cata steps away, and I'm fully prepared for us to go our separate ways for the next half hour while we get dressed and beautified, but she grabs my wrist as soon as I attempt to step toward the person who was speaking to us.

Uncertainty has replaced all other emotions on her face, and I resist the urge to cup her cheeks as I ask her what's wrong.

"Nothing," she replies, but she's digging around in her pocket until she pulls out two identical pins. They're pride flags. "A little something for during the photoshoot," she explains, offering me one. "If you'd like to, you don't have to. I know you haven't done anything like this before, but I'm so used to it, I'd feel strange not wearing anything, any message," she rambles, clearly nervous because this is uncharted water for us.

I study her with fascination because she wants to share this with me, something so very special to her. I can't quite get my mind to wrap around that fact as I take one of the pins and hold it tightly in my hand.

"Thank you. I can't wait to put it on," I say, making Catalina smile.

"Okay, cool," she replies, nodding several times. "Cool," she repeats.

I find it so adorable to see this confident woman so flustered around me at the moment because of all of the decisions I've made that have led us here. I have a feeling she isn't quite certain what to make of all of her feelings for me anymore. It was easy before. Hate me. No questions needed to be asked. She had a good enough reason. But now? Now we're growing closer, and I hope she doesn't want to cling to her hate. I hope she wants to explore this thing, whatever *it* is, between us as much as I do.

"I'll see you soon," Cata says as I continue to smile at her, watching her blush all over again.

"See you soon, *cariño*," I reply, walking with a little skip in my step because of her.

The entire time I sit in the makeup artist's chair, I think about making a page for Cata in my scrapbook when I get back home. Something to add her to it because I've never made a page dedicated to her. I was too busy pretending to hate her.

"Look up," the makeup artist says, their voice firm and irritated as if this isn't the first or third time they said that.

"Sorry," I mumble, looking at the ceiling, as instructed.

I'm itching to get back to Cata, and when I'm told I'm done, I all but jump out of my seat. The dress pants and polo they put on me are ridiculously fancy for someone like me, an athlete who only wears suits and tuxes when absolutely necessary, but I become a huge fan of the outfit when I see the fancy clothing they put on Catalina. She's wearing a berry magenta silk dress that hugs her curves in a sinful way. Her long, brown hair cascades down her back in perfect waves, and they chose to do a simple makeup look that highlights all of her stunning features, which is her whole face.

She has the pride flag pin at the left breast area of her dress. Mine is in the same spot, just a bit lower than hers. Her eyes trail down my body appreciatively, but her gaze softens when it attaches itself to the pin.

"You look dashing," she says with a grin, and I stroke a hand down my chest as a blush covers my cheeks.

"And you look exquisite, Catalina. Like you're about to storm into a castle during a dance and take the throne," I say, watching her grin stretch into a full smile because she loves her fantasy books where the female main characters actually do that.

"I think that is my new favorite compliment," she says and spins once to show off her outfit.

I almost drop to my knees.

The fabric twirls with her, hugging her body even more in some places before shifting to show off others. Her hair flies with the motion, her smile so very contagious.

I catch her once she stops turning, my hands moving to her hips.

"Now, let's get this over with," she says, nodding once in the direction she wants me to go. I follow behind her without hesitation.

The photoshoot is awkward at first, to say the least. They keep putting us in strange positions, as if Catalina and I were nothing more than acquaintances, and

I'm getting more irritated with every picture they take where I'm not looking at her, touching her, or being close to her.

I'm about to open my mouth when Catalina beats me to it.

"What is the point of this photoshoot?" she asks, standing up and crossing her arms over her chest. The photographer looks as confused as I feel.

"Well, you know, you're the first couple to play doubles in a tournament like this in a long time. It's for publicity," he explains, holding his camera to the side.

"Exactly. We're a couple. This isn't how couples look. I'm not saying to make Santiago touch my ass or anything inappropriate like that, but there should be some touching, no? Shouldn't we at least look at each other?" she says, waving a hand in my direction. I can't suppress my smile at her irritation that we're not touching each other.

"Umm, yes, okay. Maybe you can do what feels natural for you, and I'll make suggestions and adjustments," he says, and Cata spins around, her dress flying with the motion.

They put us on this uncomfortable, tiny bench, and she moves to straddle it, making me turn to face her instinctively. Her hand flies up to my hair, fixing a single strand of it. The photographer starts photographing, and I'm about to frown at him and ask to leave us alone during this sweet moment when Catalina places her hand on my neck. My attention glues itself to her lips before trailing up to her eyes. She isn't smiling at me, but fuck, I'm grinning at her, enjoying the way she's touching me so casually, as if it's the most normal thing in the world.

The rest of the photoshoot is pure heaven. Catalina and I don't stop touching. Her mouth hovers over mine for many of the photos, always shy of a kiss. And when she moves her head to the side, I follow her. When she moves it back, I lean forward, always keeping my lips near hers like metal to a magnet. It's a delicate dance, and she eventually smiles when I let out a quiet, complaining grunt after she teased me with another almost-kiss.

By the time the photographer is done with us, my entire body has stiffened. My cock is aching, pressing against the uncomfortable fabric, and Catalina hasn't stopped touching me. Her hand lingers on my left thigh as she talks to a member of the team that put this whole set together, and I barely contain myself from storming out of here to prevent anyone from seeing my awkward situation.

But I enjoy her touch far too much to leave.

"What's wrong with you?" Cata eventually asks when the person leaves. I pick up the hand that's resting on my thigh, placing it back on my neck. Her gaze catches fire as I run her hand down my chest and rest it on my abs.

"I crave you, Catalina."

She runs her nails over my abs before bringing her hand back up to my throat, her thumb caressing the side of it right above my pulse point there, the way I always do with her. My breath hitches from both the admission and the way she's touching me.

She studies me, unsure about my words for several seconds before she says something that has me fighting a whimper.

"And you've almost earned me, Santiago. Keep being a good boy, and I'll let you have me."

I nearly come in my fucking pants without her even touching me.

She cups my chin for a brief moment as she stands, but she releases me far too soon before walking away, leaving me to stare after her.

# CHAPTER 26
## CATALINA

Sage, Charlie, Matteo, Santi, Manuela, and I are having dinner together. The tournament officially started yesterday, and my back has been feeling better, even if it's still a bit stiff. Santi's and my first match is tomorrow, so we're enjoying one last quiet evening before we're going to rip each other's heads off during the match.

As soon as I think the words, I know I'm wrong.

He's not going to fight with me about silly things anymore. He wants me. He wants me so badly, he's willing to do just about anything to get me. Part of me wants to tell him to get on his knees and beg because I know he would look so pretty doing exactly that.

And I'd be lying if I said I wasn't tired of fighting this attraction between us, too.

I've kissed him twice now.

Both times were too short, leaving me needing more, but I know as soon as we do more than kiss, as soon as we make each other come, there will be no turning back. And I'm not entirely sure I'd want to. One taste of Santi wasn't nearly enough, and that was just a kiss. If all it takes to unravel me are his lips on mine, I'm scared to find out what he'll do to me with the rest of his magnificent body.

"I'm bored," Matteo says, one of his arms casually draped around Manuela, who is grinning up at his exasperated expression.

"We finished eating twenty seconds ago. Can't you at least wait until the food has left Charlie's mouth before complaining?" Santi interrupts, making my coach and trainer cover their mouth to not spit out their food.

"Charlie, I love you, you know that, but if you don't hurry the fuck up, I might die of boredom."

"You are so dramatic," I tell the Italian, rolling my eyes at him.

"You could make me less bored, Lina. We could ditch all of them and go have fun in my room," he offers, making me snort at him.

Matteo has been flirting with me for years. There's nothing new about it, nothing that makes me uncomfortable—it's almost like flirting is his love language—but the way Santiago looks at his best friend?

I shiver from the threat in his gaze.

"I could also take this knife and stab you with it, but there are simply some things people aren't allowed to do," Santi replies, but Matteo chuckles at his best friend's words.

"Relax, Santi, everyone here knows you're faking it. There's no need to keep up the pretense," he says, pure mischief in his brown eyes. He's provoking him, knowing full well Santiago has feelings for me.

"Matteo, if I were you, I'd shut the fuck up before Santi turns green and smashes you to pieces," I chime in, but I should have been paying attention to Charlie because they've taken a big sip of water that goes all over the table as they burst into laughter. Then they start coughing, the water clearly having gone down the wrong pipe.

"This isn't what I meant when I said I'm bored and hoped for something else to do," Matteo says as he cleans up the water, Charlie still clearing their throat.

"I have an idea," Sage says, jumping to her feet and running toward the room in her suite.

She invited all of us over, even ordered food and drinks. When I asked if I could chip in, she swatted my money away and told me to shove it where the sun doesn't shine. I was too busy laughing to keep arguing.

Santi simply put some money under her purse in the entrance, but when I tried to do the same, he snatched it from my hands, placed it in my pocket, and mumbled something about buying myself some more books because he gave enough to cover both our meals. Sage might be pissed when she finds the money later, but Santi was too cute for me to argue with his stern expression and the way he mentioned one of my favorite hobbies.

"Manu, are you okay?" I ask when I realize she's been sitting across from me without saying anything for... well, most of the meal.

"Yeah, I haven't been sleeping well, that's all. Alessandra and I have been training nonstop, so combined with not sleeping, I just feel a bit drained," she says and fakes a smile, staring down at her phone a second later.

I shoot Santi a look, but he's paying me no attention. He looks at his sister with worry and sympathy, clearly aware of what is bothering her. He also looks lost on how to help her, not that I think anyone but Manu can help Manu.

When he catches me staring at him, he brings a small smile to his face. I don't manage to return it because I'm too lost studying his face to remember to smile. Only once I've appreciated his full lips, chiseled face, and strong features, do I bring my attention back to his eyes.

Fourteen heartbeats pass while we stare at each other.

Fourteen.

I know because my heart is thumping against my ribcage.

When Santi looks at me this way, like there is no one else in the world but me, I can't help but feel the same happening to me. Everything and everyone else drifts away. There is only him and me, and this heat between us that has my cheeks burning and my stomach flipping.

His eyes drop to my lips, and he licks his as he slowly drags his gaze up again. I press my legs together, biting down on my bottom lip to keep from saying things I'll regret.

*Kiss me.*

*Touch me.*

*Fuck me.*

None of these words are appropriate to say during a dinner with our closest friends.

Charlie clears their throat beside me, still fighting to get the water out of the wrong pipe, breaking the moment between Santi and me. I look away immediately, reaching for my glass of white wine to give myself something to do instead of focusing on Charlie, Matteo, and Manu having witnessed yet another moment between Santi and me.

"Who's down for some tennis?" Sage asks as she joins us again, holding up her Nintendo Switch.

"Sure, but only if we make this interesting," Matteo chimes in, catching my attention.

"How?" I ask, taking another sip of my wine.

"Whoever wins gets to choose a punishment for the losers," he says, and I look at Manu, who is finally smiling, a challenge sparkling in her eyes.

"No," Santi replies. "I'm not doing that shit with you again. Last time, you made me dance naked on top of a table at one of your parties."

My jaw falls open without permission before I burst into laughter, too amused by the visual to hold it back.

But amusement quickly turns into heat pooling low in my stomach and my laughter fading as I think about Santi's glorious body without a single piece of fabric covering him.

"Let's do it," I blurt out, making everyone turn to me. Realizing what the fuck I just said after Santi's admission, I attempt to backtrack. "Or not. Whatever is fine with me."

I want to slap myself with the palm of my hand.

"Yeah, let's play. I'll team up with Sage. Matteo and Manu can play together, and Santi and Catalina can be a team. Practice for tomorrow and what not," Charlie says, throwing a wink my way before standing up and walking toward Sage. They grab her hand and press a kiss to the back of it, smirking until my friend blushes violently. "After you," they add, gesturing for Sage to go first.

I smile at both of them, ignoring the way Santi is currently watching me. He always does that. As soon as a smile touches my lips, his eyes glue themselves to my mouth. Manu and Matteo move toward where the television is in the suite, but I take my time sipping my wine because Santi also hasn't moved yet.

"Please look at me, Cata," he says softly when I put my glass down, and I reluctantly do as I'm told. He's grinning, and I hate that I want to grin back. "We're going to win, but even when we do, feel free to give me any punishment you'd like," he adds, standing and walking toward me. "I'd very much like that."

"How about getting naked again, but this time in a room full of bees?"

He chuckles, his breath coasting my ear when he moves behind my chair and lowers his head. His lips are centimeters from my ear as he replies.

"Yes to the first part, but we don't have to play for that to happen. You can have me naked any time you want, *cariño*." He brushes his lips over the shell of my ear, sending delicious shivers down my spine.

"You're so sure you'd be able to handle me, but what if I'd tie you up, overstimulate you, and make you come so hard, you'll never want to fuck anyone else?" I stand up and spin on my heels, approaching him. I would have expected his eyes to have widened, but Santi looks as interested in my proposal as I feel.

"Do it. Ruin me for everyone else, Cata." I push at his chest, guiding him toward where our friends are.

"Haven't I already?"

He doesn't get the chance to respond because Matteo wraps an arm around his best friend, dragging him away from me.

But his smile speaks louder than any words.

My stomach starts cramping from how much I'm laughing. Playing tennis on the Switch is obviously galaxies different from playing real tennis, but I'm having more fun with Matteo, Sage, Charlie, Manu, and Santi in this hotel room than I've ever had on the court. It's carefree, and we can yell out any curse or complaint we want. That's especially important for me when Santi misses yet another ball.

"Santi, you were lucky enough to be given the ability to see. Use it!" I say, pointing at the screen. Matteo falls off the couch as he bursts into laughter, Manuela joining him a second later.

Sage and Charlie are bent over at the waist, laughing too, and Santi gives me a look of utter shock.

"Me? You should have gotten that one," he says, pointing at the screen right as they replay the point there.

He missed it at the net, and my little character didn't run to it fast enough, so really, it was Santi's fault.

"Get your shit together," I say, mostly laughing, before we go back to our game.

Despite Santi's lack of skill, we win everything. Every game. But I'm too busy feeling the burn in my face from smiling so much to care. Tomorrow I can go back to worrying about everything, to doubting myself and my ability to be successful in my career. For now, I soak up this carefreeness. I soak up the love in this room. The way Manu and Matteo are whispering to each other, sharing secret words. The way Sage and Charlie are bickering. The way Santi put my legs on his lap and is currently massaging my sore feet without me having told him to do it.

I have a big family. With three siblings, a dad who loves me more than life—like he loves all his children—four grandparents, and lots of aunts, uncles, and cousins, I have more family members than I have fingers and toes. But this? This friendship which makes me feel like the weight of the world lifts off my shoulders?

I'm going to do my best to keep them all close.

Even Santi.

*Especially Santi,* my subconscious chimes in, but I ignore that asshole.

As if he heard my thoughts, he leans toward me, pressing the sweetest kiss to my cheek and playing with the necklace Mamá gave me.

"So, what are you both going to make our punishment?" Matteo asks, clearly irritated with the whole thing. I look at Santi, who turns his head my way too.

"I think the only one who should get punished is Matteo, considering it was his idea and all," I say, and Santiago nods in approval. "And I think Santi should get his revenge and choose the punishment." Santi squeezes my feet once, probably to show his gratitude, before leaning forward and grinning at his friend.

"Take it easy on me, man," Matteo says, but Santi lets out a laugh that even makes me grin.

"Clothes off, Matteo. There's a perfectly good table in here." He points at the one in front of the couch, and I burst into laughter when he adds, "Cover your eyes, *cariño*."

Minutes later, Matteo is dancing buck ass naked on the coffee table to 'Low' by Florida, but I don't get to see a thing because Santi covers my eyes, which is fine with me. With my eyes covered, I can simply think about Santi dancing naked on the table again, and I prefer that.

# CHAPTER 27
## SANTIAGO

CATALINA AND I WERE training our asses off to prepare for today, and I feel surprisingly ready to play doubles with her. My anxiety levels are lower than they've ever been before a match, and I know it's because she's with me. We're in this together, and if we lose, which we won't, we'll do that together. Knowing I'm not alone, that I'm with the woman I have feelings for, puts me at ease.

Papá and Charlie helped us warm up already, so now we're making our way to the court where we'll be playing today. Catalina has been characteristically quiet, but I can't stop talking to her.

"I'm so excited to play doubles with you. We're going to win this tournament. Oh, also, you should refrain from doing any overhead smashes and instead leave the ball to me as long as your back isn't at a hundred percent. I wanted to tell you that earlier, but I forgot. And—" I cut off when I see the amusement sparkling in her eyes.

"Santi, take a deep breath. I know you're excited, but I'm going to need you to slow down before you make my heart race any more than it already does thanks to the sight of your arms," she says, placing a hand on my arm and squeezing it. Appreciating it. "This outfit was a horrible choice if I'm supposed to not drool for the whole match."

Excitement unfurls inside of me.

"Cata, are you flirting with me again?" I ask, nudging her shoulder with mine.

"I can't seem to stop," she replies, shaking her head as I grin down at her.

"Well, the same goes for your outfit. I won't be able to focus when you're in front of me," I admit and watch a smug look take over her features.

Catalina truly looks devastating in her outfit. *Spin* has outdone themselves once more, having put her in a dark blue skirt with a matching top, but the top is tight around her chest, and the bottom flows beautifully around her trained, thick thighs. My girl is a masterpiece, made to perfection and then some, and her biggest sponsor has a way of always highlighting that very idea.

For the next tournament, I'll have to speak to *New Light* and see if they'd ask *Spin* to collab on outfits for Cata and me because not matching with her, wearing a different shade of blue, is annoying me.

"Well, you're going to have to focus because if we lose this, I'll post an embarrassing picture I took of you during one of our flights. Mouth open, eye mask on, drool coming from the corner of your mouth," she says, and I let out an exasperated gasp.

"First of all, I don't drool. Second of all, if you do that, I'll start wearing shirts with sleeves," I reply, making her chuckle.

"Fine, fine. Let's not resort to such drastic measures."

My laughter dies out when we're called to the court, the entire arena welcoming us with loud cheers and applause. I wave at all of them with a smile, and Cata does the same, but hers looks a little more forced than mine feels. I know she has a tough time with this amount of attention, so I take her hand, squeezing it comfortingly as we make our way to the seating area where we're supposed to put our bags. Towels are waiting for us there, but Cata and I always bring our own, given to us by our sponsors.

Catalina places her hand on my bicep for several seconds after she releases my hand, showing her gratitude without speaking a single word.

The mixed doubles players Cata and I are opposing today are Frederic Boutine and Inaya Klatz. They've been playing doubles for a year, so they're a bit more practiced than Cata and me, but we're the better players, at least individually. Who am I kidding? We were undefeatable when we played together as kids, and we've only gotten better in our game since. We practiced, and it's like we fell back into a comfortable rhythm.

We've got this.

We do all of the pre-match activities, flipping the coin, warming up, and so on, before the match finally starts. I'm serving first, which means Cata will be at the net for this first game. She's fantastic at volleys, so I'm confident this will be easy to get through.

"Okay, so Inaya plays with a lot of topspin, but Frederic hits the balls flatter."

"Yeah, I noticed that too," I reply, walking to the back with her to put our towels down. "His backhand is very inconsistent," I add.

"Her backhand is really strong. We should stay away from giving her that shot," Catalina replies, following me to the baseline.

"Got it. I'll serve to her forehand."

Cata lingers next to me for a tense second, not entirely sure if she should simply walk to her spot or do something else. So, while Inaya and Frederic still make their way to their spots, I place a hand on her left hip, lean down, and press a soft kiss to her cheek. The crowd cheers, and I immediately grin because they're supporting us and our relationship exactly how we'd hoped they would. Our plan is working. No one has mentioned my playboy ways in months, and Catalina's scandal is long forgotten, replaced by conversations of how dedicated we are to each other.

"We've got this," I say, squeezing her hip once more before releasing her.

The way she smiles makes me so happy.

A smile born out of a sweet gesture of mine.

I love her smile so much. I don't think I'll ever get enough of it, and not only because it's rare and I don't get to see it often. I don't think I'll ever get enough because Catalina's smile reminds me of all the good things in the world. It reminds me of my childhood, a time when she gave it to me so freely. It reminds me of what I hope my future will look like, a life filled with her smiles.

It takes me several ball bounces to ignore how gorgeous Cata looks as she gets into position at the net. It takes several more to swallow down my fear of accidentally hitting her. Only then do I manage to serve a perfect shot down the center line. Frederic is on it, though, and returns it to me. We rally back and forth until ultimately, he hits the ball to Cata, and she puts it away with so much force, neither of our opponents manages to get it.

I stand behind her, shocked into place by her amazing shot. A smile curls the corners of my mouth, and when she turns around to catch me being so surprised, she smirks and winks my way.

This woman is going to bring me to my fucking knees, and I will enjoy every second of it.

The match flies by.

Our serves are consistent. Our shots are well placed most of the time. Everything is going absolutely flawlessly. We communicate well. We listen to each other. We build a strategy that has us on top of the game.

Even though I knew Cata and I would do well, I didn't expect that we'd win the first set six games to two and then the second one six games to three. But as she serves again, she places it wide and in the corner, earning us our first win as doubles partners since we were kids.

I spin on my heels just in time to see her run my way, jumping into my arms. I catch her with ease because I was made for this woman, I truly believe that, and she wraps her arms around my neck. A victorious laugh escapes her lips, pure happiness consuming both of us as we take home this first victory.

I know people will probably have a lot to say about how we're celebrating, making such a big ordeal out of nothing. But this is important for us. It's a demonstration of our power, of our ability as doubles partners to return and play such a strong match.

Cata releases me too quickly, but I have no time to be disappointed by it because after shaking our opponents' hands, as expected, she skips toward her bag, the sight too fucking adorable to mind. I join her, both of us getting ready to be interviewed and then leave for the press conference after, cool down, and more. I'm not as physically exhausted as I would be after a three-set match, potentially five, and I hope Cata feels the same.

"How's your back?" I ask, placing a hand on it and rubbing the small of it with my hand.

"It feels good, Santi. Really good," she replies, wiping her face with one of the towels. She's not wearing a speck of makeup, and I can't describe how devastatingly beautiful I think she is, especially when she's all sweaty and happy from a match well played.

"Can I hold your hand while we do the interview?" I find myself asking, and Cata wastes no time flinging her bag around her shoulder to take my hand.

"You're a very needy man," she says, pulling me toward the interviewer.

"Only when it comes to you." I know she's rolling her eyes, even if all I can see is the back of her head.

"Everybody, let's give *the* couple of tennis a warm round of applause," the interviewer says, and the entire arena fills the space around us with more applause. "You two played a fantastic match. You had the strategy, the skill, and the communication to dominate today. Did you think you'd be playing this well during your first match back?"

Catalina looks up at me, probably because I'm almost vibrating from excitement to answer this question. She gives me a nod, as if to say "go ahead," and I waste no time doing so.

"I had no doubts. Catalina and I have been playing doubles since we were kids, and we've been training together all season as hitting partners. I know her tennis inside out, I've been studying it her whole career, and I think we fit really well together, on and off the court." I'm rambling, but there is no stopping my words. Not even as I admit something I lied to her about when we first met up before the season began.

"That's sweet. Catalina, you looked fantastic out there. Confident, strong. There were no signs your back was bothering you today. Can we take that as a good sign that you'll be back to playing singles matches soon?" the interviewer goes on, and I give Cata a proud look as she steps toward the microphone a little.

"Absolutely. I'll be back in no time, and it'll be to win my first Grand Slam," she says, and the crowd explodes into another round of cheers.

They love her so much. They always have. Catalina is the kind of person you can't help but fall for, and it shows in their support.

It shows in my feelings for her.

The interviewer wraps up their questions, and Catalina and I make our way to where Charlie and Papá are waiting to go through our post-match procedures with us. But before we reach them, she drags me into a private room, a bathroom, because there are cameras pretty much everywhere else in this area, and gives me a serious look.

"Were you telling the truth out there? You've been watching me play all this time?" She isn't angry. There is something akin to hope filtering through her eyes, and her features have softened immensely.

Without hesitation, I raise my hands to cup her cheeks, taking her face in them to keep her eyes on me as I tell her something I should have told her a long time ago.

"In my eyes, you are the best tennis player in the world. I'm in awe of you. I've been in awe of you for over a decade. You inspire me to be better, even when it was more rivalry than anything else."

I take a step toward her, bringing my chest flush against hers. Hers is rising and falling so quickly, I wish I knew why. Does she want to kiss me again? Does she want more? Are my feelings too much for her?

"I'm sorry I lied to you about that. I—" She cuts me off.

"You don't have to apologize. It was a tiny lie, and we were still angry with each other at the time," she says, attempting to avoid my gaze, but I hold her in place.

"It may have been tiny, but I'm still sorry I ever made you feel like I haven't been paying attention to you since we met. Because I have." I take a deep breath before saying something I never thought I'd say. "Cata, not a day has passed in the last decade that I haven't thought about you in some capacity. Every time I pick up a tennis racket, I think about you. I think about you during highly inappropriate moments. I think about you when I shouldn't, when I don't want to."

Our mouths keep getting closer. Our breaths are becoming one. But I won't kiss her unless she really wants me to, and she knows that.

It's why she doesn't move away.

She trusts me.

She *trusts* me.

"I think about you when I shouldn't, too," she admits, her voice hardly more than a whisper, but she might as well have screamed it for how loudly I hear her words. "I've been thinking about you even more in the last four months. And I can't stop. I don't think I want to." She grabs the front of my shirt, pulling me even more against her. "Kiss me, Santiago. Kiss me until I can finally stop thinking about your lips on mine."

She's barely done speaking when I press my mouth to hers. I hold back a sigh because I don't want her to hear how desperately I've been craving another taste of her. But considering how fervently I kiss her, she probably knows. She can probably taste it on my tongue. I want her so badly, and she's allowing me this, another piece of her.

I'll take every single one she offers me.

# CHAPTER 28
## CATALINA

I ALWAYS KNEW KISSING Santi would be heaven. He has these full lips that make my knees a little weak every single time I look at them, but I never thought it could be this amazing. Especially after he's been so honest with me again.

It feels too good when I part my lips and he slips his tongue into my mouth, exploring me, tasting me, worshipping me. When he slides his hands over my back, resting them on my lower back.

"Santi, I don't want your respectful touches right now. I need you to *touch* me," I say against his lips, and he wastes no time dropping his hands to my ass and squeezing it. A content moan slips out of my mouth, making him grin against me as he keeps kissing me.

"Don't worry, *cariño*, I'll be as disrespectful as you want me to be."

I know it's wrong, that this will complicate things even further. We're faking a relationship. We're playing doubles for the next few weeks. This can only end in chaos and drama, but I couldn't care less. This feels good. So good I might die if he stops touching me, as dramatic as it may sound.

"Fuck, Cata," he moans when I run my nails down his neck and abs. I bite down gently on his bottom lip, earning another groan before he lifts me into the air. I wrap my legs around his hips, never breaking the kiss, even as he fumbles with the handle of the door to lock it.

He sits down on a bench they have in the corner of the bathroom with me on his lap, his fingers digging into my ass as he drags me forward. I rub against him, my swollen clit sending a bolt of pleasure through me at the contact with his hard cock.

"Fuck, we can't repeat that. I'm going to come in my pants if we do," he says, but the mere thought of the power I hold over Santi has me rolling my hips again.

"But I haven't given you permission to come yet, Santi. Don't you want to be my good boy and do what I tell you to?" His reaction is visceral. His whole body shudders, his grip on me tightens, and his eyes fill with even more lust.

"I want to be your good boy, Cata. I want to be everything you tell me to be," he says as I slide my hands into his hair and tug, pulling his head back ever so slightly.

The column of his throat is exposed to me this way, and I take full advantage of the position as I lean down to kiss along the length of it. He tastes like he smells, and a bit salty from playing for a little over an hour, but I can't get enough. I nip at his skin while he keeps rolling my hips for me, rubbing me against him.

"Cata, fuck, *cariño*, I need you to stop if you don't want me to make a mess of myself," he says, panting when I trail my lips over the side of his throat.

"Make a mess of me, Santiago," I say as I lean back, arching my back when he adjusts to thrust up and against me. My breasts are in his face then, and he wastes no time nipping at my nipple where it's covered by my sports bra and shirt.

"I want to see these piercings without any clothes, Catalina. I want to admire them, play with them," he says, raking his teeth over the same nipple before moving onto the next one. "Have I earned that yet, *mi mariquita*? Or will you make me beg for it?"

"Beg," I say, even if right now I can't think of anything better than Santi removing my shirt and bra and playing with my nipples while I rub against him.

"Please, Cata. Please give me more. Please, I'll be your good boy." I shudder on top of him, the sound of his begging so fucking sweet, I roll my hips faster, chasing my pleasure.

"Remove my shirt," I instruct, never stopping my movements. I'm so close, just like him, and if I just—

"Santi? Catalina? Are you in here?" a familiar voice asks as they knock on the door of the room we're in, forcing Santi and me to stop our movements.

"Don't say anything," Santi replies, reaching for the hem of my shirt even with his father still knocking on the door.

"I saw you two go in here," Carlos says next, and I cover my mouth to hold back a laugh.

"Go away!" Santi calls back, but when I chuckle, his irritation with his father turns into amusement.

"I can't. Catalina, you have to get out here right now. Sage hurt herself during her match. They're taking her to the hospital right now."

My heart drops all the way into my stomach.

I jump off Santi's lap, rushing toward the door without a second thought. Panic has infiltrated every part of me, and I won't be able to get rid of it until I hear that Sage is going to be fine.

She has to be fine.

"I need you to tell me exactly what happened," I say to Carlos when I open the door, picking up my bag before I follow him down the hall. I look over my shoulder to ensure Santi is coming too, which he is. There's concern on his face, the same I feel deep in my chest, and it's almost a relief to know I don't have to be alone while I worry about my friend.

And I blame that as the reason for me taking his hand.

Carlos sent me the video of the moment when Sage hurt something in her back, but I've been too nervous to watch it. He told me she was serving when it happened, and I know Sage also suffers from back problems like me, but seeing it will make it all the more real.

I'll think about her getting surgery right now.

That's how horrible it must have been.

*She's getting emergency surgery.*

Tears fall down my cheeks before I can stop them, and I drag my legs against my chest on the uncomfortable hospital chair. Charlie went to get us some food, so I can't even lean on them for support. And Santi? He went to do our post-match conference so we don't get in trouble, but I wish he was here. I want to sit in his lap and let him wrap me up in his arms while he promises me everything will be okay.

My mother wasn't sick for a long time. She didn't have a disease that dragged over days and months and years, so I didn't have to sit in waiting rooms as a kid. But being here still brings up things I've been suppressing for years. Because I did sit in a hospital room with Ori for a long time the night she died. I held baby Sam in my arms, and Ori hugged Hernanda to her chest while we waited to hear any news.

Mamá had a heart condition that cost her her life. She always knew it could, but there was nothing she could do to change that. She had several surgeries to fix whatever was wrong with her heart, but they were temporary fixes. The only thing that could have saved her would have been a new heart, but she didn't get one before... well, before she passed.

Sitting here, I realize it bothers me that I don't remember what heart condition she had. It bothers me that my trauma has taken that information from me, but at the same time, I'm not sure I want to know.

It wouldn't change anything, after all.

More tears fall as I press a hand to my chest, right where the tattoo for Mamá is. She'd be so sad if she saw that I'm still crying over her so many years after her passing. It hasn't gotten easier for me like everyone promised it would be. Any memory of her saddens me deeply. Even if some of them bring me joy, it's hard to think or talk about her.

"Cata, *cariño*," Santi says, and I realize I've covered my eyes with my hands, so I lower them to look at him.

He's standing at the end of the hallway, soaking wet from the rain outside, and I have so many questions.

Why does he look like he ran all the way from the post-match conference to this hospital? Why can't I stop relief from filling every part of me at the mere sight of him? Why did he take so damn long to get to me?

But I don't ask any of them at first. No. I stand up and run all the way to him, straight into his arms. It doesn't matter that my clothes are immediately soaking wet. I need him, his touch, and even if the feeling doesn't last because one of us finds a way to ruin it, right now it's in my chest. And I can't get rid of it, no matter how much I try. Not that I'm trying very hard. Despite my best efforts and everything that's happened between us, I care so much about this man.

I always have.

I'm starting to realize I always will.

"*Mariquita*, I'm getting your clothes all wet," he says, but he doesn't release me either. If anything, he holds on tighter.

"I don't care," I reply, my fingers slipping into his hair. "Did you run all the way here?"

He chuckles as he holds me tighter, burying his face in my neck.

"Pretty much, yeah. Traffic was so bad, running was faster," he replies, and I shake my head as I fight back tears because of how relieved I am that he's here. Because my feelings for him are more than reciprocated, they're multiplied tenfold for him. Because he'd run in the rain for me, the man who never wanted to be in a relationship.

"This is getting so messy, Santiago. What does any of this mean? We keep kissing when no one is watching. We keep touching when it's not necessary. You keep saying things you don't have to. This doesn't feel so fake anymore, and that makes everything complicated," I say, finally leaning back to see drops of water dripping from his hair and onto his cheeks.

He should look exhausted. We had a match earlier and he just ran I don't know how many kilometers to the hospital. But he doesn't. He looks devastating. His heart is in his eyes, he's been wearing it there for weeks, if not months, and I can't decide if that terrifies me or settles the turmoil inside of me.

"It doesn't feel fake because it isn't fake, *cariño*. What I feel for you has been real since we met. I keep touching you because I think I'd die if I didn't. I keep saying things that I don't have to say but that are true in every way. I keep kissing you because I'm catching up on the time I didn't do so."

As if to prove his point, he leans down to lightly brush his lips over mine.

"Let's give this a shot. We won't tell anyone in our surroundings that we're not faking anymore. We will let them think we're pretending, but in private, we can try this out for real."

My heart stops beating as soon as the words have left his mouth.

It's terrifying to fall for someone who's hurt you in the past, but I see now that Santi didn't mean to hurt me. I'm realizing he was a kid. Selfish, yes, but he was *just a child*. He's grown so much, and if I'm being honest, if I had been given the opportunity to qualify for the junior tournament, I'd have taken it too. Granted, I would have spoken to him about it first, but it feels so ridiculous to continue to be upset about something that happened so long ago. Especially when Santi dropped out of the next two singles tournaments to play doubles with me. He prioritized me. He keeps putting me first, and I don't want to be angry with him anymore.

"You don't even know how to be in a relationship." I don't know why I'm still looking for an excuse, but I'm so scared.

Santi tucks a strand of hair behind my ear, not in the least bit annoyed with me for my response.

"You're right. I have no idea how to be in a relationship, but I think I've been doing a pretty good job in our fake relationship. Imagine how good I'd be in a real one with you," he replies, and it's that "with you" that has my stomach twisting in the best ways. "One chance, Cata. It's all I'm asking for."

"One chance," I echo, tasting the words on my tongue. They're as scared as I am. "But I swear to God, Santi, if you make me regret it, I'll throw you in shark-infested waters with fish wrapped around you," I warn, and he chuckles, pressing his forehead to mine.

"I think that's fair," he says, kissing my temple. "I'll take you on a proper date once this tournament is over." He goes on to kiss my cheek. "I'll show you how good I can be for you, *mariquita*." He hovers his mouth over mine, but I'm the one who kisses him. I'm the one who closes the distance and captures his lips with mine.

Santi melts against me, his hands lifting to my neck and his thumbs pressing against my jaw to tilt my head up more. It allows him to deepen the kiss, to make me forget about the rest of the world.

But it only lasts so long until reality comes crashing back in.

"Have you heard anything about Sage?" he asks after he pulls back and traces my lips as if to make sure I still feel him there, even with his mouth gone.

"Nothing yet," I reply, panic seeping back into my body. "I'm really worried," I admit. Santi's amber eyes hold me in place as he speaks again.

"I know you are. I am too. But Sage will be fine. She's too stubborn for anything worse to happen to her," he teases, but it doesn't make me smile. Not when I remember her being hurt all the time. She's already had so many injuries, so many timeouts she had to take because of them.

Sage doesn't deserve to be in that operating room right now. She deserved to win the *Indian Wells Open*, but that has been taken away from her.

Santiago and I move to sit down, but as soon as we reach the chairs, a doctor walks into the hall, looking for someone.

"Are there any family members for Sage Clark?" she asks, but the only people here are Santi and me, so all of her attention is on us.

"We are." Even if we're not related by blood, we're the only family Sage has. Well, us and her friend Tatum, who lives at Silver Creek Ranch, but Sage made us promise to never call her unless it was something life-threatening.

"And me," I hear someone say before Vanessa steps toward us in a pantsuit that looks perfectly put together.

"What are you doing here?" I ask, stepping into her arms when she opens them for me in invitation.

"I took my private jet and flew here as soon as I heard. Luckily, I was in Toronto to visit a friend, so I wasn't too far away," she says, kissing my cheek before greeting Santi with a nod before approaching the doctor. "I want to know everything in detail."

I don't often get to see this side of Ness. She's usually so comfortable letting go that the businesswoman in her doesn't come out unless she has to. Right now, she is in businesswoman mode, probably to swallow down the panic and concern in her chest.

"Because of her disc herniation and the fact that it has not gotten better but worse, we have had to do something called a microdiscectomy to remove the herniated part. It went successfully, and after her recovery, she should feel much better."

A sigh of relief *whooshes* out of me, and Santi takes my hand clearly feeling the same. His shoulders drop as the worry leaves him, and I squeeze his fingers as if to acknowledge that everything will be fine now.

"She's still sleeping, but you can see her soon," the doctor says before leaving to get back to her other tasks.

Ness pulls me into another hug, and I fling my arms around her, holding on tight.

"Yeah, you, too. Come here," I hear my friend say, and a second later, Santiago's arms wrap around both of us.

# CHAPTER 29
## SANTIAGO

SAGE IS RECOVERING WELL, even if she's very impatient about her healing journey. Things are not moving quickly enough for her, and I can't blame her. I'd probably be the same.

Between training, our matches, and Cata refusing to leave Sages' side, we haven't had a chance to do anything more than stare longingly at one another, which is fine with me for now. I have waited a long time to get a chance with Catalina. I can wait a little longer while she takes care of our friend.

Plus, I like spending time with Sage, especially when she scowls at all the nurses for giving her hospital food which she absolutely hates. Ness has been sneaking in other food for her, and I'm convinced it's the only reason she hasn't ripped anyone's head off.

Today, Catalina and I are playing in the finals of the *Indian Wells Open.*

We made it here by pretty much bulldozing through all of our opponents, never needing more than two sets to defeat them.

I don't want today to be different, but we're playing against Noah Volic and Bernadette Jowls, and they're the best doubles players in the game right now. Well, before Cata and I started, that is, and I don't care if it makes me sound full of myself—us, I guess—because we *are* that good.

We're warming up, Cata rallying with Bernadette, and Noah and I doing the same. They're both incredibly strong players, but before the match, Cata and I spent an hour studying their game.

"Noah's forehand isn't all there today. He's making a lot of mistakes," I tell Cata as soon as she approaches me after the warm-up. Noah and Bernadette are getting ready to start serving for this match.

"I suggest we aim our balls his way. He's a bit less consistent than she is in general. He tries shots that always go too far or in the net," she says, and I smile at her because watching her strategize and analyze is one of my favorite things about playing doubles with her.

"Yeah, he hits the balls really flat," I agree, taking a step closer to her to make sure no one can hear our words. Bernadette and Noah are huddled together, Noah covering his mouth with a ball as he speaks to his partner, a common tactic in doubles.

"We can do this," she says, encouraging us, and I lift her hand to my mouth to place a kiss to the back of it.

"We got this," I echo, watching a shy smile curl up the corners of her lips. She's blushing because the crowd always whistles, screams, or cheers for us when we show any kind of affection, but I think she's getting used to it.

Or maybe she's simply getting more comfortable with me so that she doesn't mind the attention being on her because she knows it's divided between us, and I will always have her back.

The first game is uneventful. Bernadette and Noah manage to bring it home somewhat easily because Noah's serve is flawless and incredibly fast. There is barely any fighting at all because even when Cata and I are on the ball, we don't manage to hit it well enough to take control of the rally.

The second game goes to us just as easily. I started serving, as I've done in every match, to give Cata more time to warm up and get ready to serve. If she knew that's what I was doing, she'd probably gut me like a fish, so I simply say I prefer serving first. It's not entirely a lie, even if it's not the full truth either. I'm worried about her, and I want her to get better as soon as possible so she can finally win her first Grand Slam.

She deserves it.

It's long overdue.

Bernadette serves next, and Cata and I are struggling to find ways to outplay them as well as outsmart them. They're both playing well at the moment, their shots are consistent and well-placed, but there has to be a way to take a service game from them.

"Santi," Cata says after we lose another point. I move toward her, lowering my head so she can whisper in my ear. "Go far left, then I'll go down the middle," she says, and I give her an agreeing nod. She offers me one last firm, determined look before moving to the net.

It's my turn to return the serve, which is why Cata told me to go left. To my benefit, Bernadette serves in the right corner of the box, and I easily hit the ball cross-court where my doubles partner told me to go. Bernadette manages to get the ball, but Catalina moves toward the center line and puts it away, straight down the middle of the court, where Noah can't reach it while Bernadette recovers.

"*Vamos, cariño!*" I call out, a bright smile taking over my face when she turns to me to show off her smug expression. She has every right to wear it after such a beautiful point.

"You see, you have to listen to me," she says, wiggling her brows at me.

"Tell me what to do, and I'll obey without question," I reply as she comes closer, and she whispers another plan into my ear.

A minute later, we get another point, making it thirty all for the score.

"You're unstoppable," I say, high-fiving her when she walks back toward me. "What's next?"

It's one set to one.

Cata and I won the first set, but Bernadette and Noah destroyed us in the second one.

Now it's five games to four.

We have had one break this set, taking a service game from Noah, and Cata and I are exhausted. The last few rallies have been a minimum of twenty shots, which is a lot. It's her turn to serve now, and I step toward her, concern slipping into my throat. I barely swallow past it to speak.

"How is your back?" I ask, placing a hand on it as if I could feel the answer there for myself.

"It's fine. Tired," she admits as she raises her hand to the bicep of the arm that's around her, so my fingers can trail over her back.

"We're almost there. All we have to do is get your game," I say while she wipes her face with her towel.

"You say it as if it's so simple. We've been struggling to get mine through the whole match," she replies with a tired laugh, her shoulders dropping as she takes a deep breath. "But you're right. We can do it. This is our match," she whispers, her determination one of my favorite sights in the world.

"Yes, we can. One more game, and we'll finally have a few days off to go on a date," I say, a sense of giddiness spreading through me at the very thought.

"Is that all you think about?" she asks, shaking her head at me.

"Not all, but like ninety-five percent of my thoughts are occupied by you." The words roll off my tongue more easily than I ever thought possible, but at this point, I can't remember a time I wasn't wrapped around her finger.

I can't even remember why I ever chose to fuck around instead of asking her to be in a real relationship with me.

"Santi, are you obsessed with me?" she asks, starting to walk back to the baseline while I follow behind her like a lost puppy.

"Undeniably."

I only see the back of her head, her braided hair as it moves from side to side, but I know she's smiling at my response. Despite not thinking we could ever make this work, I think Cata may be falling for me, too, even if it's only a little.

Fuck, I hope it's a lot.

"Okay, focus on the game, Santi. We can keep talking about this later," she says, taking the balls the ball person hands her and inspecting them.

"Promise?" My smirk has a blush settling on her cheeks, but she doesn't respond to my question. Instead, she locks in and goes straight back to talking strategy with me.

"I'm going to try and speed up my serve," she says, and I open my mouth to argue, to remind her she's been slowing it down—if only slightly—for a reason. "They won't expect it." Hard to argue with a good point, even one I don't like.

"As soon as you feel the tiniest pulling or pain, you slow down again," I say, pointing a warning finger at her. She pokes me in the stomach with the head of her racket, making me drop the finger.

"You know I'm a grown woman, right?" she asks, furrowing her brows at me, but I just shrug because yes, she is, but I'm also never going to stop worrying about her.

Not since I saw what happened when she overused her back.

Cata takes my arm and leads me to the baseline, and I realize our opponents are doing the same.

No more time to flirt.

"Trust me," is the last thing Cata says before urging me to go to the net.

We're both so tired, but I think she's even more so because her left hand trembles a little as she wraps her hands around the tennis ball and prepares to serve. Then I look at her face and realize it's not exhaustion at all.

She's nervous.

As a matter of fact, I'd even say she's anxious about losing this, and I don't blame her.

Losing when you have a fundamental fear of failure is one of the most triggering things for my mental health. I can only assume the same applies to her. Knowing

Cata, I'd even go as far as assuming it's a combination of things, and she's scared serving faster, using more strength, is going to do something to her back again. If only she'd listen to me and keep slowing it down. We don't need her to risk anything. We will win either way, but Cata is determined, and there is no stopping her now.

Worst of all, I'm pretty sure she'd risk injury if it meant proving to herself and the world that she's good enough for this sport.

"*Cariño,* take a deep breath," I say in Spanish, and she does as told as I position myself at the net.

She takes another fifteen seconds or so until her racket connects with the ball, followed by a grunt. My eyes catch sight of the ball as it goes straight down the center line. It's fast, precise, and absolutely perfect. Noah, so surprised at the sheer speed, doesn't manage to get to it, turning the serve into an ace. I shift to Cata and start clapping along with the rest of the stadium. Her nerves seem to settle a little now that she got her first ace of the set in, and I couldn't be prouder when I notice her confidence as she positions herself to serve again.

The next shot isn't an ace because Bernadette manages to touch the ball with her racket, but it goes flying into the crowd.

Thirty-love.

"One more, baby. Give me one more of those beautiful serves."

She gives me one more, another ace, making it forty-love.

The game is ours in the next rally.

The match is ours.

I hear her racket drop right before I spin around to see Catalina covering her face, her shoulders shaking as she cries into them. I waste no time running to her, and as if she senses me, she drops her hands to lift her arms so I can wrap mine around her. Her legs fling around me too, and then we're hugging, all sweaty and sticky from this exhausting match.

"That was incredible," I whisper into her ear, but Cata doesn't reply.

She merely holds on tighter.

We did it. We won our first tournament as doubles partners in years. We *dominated* this tournament.

"Good job, *mi mariquita*," I say.

"Good job, *mi corazón*," she replies, and I have a feeling that for the first time, she isn't saying it sarcastically.

# CHAPTER 30
## CATALINA

"IF THEY TRY TO feed me one more fucking tasteless sandwich, I'm going to throw a pillow at their heads," Sage says, glaring at the tray with food in front of her.

A nurse caught me bringing her food two days ago and told me this hospital has a strict policy against that. I got a warning not to do it again *lest I want to be kicked out of the hospital*, or whatever the fuck they said to me. I was too distracted by Charlie laughing at me for getting scolded and Sage's complaining grunting noises. Vanessa was frowning at the nurse because of how ridiculous it was.

"If only you hadn't been so reckless about sneaking food in," Sage goes on, and I scowl at her.

"Eat your tasteless sandwhich," I grumble, but when she smiles at me, I smile back.

It's been hardly more than a week since her surgery, but she looks much better. They're keeping her here to ensure there are no complications. According to the doctors monitoring her she's supposed to get discharged soon to fly back home. This isn't the first time Sage had to withdraw from a tournament, so she's taken the news of not being able to play for a while much better than I would have.

"What if I told you I brought you some dessert?" Charlie asks, piquing Sage's interest.

"I'd ask why you didn't bring me a bucket of chicken tenders too," she replies, but her eyes are full of amusement as Charlie walks toward her with a wicked smile.

"They would have smelled the chicken. They can't smell the chocolate bar," they say and pull out said bar, holding it up so Sage can admire it.

"Marry me, Charlie," Sage teases, and Charlie bursts into laughter.

"Eat your chocolate bar, woman," is their only reply as they shake their head, but I notice the smile on their face. The way their eyes sparkle too.

I look back at Sage, wondering if maybe there's something there I didn't notice before.

The thought leaves quickly because Ness gets up and walks to the window in Sage's room, looking out of it with a thoughtful expression on her face. Sage is munching on the chocolate bar now with Charlie watching her from the chair they're occupying, so I walk toward Ness, placing a hand on her arm once I'm close enough.

"You alright?" Her brown eyes meet mine, and she forces a smile.

"Nothing I can't fix." I furrow my brows at her non-committal answer, and Ness lets out a sigh. "I'm having some trouble with one of my biggest distributors, but it'll be okay. Once I figure that out, I can get back to designing your next outfit for the next tournament. I'm trying to figure out what message we can send this time. Any ideas?"

I smile softly at her.

"Hundreds," I reply, and she grins back at me, leaning forward to wrap me up in a hug she needs very badly. And I hug her back because I'll be damned if I didn't give my friends the kind of comfort they're always so happy to give me.

Santiago: Hey, cariño. I know we were meant to go out on a date tomorrow, but I have to reschedule. I'm having an episode, and Manu isn't home to help me through it. Please don't hate me. I promise to see you as soon as it passes.

Ever since I received the message an hour ago, I have been running to get all of his favorite things. His favorite croissants from the café. Some iced tea from his favorite brand. Some *Lebkuchen* from the grocery store. A bunch of other snacks he always talks about. I also got him a plushie of a bunny that looks like Tornado, bought a new game for us to try out together, and in case he doesn't want to do any of that, I've taken my car to his house so he can drive it and cheer him up. He may have been sponsored by Spark Racing with his Lightning Bolt, but my Ragna Velocità Rossa is still one of his favorite cars in the world.

If Santi hadn't told me he needs to be distracted and talk through these episodes, I wouldn't be on my way to him. Other people prefer to be left alone when they have episodes of depression, but my sunshine man isn't like that. He needs to be around people he cares about, and if he didn't think he'd be a burden to me, he'd have asked me to come to him.

But I don't mind him not saying anything. He's done so much for me without me saying a single word, like all of the dates he took me on. Playing doubles with me. Getting me tickets to the Monaco Grand Prix where I will meet Valentina Romana in person for the first time.

I'm still annoyed with Santi for meeting Adrian Romana and Nevaeh Fuchs-Romana all those years ago for a tennis session. I knew he had history with Nevaeh, but I hated him for meeting her and her husband again without me present. I admire her, and I'm a big fan of Adrian. His performance at Velocità Rossa in Formula 1 is unlike any other, except for his sister's, of course.

"Hi, I'm here to see Santiago Castillo. I'm his girlfriend," I say to the security person at his apartment complex.

"Name?" they answer, their broad shoulders and muscular, tall frame intimidating me a little.

"Catalina Sanchez." The security person nods, then crosses their massive arms over their chest.

I swallow hard.

"What does he call you?" they ask, and I almost stutter out a wrong response. They're intimidating me so much, I'm not even sure anymore if I really am Santiago's girlfriend.

*Fake* girlfriend.

"*Mariquita* since childhood. *Cariño* more recently," I blurt out, and they give a satisfied nod as they finally let me through. The valet takes my key and gives me a ticket, and when I walk inside, I find a person in the lobby of the apartment complex already waiting for me.

"Ms. Sanchez, please follow me. Mr. Castillo gave us very specific instructions on what to do when you finally came to his apartment," he says, gesturing toward where the elevators are. He brings me all the way to Santi's floor, then leads me to his apartment number. "He has given us this spare key to give to you as well." He hands me a key, then leaves me standing in front of Santi's door, dumbfounded and baffled.

For someone who's never been in a relationship, Santiago sure knows how to make a girl feel special.

Even though I have a key, I knock first. It's only when several minutes pass and there is no answer that I decide to use the key Santi intended for me. I unlock the door, finding his apartment completely silent and dark. Tornado welcomes me by the door, spinning in a circle. He has his own little area in Santi's apartment, but he must have left him out to run around, something he always does when he's home. I pick him up and carry him with me as I walk through the rest of the apartment, enjoying the way he nuzzles into my arms, his cute, little nose wiggling from side to side. Santi can't take him with him to most tournaments, and he usually stays with a friend who has a few bunnies himself.

The curtains are shut, there are no sounds, and I know exactly where he's hiding before I walk through his apartment and down the hall to where his bedroom must be. The door is wide open, and I find Santi in his bed with the blanket wrapped around his entire body, even his head. The only thing peeking out is his face, but

I think that's mostly so he can watch whatever show or movie he put on, on his phone.

I place Tornado on the bed, and he wastes no time in hopping toward Santi.

My knuckles brush against the door, finally catching his attention.

"Catalina?" he asks, slowly sitting up in bed and rubbing his eyes as if he can't quite believe I'm standing here.

"I'm sorry, I just came in. I knocked, but there was no answer, and I was given a key," I explain, rubbing my left arm as a nervous laugh escapes me. "Is this the wrong thing to do? I thought maybe... I don't know. I thought you might need me."

Santi's amber eyes study me for several long seconds, his mouth opening and closing as he looks for the right words. All I can focus on are the circles underneath his eyes. He looks less like himself. His tanned skin is unusually pale, which isn't from not being in the sun. We only came back from Australia yesterday, and up until we left, he was on the court, beneath the sun, every spare second to train with me. So, I know it's something else. I know it's him genuinely not feeling good.

"I do need you. I need you more than air right now, Cata, but you shouldn't have to see me like this. You shouldn't have to deal with me when I have no idea how to crawl out of this hole I've fallen into," he explains, which spurs me on to close the distance between us. I sink onto his bed, my hand finding his before I snake my fingers around his.

"Let me be the ladder to help you climb out of it, Santi." His eyes soften visibly, his shoulders untensing as his eyebrows also unforrow. A look of relief covers his features. "I promise if you let me be there for you, I will be. I'll always be there when you need me." Santi lifts his hand to my cheek, the adrenaline of the surprise of seeing me slowly slipping out of him, leaving him entirely without energy.

"I'm sorry," he says, his hand shaking a little as he lifts it to my face. "I need to brush my teeth and shower, but I can't find the strength to. I feel so unmotivated to do anything but stay in bed, but at the same time, I'm so uncomfortable because I haven't washed myself." His hand drops from my face, but I take it in both of mine, pressing it to my chest as tears fill his tired eyes.

"I can help you." He gives me several slow nods as the tears drop down his cheeks. "Come on, Santi. I'll help you feel better," I say and stand up, pulling him with me.

As soon as he's on his feet, he wraps his arms around me and drags me against him. I feel his tears streaming down the side of my head, but I hold him close because I know he needs me. He probably needs me more than he ever has before.

"I'm sorry. I just really needed a hug from you," he says, attempting to step away when I hold him even tighter.

"Don't be sorry. As a matter of fact, you're not allowed to say those two words to me anymore today. You've reached the limit," I say, stepping back to look up at him and give him a scolding look. He brings his forehead to mine, but I see the tiniest hint of a smile before he does so.

"I'm so happy you're here. Thank you for coming to me," he replies, and I tilt my head only enough to press my lips to his cheek.

"There is nowhere I'd rather be, *mi corazón*." It was supposed to be a fake pet name, something to sell our fake relationship, but it sounds too right for me to use anything else. Santi seems to agree because his shoulders relax even more.

I lead Santi into his bathroom, grabbing his toothbrush and applying a layer of toothpaste to it. Santi's exhausted eyes focus on the thing in my hand, and I guide him to the rim of his bathtub to sit him down. He spreads his legs so I can step between them, opening his mouth for me when I bring the toothbrush to his lips. His hands lift to my thighs, gripping the backs of them while I brush his teeth.

"You know, Ori called me this morning and told me Sami won another award for best project at another science fair from his school, and Hernanda received her tenth golf trophy. Ori is also nearing a breakthrough in her research, according to her, so I'm pretty sure my siblings are going to take over the world soon."

Santi's eyes sparkle at my words while I continue using circular motions to clean his teeth. There is something incredibly intimate about doing such a normal task for someone else, but from the way Santi is looking at me right now, I can tell he's enjoying this as much as I am. Being close to one another. Having each other's back no matter what. Being taken care of during a very hard time.

"My back has been feeling much better, by the way. I think taking it slow has been helping a lot, and I'll be able to participate in the Stuttgart Open as a singles player again. I'll be able to start catching Layla again," I keep going, knowing he prefers conversation when he's feeling this way.

It's when he gets lost in his head and loses his firm grip on reality that he spirals into darkness.

Santi spits out his toothpaste and rinses his mouth.

"Didn't you want to go visit your family today?" he says when I wash off the toothpaste from his toothbrush, placing it back in the holder.

The bathroom is a mess. The rest of his house is clean because he clearly didn't do more than lie in his bed since he came back, but his bathroom has clothes everywhere, his suitcase half-opened in the corner along with tennis balls, rackets, and bottles of electrolytes. It's not dirty, but it's messy.

"I was going to, but—" I cut off, biting down on my bottom lip.

"I sent you that message," Santi finishes, and I meet his gaze to see the sadness in his eyes. "I'm so sorry, Catalina. I didn't mean for you to have to change your plans. I'm sorry." Tears return, but I grab his face in my hands and force him to look at me as I shake my head.

"My day trip to see my family can wait. You're mental well-being is more important to me right now," I say, but tears drop down his cheeks.

"It shouldn't be. I'll be fine. You should go, Cata. I know you miss them. I don't want to be the one to—" I kiss him to cut him off. It's barely more than a press of my lips to his, barely anything at all, but Santi melts against me and the tension finally leaves his body again.

"Don't make me say it out loud, Santi. I'm not ready to," I whisper, even though I know that my actions speak louder than any words. I may not want to say it out loud, but that doesn't make it less true. I care so much about Santi. He's one of the most important people in my life and if he doesn't feel well, then I'm going to do everything in my power to make him feel better.

"Then kiss me again. Please. Kiss me so I can feel what you feel."

I press my mouth to his.

Kissing isn't necessarily linked to vulnerability. Being naked is. Having sex is. But kissing? Kissing isn't considered as meaningful, but I think that's wrong because kissing Santiago makes me feel more vulnerable than I've ever felt in my life.

It feels as if I'm baring myself to him. As if he can look into the deepest parts of me and study them, analyze them, determine if they're something he likes or doesn't like. As if he's tying his soul to mine and there is nothing I can do to stop it.

If I'm being honest, I don't want to stop it. I want him tied to me in every way possible. I want him to feel everything I do as deeply.

So as my mouth glides over his, I'm ensuring I'll never leave his mind. I'm ensuring he'll never want to kiss anyone else but me. I'm ensuring he knows kissing him is addictive for me.

He tastes like his toothpaste, which only makes me deepen the kiss. Santi's hands roam upward, stopping at my hips to squeeze them once. I think if he had energy, he'd be lifting me onto his lap, but this kiss isn't meant to lead anywhere. He's finding comfort in it, comfort he very desperately needs at the moment. Comfort he will also get by showering. So, I kiss him once more before leaning back and urging him to wash.

"Will you shower with me?" he asks, the tiniest of smirks covering his mouth.

"Do you need me to because you don't have energy or because you want to have me naked in your shower?" I ask, and he places his forehead against my stomach.

"Can't it be both?" he replies, and I let out a small laugh.

"Is that really how you want to see me without any clothes on for the first time?" His head snaps up again before he shakes it. "Well, then there you go," I say, running my hands through his hair. "Go shower. I'll be outside with more things to do for us," I promise, kissing his forehead once and then leaving his bathroom.

It takes him a while to shower and get dressed, but I don't rush him. It's clear that when a depressive episode hits Santi, he needs more time to do things other people consider small tasks, so I'd never, ever stress him. Instead, I set up our food and game, then start playing with Tornado.

"This is the most beautiful sight I've ever laid my eyes on," Santi says right as I scratch Tornado's big, fluffy ears.

Santi is leaning against the doorframe leading into his living room, his head tilted to rest against it. He takes in the image in front of him, all of his favorite foods spread out on the table, as well as a new board game, and a bunch of candles I found because I didn't want to open the curtains or turn on the light if he wants to have it a bit darker in here. It gives it an awfully romantic vibe, but I don't mind it as much as I thought I would. For my ex-girlfriend, I used to do something like this every week. I just never saw myself doing it for Santi.

Tornado hops to Santi as soon as he sees him, but I don't quite manage to break eye contact with my fake boyfriend as he studies me. There is a new look on his face, one I haven't seen in years, and I welcome it back with open arms because this is how he used to look at me. Without our past hanging between us. Without a filter. Without trying to hide that it's always been me. He's said he wants me, but it's another thing entirely to see how desperately in his eyes.

"Come, sit. I thought we could eat and play this game that I found," I say and gesture toward the board. Santi pushes off the doorframe and picks up Tornado, sitting down with him across from me a second later.

"I wanted to be the one to take you on our first real date, but I have to admit, this is really nice," he says once we start eating.

"Of course it is. I'm amazing at this," I say with a small smile that has Santi's tired face lighting up.

"You are." He takes a sip of his iced tea, shaking his head in disbelief. "You're amazing at everything. It's annoying." I snort, but he seems to truly mean those words, so I clear my throat as a cover-up.

"I'm sorry?" Santi's still smirking, and it's my turn to shake my head at him.

Silence engulfs the room as we eat and drink, but as soon as we get to the game, we can't stop talking. About the game. About life. About everything. We talk and talk and talk until hours pass, and we play several rounds of *Mensch Ärgere Dich Nicht*. It's a brutal game, and every time we kick each other out, we start yelling at each other—not seriously, but in a teasing kind of way that leads to us bursting into laughter.

Afterward, we go for a walk because Santi told me it helps his mind a lot. I don't even mind him taking my hand as we take step by step as a couple. And not a fake couple. No, this feels very real.

Monaco is very beautiful by day. It has that old-money kind of feeling to it. I find it even more beautiful at night. When the lights all around us illuminate this tiny country. When the people are strolling down the streets, talking about nothing and everything. When I get to admire all the fancy cars that drive by.

Most of all, I love the way the night paints Santi in a very specific light, dark, yes, but light enough to see his bright eyes and chiseled face.

"Santi, can I ask you something about your depression?" I ask, and he tilts his head down to bring his attention back to me.

"Of course." I chew on my bottom lip while I think about how to phrase my question.

"Do you know when your depression started?" I ask, and he squeezes my fingers, telling me he's surprised by my question.

"Not entirely. I...I don't know. I think I realized I had depression when I stopped enjoying things in life that I used to love. For example, when I went to Christmas markets as a kid, I was always so excited, but then all of a sudden, I didn't enjoy it anymore. I didn't enjoy anything. I wasn't sure what was wrong with me. I didn't understand why I wasn't enjoying life, and then my anxiety started because I also didn't want to die. I never wanted to die, but my depression made me think I couldn't enjoy anything in life anymore. It was a vicious cycle that I spiraled through over and over," he explains, holding onto me a little tighter as he shares his story with me. "Manu helped me figure out what was happening. We found things I enjoyed. Actually, there is something I can show you that made me realize there were still things I loved doing."

As soon as he's finished speaking, he pulls me back toward his apartment. He's so excited about whatever he wants to show me. Santi brings me all the way into his bedroom, where he gently guides me to sit. He rummages around in his closet before pulling out a box and carrying it to me. He settles down on the bed beside me, the box between us.

"Don't laugh," he says, a shy laugh of his own escaping him.

Then he lifts a notebook-looking thing out of the box, handing it over to me. On the front, in letters clearly cut out of a magazine of some sort, the words "Santi's Private Thoughts" are spelled out. There are pages and pages covered with his, well, private thoughts. A page covered by his dream house. A page filled with his dream car—mine. A page dedicated to all the places in the world he has traveled to and another for all the places he still wants to go.

A page for all of his victories in tennis.

A page for... me.

"Santi—" I start but cut off because I'm not entirely sure what to say.

He doesn't force me to finish my sentence, simply places his fingers on my chin, lifting it to bring my mouth to his. He kisses my lips, my cheek, my temple, and then smiles down at the page covered with pictures of me and us together.

"That's my favorite one," he says, but I don't manage to reply. All I can do is lean my head against his shoulder and snake my arm around his as he explains more pages of his scrapbook to me.

And it's the first time I feel it deep inside of me.

Deep in my chest as a wave of emotion hits me.

I'm falling in love with Santiago Castillo.

Again.

# CHAPTER 31
## SANTIAGO

Catalina took care of me.

She chose me over going to her family.

She organized a date for us.

All of these things are so difficult to wrap my head around. Not because I believe Cata is a horrible person. On the contrary. But it still surprises me when she offers me that level of kindness because I most certainly haven't deserved it in a very long time.

It's been over ten days since it happened, and neither one of us has spoken about it because we've been so busy training and winning matches at the Miami Open to get a second to be truly alone. Charlie and Papá have been on our asses to focus more on the tennis aspect of our fake relationship/hitting partner agreement, so Cata and I are on the court for so long, neither one of us has energy to do anything but pass out on our beds.

Even when there is so much I want to do with her. While I can still study her as much as I want—I can't be blamed, watching Cata do the littlest things brings me the utmost joy—I also want to take her on more dates. I want to kiss her until she's sick of me. And fuck, I finally want to take my time exploring her body, find all the ways her body quivers in pleasure. I want to make her come for the first time, then repeat it a million more times.

Because I'm in love with her.

My father was right. Manu was right. Matteo was right. Thomas was right. Everyone in my life was right when they told me I was in love with Catalina. I was

211

too blinded by my supposed hate for her to see it, but it was never truly hate. It was my heart fearing her rejection, after she rejected me so suddenly when I fucked up, so it convinced itself it hated her, too. It never did. It loved her from the very first moment I saw her play tennis all those years ago.

And I'm a million percent sure it is going to love her until it stops beating.

"Sage is being a very difficult patient, according to Ness," Cata informs me as she joins me in the gym room where we get to warm up for our finals match.

A smile immediately brightens up my face at the sight of her.

Catalina is wearing the matching dress to the outfit I have on, thanks to *New Light* and *Spin* teaming up to make this happen. I'm wearing a magenta shirt with black pants that have stripes of the same color on either pant leg. There is a symbol for gender equality in sports printed on the left pocket area, the same as for Cata, and I love the way the dress is backless for her, showing off her trained, strong back. I know she's a bit insecure about the width of her shoulders and size of her back, even if she'd never admit it to me, so I love the way she's showing it off during this tournament.

"What's she doing?" I ask as I stand up to stretch out my hips.

"She complains every time she needs to fix the bandages. She doesn't like sitting still. She won't eat anything healthy Ness prepares for her," she replies, stepping in front of me to watch me stretch.

"Sounds like Sage," I reply with a laugh.

Cata furrows her brows, then adjusts my position, making the pulling feeling go from my leg to everywhere in my lower body.

"Holy fuck," I breathe out, cursing even more as I hold the position.

"Atta boy. Good job," she praises, and I flush immediately under the heat of her compliment.

"Can you say that again, but next time, can we both be naked while I put my mouth on you?" I ask, watching a small smirk cover her face in response to my dirty question.

"If we win today, yes."

I stop stretching, stand upright and take a step toward her, bringing our chests almost flush together. She tilts her head to look up at me, but even with our height difference, there is no doubt about who is in charge.

Cata is.

And when she licks her lips and smirks, my knees go weak.

"And if we don't?" I ask, my voice practically shaking because of how turned on I am.

"Then you'll watch as I make myself come," she replies, running a single hand from the side of my neck down my chest, stopping at the waistband of my pants.

My cock is painfully hard. So hard, I have a difficult time not begging her to wrap her hand around it so I can thrust into it and ease the tension.

"I think I'll die if you don't touch me soon, Cata. If I don't get to touch you."

"That's a bit dramatic, don't you think?" she asks, her smirk still in place as she closes the distance between us fully. Her lower stomach is pressing against my groin, and I groan as she steps on her tiptoes, rubbing against me as she brings her mouth to my earlobe. She bites it gently before saying, "Let's go get that trophy so I can find out how this—" She cuts off to push her hips into me, rubbing even harder against my cock. "—feels inside me."

Cata shoves away from me without another word, leaving me to shiver in pleasure and trying to figure out how to get my dick to calm down. Especially because Cata bends over to stretch, putting her glorious ass on display for me, and I just about come in my fucking pants *again*.

*Trash cans.*

*Rotten vegetables.*

*Mathematical equations.*

I think of all the unsexy things my brain can conjure, looking at the ceiling in the room as I take several deep breaths.

Nothing works.

Nothing's going to work until we win this tournament and I finally get my alone time with Cata back.

But that'll have to wait until after Cata's surprise, too, and I have a feeling she's not going to spend any time with me once she sees it.

The thought makes me smile.

Stepping out onto the court is always a fun experience with the crowd cheering my name, but if anyone asked me if I prefer doing so on my own or with Cata, I'd tell them I'd sell my left arm if it would guarantee she walks out with me every single time. There is something about the way Cata demands attention, attention she absolutely despises, that mesmerizes me every single time. Especially because even though she may hate it, she glows under it. It's as if she could absorb the crowd's love for her, and in turn, it makes her shine brighter.

And I'm so happy there are cameras filming us because the look on her face when she spots her family sitting in the box dedicated to our team is priceless. She grabs hold of my arm and stops walking, covering her mouth with her other hand. Tears fill her eyes as Ori and Hernanda stand up to wave at Cata, her dad places a hand on his left breast, and Samuel lets out a *whoooooop* for his sister.

Cata waves back at them, doing her best not to burst into tears.

"Santi, what are they doing here?" she asks as I take her hand to guide her to the bench where we're meant to put our things.

"They're here to surprise you," I explain, running a soothing hand down her bare back. Cata brings her tear-filled eyes to my face, then shifts them to her family again before waving and smiling. I know she must be in disbelief, but I can tell how happy she is simply by the real smile covering her lips.

"I hate you so much for making me cry on a tennis court again," Cata says as her tears fall, but I wipe them away for her before anyone realizes what's happening.

"I know, but it's worth it," I reply, grinning at her. "Go to them. I'll distract the umpire," I say, nodding in their direction.

Cata steps on her tiptoes to press a kiss to my cheek, then sprints toward her family. I rush over to where the umpire is standing, putting my most charming smile on.

"Weren't you the umpire at my match in France two years ago?" I ask, feeling a little awkward.

"Yes. You lost that one, if I recall correctly," they reply with a frown, and I let out a nervous laugh.

"Yeah." Another nervous laugh escapes me, and I realize how fucking horrible I am at this. Take away my flirtiness, and, apparently, I have no idea how to distract someone.

But I'm not flirting with anyone.

No one but Catalina.

"I didn't know you were also an umpire for doubles matches. Is it very different from singles?" The umpire furrows their brows at me, but the amusement remains on their face.

I might die of embarrassment.

"I think you should be getting ready. We have to get started," the umpire says with an amused look, and I feel my cheeks flush because of how embarrassed I feel. I look over my shoulder to see Catalina rushing back to our bag and almost let out a sigh of relief.

Thank fuck.

I think that was the most awkward minute of my life.

"Yeah, right," I reply and give them a thumbs up, then mentally smack myself because *what the fuck was that?*

When I walk back to Cata, she's grinning at me in a way that lets me know she's not grinning with me but at me.

"What?" I ask, poking her side.

"Nothing. You're just—Well, you're as red as a tomato, Santi," she replies, chuckling to herself as she takes out her racket. I place a hand on my left cheek, feeling the heat beneath my palm, which only makes me blush harder.

"Sometimes it's nice to keep thoughts inside, *mariquita*," I say, covering my cheeks with both hands.

My woman merely chuckles again.

"You don't enjoy my pointing out the obvious?" she teases, and if we were alone, if we weren't being watched from every angle, I'd throw her over my shoulder and carry her to the nearest empty room.

"Let's win this game so I can go back to kissing you to give your mouth something else to do," I say, but she simply keeps snickering to herself.

I hate that I can't even be mad because Catalina is so beautiful when she's happy.

# CHAPTER 32
## CATALINA

MY FAMILY IS CHEERING for us every single time Santi and I make a point, and when we don't, they yell out encouraging phrases.

From afar, I hadn't noticed their shirts, but when I got closer to them earlier to greet them—while Santi distracted the umpire and made a fool of himself to give me time with my family—I noticed they were all clad in matching shirts that said "Catalina + Santiago = Best Team."

It's hard being away from them for months and months on end. I chose this life, to be a professional tennis player, but I didn't understand just how busy I would be. How little time I'd have to see my family. It isn't easy for them to fly out to where I am. They all have their responsibilities and schedules. They can't drop everything all the time, but I'm so grateful they did to be here.

It's a boost of encouragement I didn't think I needed, but that has me playing better than I have in months.

Santiago and I are always a good doubles match-up, but today we're unstoppable.

Our opponents have no chance against us while I feel invincible and Santi plays like some sort of tennis god.

"How's your back?" Santi asks halfway through the second set. We won the first one six games to three and are leading the second three games to one.

"Fine. How's yours?" I reply, but I responded too quickly, and my question certainly doesn't convince him.

Because if I'm being honest, it is a bit stiff, but I can hardly feel it with all of the adrenaline coursing through my veins at the moment. Santi opens his mouth to protest, to tell me to slow down, but I beat him to it.

"Three more games, then I have a break," I reply, and his mouth clamps shut again. Two weeks off is what I'll have before Stuttgart. Two weeks in which Santi and I will be attending the Monaco Masters, where I'll watch him win.

"Fine, but let me take more of the shots, Cata. You're taking most of them, and I need you to give me the chance to make points too, okay?" he asks, and it's only fair that I nod in agreement because we are a team and he is right.

"Okay," I reply with a nod, and he offers me a bright smile, his full lips stretching to reveal his teeth. His amber eyes are sparkling in the noon sun filtering into the arena.

"Last set as doubles partners for now," he says and nudges my shoulder, placing his towel back down. I glance up at my family, at the way Charlie keeps making Hernanda laugh during the breaks between the games.

Only a few games left before I get to be with them.

Well, a few games and a press conference.

Almost there.

My eyes drift to where Santiago's parents and Manuela sit, and his twin sister gives me a cocky smirk as if to say that Santi and I got this, that she isn't the least bit concerned if we'll win this match.

It's Eunice's turn to serve, and our opponent looks as frustrated as I would feel if I was losing a match this badly.

Her partner, Colin, looks pissed.

Santi is the first one to return so I make my way to the net. I glance at Colin again, but he's staring at Santi. I think if he could, he'd rip his head off, and suddenly, I'm angry because no one gets to look at Santi this way.

No one but me.

If it wasn't a ridiculous thing to do, I'd growl at Colin, but I think my deathly glare is enough because he turns his head to me, and surprise covers his face as he takes a step back, away from the net.

I force my attention to Eunice, content with hopefully putting Colin a bit off-balance for the way he looked at Santi.

Eunice finally serves, a perfectly placed shot in the right corner of the service box, but Santi was anticipating the placement and returns it effortlessly. They rally back and forth while I stay ready at the net, waiting for the ball to get to me, but it never does. Santi goes wide, forcing Eunice to make an error and hit the ball in the net.

Love-fifteen.

Colin stalks toward Eunice and starts whispering something to her, waving his hands around angrily as if it's her fault they lost the point when it was merely Santi's phenomenal shot. No one could have gotten it.

Colin doesn't seem to care about that, though.

"Why is he so angry?" I ask Santi.

"Colin is usually a singles player, but because of the domestic abuse allegations against him, he was not allowed to play in any singles tournaments this season," he explains, and my jaw just about drops to the floor.

"How the fuck is he playing doubles? Shouldn't they have kicked him out of the sport entirely?" I ask, resisting the urge to take my racket and hit Colin with it to avenge the people he hurt.

"For now, allegations are all there is. It's already a wonder they disqualified him from singles. Most of the time, they wouldn't even have done that, but the evidence against him is too indisputable. There is a video, apparently."

All words leave me because I know he's right. I know money comes before all else, even morals, in so many sports. I simply wish it wasn't like that in the sport I love so much. The one I dedicated myself to for so many years. I've been trying to change mindsets since I got here, but in a sport as old as tennis, it's hard to do that.

Clearly, considering a man accused of domestic violence with video proof is currently our opponent.

It disgusts me.

"Let's beat his ass," I say with gritted teeth, and Santi gives me an agreeing nod, the topic having affected him so much, his smile is nowhere to be seen.

My sunshine man looks downright murderous.

It's my turn to return the serve. After missing her first serve, Eunice places her second one in the center of the service box, but she puts a spin on it that has me jumping in the air a little to get a good position on it. My ball goes straight to her, and we rally back and forth until I place my ball too far toward Colin's side. He doesn't hesitate to step toward it, hitting a volley that goes straight into Santi's stomach. And he put so much force behind it, my partner lets out a pained *oomph* and bends over at the waist as he clutches his stomach.

I see red.

I storm toward the net at the same moment Colin backs away, not even raising his hands to apologize. It's the most unsportsmanlike behavior I have ever witnessed in my professional tennis career. The crowd seems to agree because they start booing him, and I would smile at Sami being the one to boo the loudest if I wasn't so worried about Santi.

"Are you okay, *mi corazón*?" I ask, my heart racing because of how angry I am. The tears that usually come with this type of anger combine with my worry, making me swallow hard to get them under control.

My hand slips onto his back, but he only very slowly straightens it out again. I notice tears have appeared in his eyes, and it makes even more anger spread through me.

"Fuck, that hurt," he mumbles, letting out a strained breath. It's nothing new for a tennis player to get hit with a ball, we're used to it, but not so hard from so close up and then straight into the stomach.

"Do you need ice?" I ask, lifting his shirt to see the red spot on his stomach from how hard Colin hit him.

"I'll be fine. It doesn't even hurt that badly," Santi assures me, but I don't believe him. Not even a little.

I stare at the red spot on Santiago's stomach for a second longer, wondering if I could rip off Colin's head and feed it to Tornado.

"It's okay," Santi says, caressing my jaw before he steps away and goes to line up at the baseline.

Red is still clouding my vision as I step toward the net on my side. Colin is already on his, the crowd still booing. He catches me staring at him, so I offer him a threatening smile that has his eyes widening.

"If you hurt Santiago again, I'm going to beat you with my racket until I'm sure your career is over. As a matter of fact, if you ever hurt anyone physically again, I'll do that. I don't give a fuck about what happens to me if it means one less prick like you is part of my sport," I warn, quietly enough to ensure the crowd can't hear me, but loud enough so Colin can.

He has no time to respond before Eunice serves again, and Santi hits the ball back to her, but the look on his face, anger and surprise, is enough to satisfy me. He seems scared of me, and he should be. As much as it seems like an empty threat to him, I've once punched a guy in the throat and kicked him in the balls after he grabbed my ass at the club and rubbed his bulge against me non-consensually.

I'll do the same to Colin, maybe even worse.

Santi and I fight for the point until finally, we secure it through an overhead smash on my part.

Fifteen-thirty.

Santi is at the net again, but for this point, I make sure not to let the ball get anywhere near Colin. I don't trust my warning to have been enough for him to get the message.

Fifteen-forty.

Colin is getting more frustrated, yelling at Eunice like it's her fault. She doesn't take his bullshit, though, and instead yells right back at him, telling him how useless he is. It's quite unprofessional from a tennis standard perspective, but I almost want to applaud her for standing up for herself.

"A wrongly matched pair," Santi starts, and I nod several times, my stomach clenching from nostalgia as I finish the sentence.

"Will never reach the top." His father used to say this to us before every match as children, and I will never forget those words. "They're not going to recover from this tension," I whisper, and he nods several times.

"They won't have a comeback. This is ours."

And it is. Colin and Eunice fight each other until the end, but the battle against us is long lost. No matter what they try, a new strategy or having both players stand at the baseline after the serve, nothing works.

The match goes to us.

As soon as the final point is ours, I spin around to run to Santi. He opens his arms for me to celebrate, but I have another mission: making sure his stomach is okay. The crowd screams for us, but I drown everyone out as I focus on Santi.

"It's already bruising. We need to put some ice on it," I say, placing my fingers around the area gently. "How hard did he fucking hit you?" I mumble, but he tilts my head up to get me to look at him.

"Forget about the stupid bruise and kiss me, Cata," he says, but he doesn't give me the chance to tell him we need to ice it again before putting his lips on mine.

Sharing a win with a doubles partner is always wonderful, but sharing it with Santi makes it all the sweeter.

And when we accept our trophy, and he says, "My half of the paycheck is going directly to a charity for domestic abuse victims," I know falling in love with him again isn't just a possibility anymore.

It's a fact.

And it's about damn time I take what I want.

# CHAPTER 33
## SANTIAGO

CATALINA IS DRAGGING ME somewhere. With our trophy in her left hand, my hand in her right, she is pulling me and dragging me until she stops abruptly in front of a room I've never been in.

"Cata, we have to get to our press conference," I say, but she opens the door and guides me inside anyway.

"No, Santi, I have to get you inside me. Now," she replies, almost making my whole body whimper with need.

The words have hardly left her mouth before I grab her wrists and pin them above her head against the door. I capture her mouth at the same moment, making sure her head is away from the wood as she desperately clings to my mouth with hers. I shift one of my thighs between her legs, leaving it there while I explore her mouth, taking in the taste of her.

"Tell me what you need," I say, practically beg, because I want to give her everything she desires. I want her to never need anyone but me again because I'm too good at being everything she ever hoped for in a partner.

"Make me come, Santi. Make me come as often as possible," she replies against my mouth, her demand like liquid pleasure coursing through my veins.

"Say 'out' if you want me to stop at any point," I say, using a tennis phrase I think fits well and is easy to remember. Cata laughs against my lips, but it's a breathless sound filled with pleasure.

"Okay. Same goes for you," she says, going back to kissing me.

I move my leg a little, bringing the top of my knee and lower thigh flush against her pussy. Cata moans instantly at the contact, and my cock gives a needy throb at the feel of her warmth against my skin.

"Ride my leg, Cata. Let me see you fall apart," I say, pushing it even more against her clit until she's frantically rubbing to chase her pleasure.

Part of me wants to kiss her through her orgasm, while the other is too busy being mesmerized by how devastating she is this close to her orgasm. Her wrists are still pinned beneath my hands, but I shift them around so that both of them are only covered by one. My other hand drops to her throat, not applying any pressure but merely holding her there like the possessive man I am when it comes to Cata. It also forces her eyes to stay on me as she rolls her hips, getting closer and closer to falling apart.

I finally apply the slightest bit of pressure to either side of her throat, and Catalina moans so loudly, I kiss her to swallow the sound.

"Does that feel good?" I ask once I pull back, watching her bottom lip slip between her teeth.

"Mhm."

"Mhm?" I ask, smirking when she whimpers in pleasure. She's so fucking gorgeous when she's like this. Unrestrained, frantic with need, and desperate for me.

It's exactly how I feel about her.

"I'm gonna come, Santi," she says, moaning as she picks up speed and grinds against my leg faster than before.

Her eyes keep fluttering shut as she rolls her hips forward, bolts of pleasure probably shooting through her. Fuck, I'm so desperate to chase my own pleasure inside of her. I add even more pressure against her clit as I lift my leg higher.

Cata falls apart in my arms, and I let her moan my name as loudly as she wants because, for all I care, the whole world could hear her scream my name. Mine. No one else's. Maybe then they would all understand that we belong to each other.

I release her wrists and guide her arms around my neck, but she's so limp from her orgasm, I have to hold onto her hips to keep her upright. I kiss the corner of her mouth, the middle of it, and then the other corner as she comes back to reality.

"That was fun," she says, dragging her nails over my nape and making my whole body tense with need. "You know what would be even more fun?" she asks, leaning forward to rake her teeth down my throat.

"Cata, I'm going to come in my pants before you even touch me if you keep this up," I warn, but she doesn't stop. Instead, she lifts my shirt, urging me to take it off while she removes her dress, and as soon as it hits the floor, she trails her nails down my chest. "Catalina," I warn because the pressure in my cock is building in the way it does right before I come, and I don't know if I can stop myself.

It's been too long, and Cata feels too good, and fuck, I don't want to stop it. I want to come. I want her to make me come.

"Santi, you didn't answer my question," she reminds me as she drops her hand to my bulge and cups it.

"Fuck!" I groan, slamming my hand against the door behind her as my head falls back. Pleasure explodes through me, and I barely keep from embarrassing myself.

"Answer my question," she demands, and I let my head fall toward her again to look into those blue eyes of hers that I love with my whole heart.

"What would be more fun?" I manage to croak out, and she rewards me by giving my cock a firm palm through the fabric of my pants. Well, reward, punishment, it feels like both, considering how hard I have to fight against coming with every rub.

"Riding your cock," she says and brings her mouth to my nipple to kiss it.

"I'm not going to last right now," I admit, even though there is nothing I want more than what she's describing.

"Yes, you are. You're going to last because you want to make me come again, don't you? Don't you want to know what it would be like to feel my pussy clench around your cock as I shiver through my orgasm?"

"Yes, I want that." Cata releases my cock, and I almost sigh in relief and whine in complaint at the same time.

"Then be my good boy and last long enough to make that happen," she says, and I lift her off the ground, guiding her legs around my hips as I carry her to… well, I have no idea where the fuck I am, and I can't see past Cata's stunning breasts, so I'm going nowhere.

"There is a table to your left. My bag is underneath it, so we can get a condom from there, too." It's all the instructions I need.

I guide her to the table and place her down on it, but Cata isn't having it. She wants to be in charge, and I'm more than happy to do as she tells me to.

She slides off the table again.

"Undress, Santi, then get on the table." I drag down my pants, leaving us in only our underwear and her in her safety shorts. I see the imprint of her nipples with her piercings, making my mouth water.

"Can I take your bra off first?" I ask, stepping toward her, pulling her in by her hips.

Cata smiles as she lifts her arms, inviting me to drag her sports bra over her head. I bring my fingers to the band at the bottom of it, slowly dragging it upward and exposing her breasts to me.

I've fantasized about them more often than I care to admit, but I could never have predicted how perfect they are without any fabric covering them. The piercings going through her nipples have me damn near coming at the mere sight of them, and the shape of her full breasts, one slightly bigger than the other, has my hands twitching, begging me to cup them.

"You can touch me, Santi," she says, reaching for my hands before placing them on her perfect tits.

A groan escapes me as I palm them, stepping into her to push my hard cock against her stomach in search of any sort of friction, no matter how dangerous that is. I drop my mouth to hers, but she leans back, arching herself into my touch.

"Put your mouth somewhere more useful, *hermoso*," she instructs as she lifts her hands to her hair to take it out of its long braid.

I lean down, flicking my thumb over her piercing with anticipation licking up my spine. I watch her nipple harden with fascination before finally sucking it into my mouth.

"Fuck. That feels good." Her moan has a wave of pleasure coursing through me, snapping the last bit of restraint I had left.

A sort of frenzy takes over as I keep kneading her breasts while I play with her nipple piercings. My hands work on shimmying down my underwear, then move on to drag her safety shorts and panties down.

I'm about to kiss her mouth again when she pushes me backward, the backs of my knees hitting the wood. I lift myself on it, positioning myself far enough in the middle to give her space to ride me.

"You look incredible sprawled out on the table like that," Cata says, and I watch as she gets on the table too, her gloriously naked body crawling to where I am.

"Like a meal ready for you to devour?" I ask with a breathless laugh because watching Cata crawl to me, having her naked and about to sink down on my cock, has me as excited as it has me nervous.

"Yes, Santi, exactly like that," Cata replies as she brings her hands to my thighs, a condom resting between her left index and middle fingers. "We have to be quick. People are waiting for us," she reminds me, but there is no way I'll last anyway.

Not when she dips her head down, keeping eye contact as she wraps her fingers around my dick and strokes it gently while her lips press against the head of it. Precum is leaking from my tip because of how turned on I am, but she licks me clean, then sucks on the tip for good measure. I whimper in a way I never have before, too sensitized to hold it back.

"Please put the condom on and get on top of me, *cariño*. Please," I beg because I'm desperate to make her fall apart again, this time with her walls squeezing my cock to drag me over the edge with her.

"Hearing you beg may just be one of my favorite things in the world, Santi," she says as she slides the condom down my length torturously slowly.

Catalina crawls up my body until she can put her mouth back on mine, and stars appear in my vision as she guides the head of my cock to her wet entrance. My whole body shakes, and I'd be embarrassed if I didn't see the fire in her eyes from my reaction. Cata loves being in control, she loves that I'm so visibly affected by her and everything she does, and I'd be a fool to do anything to take that away.

Especially because I love how much pleasure it brings her to top me, figuratively and literally.

"Don't come until I tell you to," Cata says, sinking fully down on my cock.

"I'm gonna come," I blurt out as my head falls backward. Feeling her wrapped around the length of me is too good.

I clamp my eyes shut so at least the visual of Catalina bouncing on my cock is taken away, but her chuckle because of my words is a different type of torture in itself.

"Has it been too long for you, Santi? Is your cock too sensitive?" she asks, the teasing tone she's using makes my cheeks flush. I hate that it only makes this hotter.

"It's been too long. I've wanted you for too long, and you feel so much better than I could have ever imagined," I admit. "I fucked my own hand more times than I can remember thinking about this very moment, but none of my fantasies compare to you," I go on, my hands reaching for her hips as I lift my head again, looking at where Cata is sitting on me. She's waiting for me to be ready, to not be a one-pump chump, or whatever they call it in English, but I'm still fighting my orgasm with every fiber of my being.

"I'd be lying if I said I didn't think about you when I slid my toys between my legs, Santi. If I said I didn't think about you filling me instead to make myself come."

Fuck me.

Fuck me, fuck me, fuck.

"Cata, if you keep talking, I'm going to come without you even moving." Because that's all it would take. That's how much I want her.

"Play with my clit, Santi. It's really sensitive because of the piercing there, so if you work it well, I'll come quickly too," she assures me with a soft kiss on the lips, but I'm too focused on her words to enjoy the kiss or the reassurance.

"You have a clit piercing too?" I ask, and amusement flickers through her eyes before she nods. "Fuck, Cata, you're going to kill me." She chuckles again as she lifts off my cock halfway, only to slam down again. "Oh my f—"

My words cut off as I groan in pleasure.

Cata keeps riding me, rolling her hips forward, then to either side to find the spot inside of her where she needs me the most. And I'm more than happy being her toy that she can use to chase her own pleasure.

I'm drunk on her.

My fingers find her clit, the metal of her piercing so hard in contrast to her skin. I rub my thumb over it, making Cata slam her hands on my chest and throw her head back. Her breasts bounce with her movements, and I take my time studying the way they almost hit my lips as she rides me before dropping my gaze to where my finger is.

My balls tighten, bringing me even closer to my orgasm when I first spot her piercing and then stare at the spot where we're joined. I pick up my speed, desperate to make her come because I won't fucking last. With Cata's walls squeezing my cock, her hair wild and free, and her nails digging into my chest, leaving marks, there is no way I can resist this paradise.

"Yes, oh yes," she chants as I press down on her clit. She fucks me harder and faster, taking me as deep as possible, and when she slams down on me again, I come so hard, my vision goes black.

Catalina's entire body shakes on top of me while she rolls her hips and calls out my name, riding out her orgasm and elongating mine to the point where I have to hold onto her hips to get her to stop. Wave over wave of pleasure rocks through me, and I love that she kisses me right then and there. I love that she kisses me as we both come apart because it feels like she's putting me back together with that single kiss.

"Cata," I moan when she keeps rolling her hips, grinding her clit against my thumb. A weird combination of pain and pleasure shoots through me, and I can't decide if I want her to stop or keep going.

"You're still semi-hard," she says, leaning backward to cup my balls.

"Fuck, Cata. No more," I beg, but I have a safeword I'm not using.

"Are you overstimulated already?" she asks with an amused lilt in her voice.

"I don't know. Fuck, keep going." I'm contradicting myself, I know I am, but I don't ever want this to end, and the pain only makes me fully hard again.

"Keep going? Stop? What do you want?" She kneads my balls, and my head falls backward onto the table again.

"I want more," I whisper because all strength has left my voice.

"Good boy," she praises, and I moan so loudly when she tightens her grip on my balls and slams down on my cock again. "Sit up, Santi. Put your hands on my clit and tits as I ride you the other way around," she instructs, releasing me entirely as she spins around.

Her ass is perfectly on display as she reaches for another condom and a small towel, throwing them both my way. I clean myself up and slide a new condom down, my cock so sensitive that my legs shake with the motion of rolling the tight latex down. Cata doesn't waste a second, lining my dick back up with her entrance, then sinking down.

I just about lose it.

Bringing one of my hands to her clit and the other to her left breast, my arm banded around her so both of them get attention, I give myself over to the pleasure. Cata rides me like I've never been ridden before, hard and fast and precise to make sure she hits the perfect spot inside of her while bringing me more pleasure than I ever thought possible. I play with her nipple and clit piercings, making her writhe on top of me until her movements become frantic.

I don't know how much time passes. It feels like an eternity and yet no time at all, and when she finally clenches around me again, crying out as her body trembles, I hold onto her and fuck up into her.

My pleasure is bliss, sending me straight to paradise.

"We should have been doing that for years," I blurt out minutes later, her breathing as uneven as mine.

"You would have gotten sick of me by now," she replies with a laugh, but it sounds as unamused as I feel.

"I don't think I'm ever going to get sick of you, Catalina. You're my favorite person in the whole world."

*Fuck me, why the hell did I say that?*

*Why would I bring up something so deep after we've just had sex for the first time?*

She's not going to believe me, something her next words prove.

"Tell me that again after your post-orgasm high disappears," she says, bringing her lips back down to mine for one last, sweet kiss. She gets off my spent cock, but my limbs are still jello, so I don't move a centimeter. "Until then, let's get this stupid press conference over with so I can go see my family." She picks up her clothes and dresses in record time, and I make a mental note to tell her she's my favorite person again when we have a quiet moment.

Because it'll be as true then as it is now, if not more.

# CHAPTER 34
## CATALINA

I HAVEN'T FOUND A way to stop hugging Hernanda and stare at Sami with tears in my eyes. They both have grown so much since I last saw them, and the fact that I'm missing it makes me never want to let them out of my sight again.

"You're suffocating me," Hernanda says when I squeeze her a little harder, making Sami laugh.

"You have to deal with it for a little longer," I reply against the crown of her head where her dark blonde hair tickles my nose.

"Can you go bother Samuel?" she asks, pushing against me to get me to stop hugging her.

"I already did for half an hour. It's your turn now," I reply, and even though I know she doesn't want to, she giggles in my arms.

"Okay, Lina, come here. Let's give your siblings some space," I hear Dad say, so I turn my head just enough to see him standing behind us with open arms. I kiss Hernanda's head one more time before releasing her, grinning as she runs away to make sure I don't hold her captive in my hug again. Then, Dad's arms wrap around me, and I melt into his chest.

"I missed you," I say as the tears finally drop, my arms flinging around him as he holds me close.

"I know. We missed you so much, too, Catalina." With my face buried in his chest, I let more tears fall.

Nothing could help me hold them back.

Ever since Mamá's passing, I've held the rest of my family so much closer in my heart because I don't ever want to have to regret not loving them enough, not loudly enough. They mean everything to me, and I don't want them to doubt that fact, no matter how far away I am. No matter how long I am gone from home.

They are my reason for everything. The reason I do the things I do. Mamá was what got me started in tennis, but I keep going for my family. To keep earning the money that will make sure my father doesn't have to work as much as he used to, to afford Sami's and Hernanda's hobbies, medical bills, or anything else they need. Ori has been sustaining herself for a long time, but taking care of my other two siblings brings me joy, and I'm going to keep doing so until they either don't need me to anymore or I physically can't.

"You played so, so well today, my darling girl. I'm so proud of you," Dad says before pressing his lips to my forehead and stepping back.

He squeezes my arms one last time before nudging my chin with the back of his fingers and stepping toward where Hernanda flopped down on the couch in my hotel room. I move over to Sami, stroking his hair once as he looks up at me with that big, bright smile he's had ever since he was a baby. He's always been such a happy kid, through all the tough and sad times, his smile has never faded, not in the way it did for Hernanda when she was old enough to understand what it meant to have met your mother but be incapable of remembering more than perhaps the smallest of memories about her. All they know are the stories we share, and that knowledge hardened her a little in a way that I wish I could undo.

I don't want my siblings to know that type of pain. I know it inside out. I breathe it most days. Being in tennis makes me so painfully aware of everything I'll never get to share with her, everything she wished for me in the sport we both loved, and I know my siblings feel the same about their accomplishments. Whenever Sami or Hernanda win a trophy, they go with Dad to where Mamá is buried just so they can show it to her. Whenever Ori has a breakthrough in her work, she talks to Mamá in her room.

I...

Well, I haven't found a way to feel connected to her in that way. To speak to her. To feel like she's listening.

Ori and Santi step back into the room right as Sami tells me about the new robot he's working on for another science fair, but he cuts off to clap excitedly.

My brother loves food more than he loves me, I'm sure of it.

"Catalina, can you come help us?" Ori says, and I notice Santi's pale face as he walks silently beside her.

*Uh oh.*

I rush toward the kitchen area of the suite where Ori and Santi put the food they went out to get, feeling my heart race. My older sister usually doesn't get involved in my business unless I ask her to, but I have a feeling that is exactly what is about to happen.

"You two aren't faking it anymore," she says quietly as soon as we're somewhat alone, and I feel my heart skip a beat.

"What?" It's a stupid thing to ask. I heard her perfectly fine, and she's a hundred percent right, but asking it buys me some time to collect my thoughts.

Ori inspects me, then looks at Santiago, studying how close he's standing beside me now that I've approached them. I doubt he even noticed he came so close. Santi has this way of being drawn to me. If we were openly really dating, I think he'd constantly be touching me, but we haven't told anyone we're not faking it anymore.

At least it doesn't feel fake anymore.

Not after what happened earlier.

After I came harder than ever before while Santi worshipped my body. After he told me I'm his favorite person. After I realized I'm in love with him.

"You two fucked." I almost choke on my own spit.

"How in the world would you know that?" I ask, but my sister's brown eyes drift to Santi.

"He told me," she replies, and I spin on my heels to swat Santiago's bicep. He lets me do it even though he probably sees it coming.

"Why are you telling my sister we had sex?" Santi's mouth falls open, but before he gets the chance to respond, my sister speaks again.

"He didn't. You just did." The color drains from my face, but Santi simply starts chuckling as I cover my face with my hands.

"I hate it when you do that," I mumble because it isn't the first time in my life my older sister has tricked me. I think it's part of the eldest sibling's job to trick her younger sister.

"I know. Now, tell me, how the fuck did this happen? I thought you two hated each other?" she asks, but she looks more amused now than anything.

"You know how it goes. A dry spell makes you do stupid things," I reply to take the tension out of the question, but Santi lets the joke roll off his back as he takes my hand and steps toward Ori.

"It happened because I stopped being an idiot and because Cata's heart is big enough to give me a second chance."

Santi's words have my shoulders dropping as the tension leaves them, and I look up at him to see he's already staring down at me.

It's entirely irritating that the man who still has my legs shaking from fucking me so well earlier can also make my heart turn to putty with a few simple words.

"Santi," I start, but he kisses my forehead before I can come up with a response. He turns his head to look at Ori, offering her a nervous smile.

"I think the better question you should ask is why didn't it happen sooner? Or why did it take me so long to realize what I thought I felt for Cata was the very opposite of what I actually feel?"

My heart shrieks in fear at his words. Not because I don't think they're some of the most wonderful words I've ever heard. No. It's because I love him so much, too, and I'm scared we're going to have another fall-out that will make us stop speaking to each other for years.

"Aww, that's gross," Ori says, but her smile is telling. My sister always pretends she hates romance, but I know it's because she's never had anyone love her the proper way.

I don't think anyone's ever loved me the proper way.

Until Santi.

Which is a bold assumption to make, thinking he's in love with me, but I've always believed actions speak louder than words, and Santiago's actions have been screaming one very specific thing at me: I love you.

I lean into his side as soon as the thought enters my head, and Ori scrunches her nose at us before forcing another smile. But no matter how much I don't want to be at times, I'm a romantic through and through.

I melt at the little things.

I giggle internally when Santi looks at me, even when someone else is speaking.

I blush when he tells me how beautiful I am every single day.

Romance, to me, isn't the big gestures. They're part of it, sure, but I love to be loved quietly, too. In the little things. In the way I am looked at. In the way I'm admired for who I am.

Deep inside, I want the person who loves me to be able to make a list of a thousand reasons why they love me, not superficially but deeply. I want them to see my soul and think it's the most precious thing in the world.

Santi offers me that in his own way. In his scrapbook, he put parts of me I never thought anyone would truly see.

"We should eat before the food gets cold," Ori says, and I force my eyes open and to step out of Santi's arms.

His fingers linger on me like he isn't quite ready to let go, but I don't give him a chance. I simply walk back to where my family is with Sami and Hernanda's food in my hand, helping my little brother rearrange so he has everything he needs while eating. Santi returns with Dad's food, but Ori tilts her head, telling me there is one more thing she wants to discuss, but this time, only I'm supposed to hear it.

"Go ahead and start without us. I have a feeling this could take a second," I tell my family, shooting Santi a hint of a smile to ease the concern I see building inside of him through the expression on his face.

Ori takes my hand and leads me into my hotel room. She closes my door gently, then turns to look at me before leaning against it, her hands behind her back. Her gaze is enough to make me shuffle my feet nervously.

"Spit it out, Ori. You know I hate that look. Just say whatever it is you need to say," I blurt out, gesturing more with my hands than is necessary, but I can't help it.

"Where is your focus, Lina?" I take a step back out of pure surprise.

"What?"

"You heard me. Where is your focus? Because at the beginning of the season, it was on becoming number one and winning your first Grand Slam. It was on your dreams and goals, not on winning doubles tournaments with Santiago," she says, and I feel tears of shame fill my eyes before anger takes over.

"I told you my back wasn't doing well. I told you I needed to take a break, and it was between taking a complete break and still being able to play tournaments. Tournaments that, by the way, pay for a lot of the things Dad, Hernanda, and Samuel need. I know you're doing important, life-saving work, but it's not paying the bills in the same way my career is. And it isn't fair of you to make me feel bad about myself for a back problem I've had since I was a child, and finding a way to still play and be able to pay the bills."

The words spill out of me in a quick rant that leaves me breathless, but Ori's expression doesn't change. I'd expected her to feel remorse for what she said, but she looks as convinced by her words now as she did a minute ago.

"I don't want you to lose sight of your goals because of this fake relationship with Santiago, Lina. I'd hate to see you lose the chance to fulfill your dreams for another season, and I'm not saying this to be cruel. I love you so much, you know that, but you also know sometimes you need some tough love. If this is not one of those moments, then I'm sorry." I feel my anger drifting away at the sight of genuine worry filling her eyes.

"I promise you, my goals are my top priority. I took a break for my back, but I'm going to use the rest of this season to achieve everything I have ever wanted to achieve," I assure her, so Ori takes a step toward me. Her legs are incredibly long, but apart from our height difference, we look the same. Same eyes, nose, hair, and lips, except Ori's features are sharper than mine. I've always had a softer face despite the scowl resting there most of the time.

Ori's fingers wrap around the necklace Mamá gave me before she offers me the saddest of smiles.

"She would be so proud of you," Ori whispers, tears shooting into her eyes at the mention of the mother we both loved so much.

"She would be so proud of *you*, changing the world for the better," I reply, but my big sister shakes her head.

"I haven't accomplished much in the way of changing things, but you have. You've changed so much in the world of tennis, in the world of sport, not only through your advocating of important issues but also by being who you are. A kind person with a big heart. Never forget that."

The tears finally fall as I hug my sister, letting her strong arms wrap me up in a bear hug that settles everything inside of me.

She's right. A lot is on the line. This is the season I want to become number one, that I want to win my first Grand Slam, and it's far from over. My back is feeling better, and I will do everything I can to snatch that number one spot for myself.

And no one can stop me.

# CHAPTER 35
## SANTIAGO

AFTER I WON THE Monte-Carlo Masters, Catalina and I made our way to Stuttgart, where she won her first singles tournament since taking a break. She won the finals match against number fifteen in the world, Corinna Ginzler, which was a huge confidence boost for my woman. She needed it so desperately after returning, and she's been in a really good mood since. Layla didn't compete in that tournament, so Cata took a big chunk out of the point difference that was between them. Then, she did it again in the Madrid Open, winning the tournament a day before I won the men's.

Cata and I have both fought our way into the finals of the Italian tournament, and I need her to win this one, too, because directly afterward, we're making our way to France for Roland Garros, the French Open.

The second Grand Slam tournament of the season.

I brush a strand of hair out of her face, studying the peaceful expression on her face as she sleeps in my arms. My body is spent from all the training we've been doing during the day and losing ourselves in one another at night.

There is nothing quite as sweet as making Catalina come. If it were up to me, that's all I would do, but I have responsibilities. And as much as I'd like to wake and beg her to let me go down on her to wake her properly, we have to go train before her finals match later.

"Cata," I say quietly, brushing the backs of my fingers over her cheek. "You have to wake up, *cariño*. We're going to be late," I add, making her stir in my arms.

"Five more minutes," she mumbles, and I can't help but chuckle when she buries her face in my side.

I've slept beside Cata a dozen times by now, but I don't think I'll ever get used to how right this feels. With her limbs tangled in mine. With her hair all over the place. With the steady beat of her heart calming mine. I'd never slept beside someone I was in love with, most likely because the person I've been in love with most of my life—another fact I can't wrap my head around—didn't want me in the way I wanted her.

"Santi, can you relax? I'm trying to use you as a pillow but you're already as hard as a bag of bricks. You're even more so when you're overthinking and your body tenses," she says, but I see the little smile playing on her lips.

"I am as hard as a brick, *cariño*, but you can't blame me. It's the morning and the sexiest woman in the world has half her body draped over mine."

Her hand instantly drifts down my body, a torturously slow caress that has my already hard cock swelling in my boxers.

"We have places to be," I remind her, but Cata merely smiles as she slips her finger mere centimeters beneath the waistband of my underwear.

"Does that mean you don't want me to take care of my favorite toy?" A breathless laugh escapes me as she traces my lower abdomen.

"Is that what my cock is to you? A toy?" I ask with another laugh because I'm so hard, I can't breathe properly.

"My *favorite* toy," she corrects with a wicked smile.

"As long as it's your favorite," I croak out, trying to hold eye contact with her, but my eyes flutter shut when her fingers slip back under my boxers, getting closer to my dick.

"It is," she whispers, her lips finding my earlobe and gently biting down on it. "Will you let me play with it, Santi? Just for a few minutes until we have to leave," she says, her voice barely more than a whisper, but she has that seductive lull to her voice that would make me give her anything and everything she asks of me.

"Touch me. Fuck me. Do whatever you want with me, Catalina. I am yours."

In more ways than I will ever be able to express.

My eyes open to see her rip the blanket off us before she makes her way down my mostly naked body. She tugs my boxers down at the same time, leaving me completely naked and on display for her. I barely have time to admire how fucking attractive I find it when she wears my clothes while I wear nothing at all, but then she wraps those perfect lips of hers around my cock and all thoughts leave me.

"Fuck me," I moan, my hips arching to get deeper. Cata pins them down before I have a chance, leaving me powerless to do anything but take what she gives me.

I almost come from the thought alone.

"You feel so good, Cata. Please give me more," I beg, and she looks up from between my thighs as she swallows me down completely. "Fuuuuuuck."

She chuckles against my cock, making me see stars as more pleasure rolls through me. She runs her tongue along the length of my dick, cupping my balls in a way that has me moaning louder than ever before.

But it doesn't last. She doesn't make me come. She brings me to the very edge and then her mouth disappears, leaving me to whimper at the loss of contact.

"You look so good sprawled out like this, Santi, with your cock hard and begging to put my mouth back on it." Her hands trail up my stomach, and she moans at the contact. "Look at you, *corazón*. Look how perfect you are," she says, and I obey because of course I do. I'll always obey Catalina when she tells me what to do.

I try to see myself the way she does, see my abs, muscular and thick thighs, my cock with its slight curve and wide built. I try to see myself through her eyes, but I'd much rather have her see herself through mine because she'd never, ever feel insecure about anything again. She'd see just how perfect she is, and I don't mean simply her appearance.

I mean everything about her.

"Cata, what do I have to do so you finally ride my face? Do you want me to get on my knees? Because I will. I'll do anything," I say, sitting up to reach for her.

"As much as I'd love to see you on your knees, Santi, I want to ride your face more than I want to breathe," she replies, and anticipation licks up my spine as I position myself down on the mattress, making it easier for her to straddle my face.

"That makes two of us," I say and bring my hands to her hips as she comes closer, lifting her onto my face. "You know what I was dreaming about right before I woke up?" I ask, caressing her magnificently thick thighs as she hovers her pussy over my mouth. Her eyes catch mine, but I don't miss the way she trembles in the way she always does when she's turned on.

"What did you dream about?" she asks, and I inhale deeply, taking in the scent of her arousal.

"About shoving my tongue deep inside this beautiful pussy, tasting it, and then making you come so hard, you'll never want another's mouth on you," I reply, my grip on her tightening as I pull her pussy down and toward me.

"I already don't want another's mouth on me, Santi. You've ruined me for everyone else."

I lick along the length of her pussy, a reward for both of us.

"Oh my God," she breathes out, sinking down fully on my face.

"Hold onto my hair and don't worry about letting me breathe. I'll breathe when I've made you come," I say, flicking my tongue over her swollen clit with its pretty piercing and making her moan my name.

"Santi, I need you to tap my leg twice if you actually can't breathe," Cata says breathlessly, but I don't tell her that I think breathing is entirely overrated when I could spend an entire lifetime between her legs and never be satisfied.

I eat her out like a starved man, sucking on her clit, then licking along the length of her again before sliding my tongue inside her. Cata is enjoying every second of it, moaning my name as she rides my face, using my nose to rub against her clit too. She's soft in her movements, not grinding hard to hurt me, but I'm digging my fingers into her ass to get her to push down harder. To take what she needs and give me everything I want.

And what I want is to taste her, my sweet Catalina, for as long as possible before she comes on my face.

Cata rolls her hips, her fingers digging into my hair as I use the flat of my tongue to let her rub against. She's in control the whole time, chasing her pleasure at her own tempo, until I can no longer handle the slowness. My cock is so hard, it's painful, and I want to bury myself deep inside of Catalina again. Her mouth is heaven, but kissing her while her pussy hugs my cock and her eyes are on mine is one of my favorite things in the world.

"FUCK!" she screams and tugs at my hair when I flick my tongue over her clit and play with her piercing over and over, faster and faster. She stops her movements to let me fuck her right through her orgasm, and it takes everything inside of me not to thrust into my hand and get me off at the same time.

She tugs on my hair again as she starts grinding down on my face, desperate to ride out her pleasure for as long as possible, and I lick her clean, the taste of her orgasm so addictive, I can't get enough.

"Put a condom on and fuck me, Santi. Please," she says, her body still shaking from her orgasm, and the sound of her begging has me moving without hesitation.

I use my hold on her ass to lift her and maneuver us around until she's on her back on the bed. The sudden movement has a gasp of surprise leaving her, but it soon turns into a giggle when I kiss her lips, cheek, jaw, and then neck. She still tastes like me, and I taste like her, and it's the realest piece of heaven I've ever felt.

My fingers reach for the condoms on the nightstand, grabbing one before opening it and sliding it down my length. My mouth stays on her body the whole time, playing with her nipples and moving back up to her neck to lick along its length.

We both got tested, and Cata is on birth control, but she said she didn't want to have sex without a condom yet, and I respect her decision. Birth control is only so safe, and if she doesn't want to have sex without the safety barrier of a condom, then that's how it'll be. If she changes her mind, we'll lose the condom. Anything Catalina wants, she gets. I'll treat her like the queen she is, and I'll worship her until I die.

Cata wraps her legs around my hips, urging me toward her by pressing the heels of her feet into my ass. She's usually the one in charge, but I also want her to know that I can fuck her into paradise without any instructions needed.

I sink the head of my cock inside of her, the sensation so wonderful that I grab hold of her legs to steady me as pleasure courses through me in waves.

"More," Cata says, begs, clawing at my chest as if it would make me do as she said faster.

"Spread your legs, *cariño*. Let me go deeper," I say, pressing her legs wide and up. Catalina is completely spread out, and the smile on her lips as she reaches for the headboard to hold onto is all the encouragement I need to keep going.

I sink all the way inside of her, my cock buried inside to the hilt. We both moan as soon as I've filled her up completely, Cata's eyes closing as her back arches off the bed.

"You feel so good, Santi. So hard and big," she says, her fingers wrapping around the columns that make up the headboard. I shiver all over from her words, slipping out to thrust back inside her as hard as I can. "Yes, fuck!" she pants out, and I push her legs even higher to go even deeper.

I almost lose it as I watch her breasts with those pierced nipples bounce with every thrust, but it feels too good to stop. I don't ever want it to stop. I don't ever want us to stop.

"Look at the way your pussy hugs my cock, Cata. Look at how perfect this view is," I say, driving into her hard and slow, finding that one spot inside of her that has her screaming my name. Her hands drift to her thighs as she stares down the place we connect, and when I place my hand on her clit to rub circles, playing with her piercing, her orgasm explodes through her, catching both of us by surprise.

I don't slow down. I don't remove my hand. I fuck her through it and then keep going, chasing my own pleasure.

"Santi, fuck, shit," she says, followed by more curse words in our mother tongue.

I'm a moaning mess on top of her, trying my best to find a rhythm that makes me come but also makes her come again because I want another from her. I need another. Watching Catalina come undone is pure bliss for me.

"Fuck, you feel so good," she says, moaning as I increase my speed and angle her hips up, aiming for her G-spot with every stroke.

I've studied Cata's body closely enough to know where to touch her and fuck her to have her coming harder than she ever has before.

I'm in tune with her pleasure.

"Right there. Yes, fuck!" she chants as I press down on her lower abdomen and the top of her pussy, feeling myself slipping in and out of her.

"Shit, Catalina," I breathe out, my movements turning frantic.

She squeezes her walls around my cock seconds later, unraveling me.

I come so hard, my entire body trembles. My cock pulses inside of her as I fill the condom, her pussy fluttering around me as she comes again, too. If I could, I'd keep slipping in and out, but I have no strength left. Cata, on the other hand, rolls her hips to keep her pleasure going, dragging out mine too.

I'm a fucking goner.

For her body.

For her mind, heart, and soul.

For *her*.

Catalina pulls me down to bring my mouth to hers, and I use the proximity to massage her breasts in my hands, scolding myself internally for forgetting to give them any love.

"We don't have time for you to make me want more, *mi corazón*," she reminds me, nipping at my bottom lip before she smiles.

"Then let's get you cleaned up," I say, using all of my willpower to slide out of her.

Cata watches me from the bed as I rip off the condom, hunger in her eyes as she studies my half-hard cock like it's exactly what she said it was.

Her favorite toy.

A chuckle escapes me as I lift her out of the bed, carrying her to the shower with me. I take my time washing her, then wrapping her in a towel and placing her on the empty area beside the sink. I hand her her toothbrush with toothpaste on it, and I do the same for myself, brushing my teeth even if it means getting rid of Cata's taste for a little.

"Are you ready for today?" I ask once we're done.

Cata hands me a cotton swab and some cleansing toner that she uses for her face. The message is clear, and I waste no time putting some of that liquid on the swap and swiping it across her face.

Fuck, but I love these moments more than anything else in the world. The quiet ones. The ones just between us when she's entirely mine and no one else's. When she wants me to take care of her. When she lets me in.

"I'm ready for today, but Santi..." She trails off, uncertainty covering her features.

"What, *cariño*?" I ask softly, placing my hands on either side of her thighs where they rest on the marble.

"I don't know if I'm ready for Roland Garros. I need to win that tournament, and I—I just feel so hopeless. Maybe if there was a way I could feel closer to my mamá again, I'd feel more confident, but right now? I'm so lost," she admits, placing her hand on the spot between my neck and collarbone, her eyes trained on her fingers. "I'm so lost without her in the world of tennis," she whispers.

"What can I do to help you find your way again?" I ask, but she simply presses her lips to mine, lingering there with her eyes closed. Mine are half-open, too desperate to take in the sight of her to close them fully.

"I don't think there's anything you *can* do, but thank you for wanting to try," she says before pushing herself off the sink, her hand trailing across my naked stomach before it disappears entirely as she leaves the room.

"I'm going to find a way," I mumble, even if she can't hear me anymore.

# CHAPTER 36
## SANTIAGO

THE SCORE IS ONE set to one, with Cata leading the third set three games to two. She's been strong since losing the first set, but she has yet to take a service game from Hallin, her opponent, in this set.

I can tell she's nervous, no matter how much she's trying to hide it. Charlie hasn't said a word in an hour to me, so I know they're as anxious for Catalina to win as we all are.

Layla has been absent from yet another tournament, this one, because of an injury, so if Catalina manages to win today, as she has done for the last couple of tournaments, the gap between her and Layla in the standings will close immensely. And when she wins Roland Garros next, which I know my girl will, she will be number one in the world.

She will have accomplished everything she set out to do.

"Her confidence is going to crumble if they go into the tiebreaker," Charlie says, and I tilt my head to look at their worried expression.

"It's not going to go into a tiebreaker. Cata is going to get a break," I assure them, but they use their chin to gesture toward Hallin, who looks ready to eat someone for lunch.

"With a serve as strong as hers, it's going to be difficult." I throw Charlie the look that statement deserves. They simply chuckle at my expression. "Okay, relax, Mr. I-Would-Die-For-Her. All I mean is that Cata needs to readjust for her return. She needs to back up a little, but she will figure it out. If not, I will tell her," they add, patting my back before leaning forward by putting their elbows on their knees.

"I'm so nervous," I say as I place a hand to my chest, doing my best to take deep breaths.

"Stop that. If she sees you're nervous, she's gonna get nervous," Charlie says and swats my arm.

"That's ridic—" They cut me off before I have the chance to finish my sentence.

"Why do you think she always has that stoic expression on her face when she watches you?" they challenge, but as much as I try to bite back my answer, I can't.

"Because Cata is my little rain cloud. She always frowns. It's one of the reasons I love her so much." My eyes widen at the admission, but Charlie seems as unsurprised by it as everyone else in my life.

"No, dumbass. It's to calm you when you're feeling nervous. It's to let you know she doesn't have a speck of doubt inside her about your ability to win," they say, and I sink back in my chair as I do my best to bring the same kind of determined look to my features.

Because they're right.

And I finally understand why I feel so steady whenever I see Cata during my games.

It isn't just because of my feelings for her, which is a big part. It's also because of her unwavering faith in me that she communicates with nothing more than a simple look.

Fuck, I love her so much.

It makes breathing harder and easier at the same time every time I realize it. And I can't stop realizing it.

Hallin gets up from her bench to walk toward the baseline. This tournament is held on clay courts, which Catalina excels on. Every type of court makes the ball bounce differently, and on clay, it bounces higher and the shots are usually slowed down. Cata is also taking advantage of her spin because the clay is made for those shots. It's why Hallin's serve is so strong. She puts a lot of spin on it, making the ball bounce even higher. It makes it almost impossible for Catalina to hit it back.

My girl positions herself at the baseline on her side of the court, which is closest to where we're sitting. She moves back in place where she was the whole time, but right as Charlie opens their mouth to say something, she holds up her hand to silence them. I don't know how the fuck she saw them attempting to speak out of her periphery, but it has me cracking a smile.

"Don't tell her what to do," I whisper a second before Hallin serves, and Catalina jumps into the air to get under the ball and follow through properly. She returns it down the line, and Hallin is too surprised by her strong return on her first serve to be fast enough to get to the ball.

"Love-fifteen," the umpire calls out, and I start clapping louder than anyone else for Catalina because, fuck, that was one of the most beautiful returns I've ever seen in my entire life.

She moves to wipe her face on her towel, her game face still on despite having won such an impressive point. Cata never really shows her emotions unless she's too frustrated to hold them back. But she's locked in right now, and nothing is going to stop her.

Catalina wins the second point after an excruciatingly long rally that ends with her using an overhead smash to place the ball deep into the court, making it bounce too high for Hallin to reach it.

"Love-thirty," the umpire says, making hope bloom in my chest.

All it takes is two more points, and she'll get the break she needs. Then, all that's left for her is to bring her games home.

Cata is so close.

Hallin takes as much time as the clock allows to get ready for her serve, and I take a moment to admire how stunning Cata looks in her red dress. Her long, dark hair is braided and her baby hairs are pinned down by clips. She's wearing one of those visor caps to hide her face from the sun, and her strong back is fully on display again, making my mouth water with every movement of hers.

Cata doesn't manage to get the next serve, but she wins the point after because Hallin makes an unforced error.

"She's so close," I whisper to Charlie, who nods several times. "One more point. She can do it." My words are followed by more clapping, trying to encourage Catalina.

She ignores me because she's in her zone, but I know she heard me, and that's all that matters.

I hold my breath as Hallin serves. Hold it even harder as Cata straightens out and jumps, getting ready to return the ball. She hits it into the net.

"Thirty-forty," the umpire says, their voice travelling through the arena.

"*Vamos*, Cata," I call out, scooting to the edge of my seat to get closer to her. "*Tú puedes, cariño. Respira y concéntrate*," I say, and she looks up at me and places her index finger to her lips before winking at me. A tiny smirk covers her lips, and I wish her confidence would settle me, but I'm nothing more than a puddle of nerves.

Hallin prepares to serve again, and I hold my breath once more.

This time, Cata is further behind the baseline, and she attacks the serve, sending Hallin running to the other side of the court. Cata takes the chance to sprint to the net, volleying a winner down the same side of the court Hallin was, and since she wasn't expecting it, running in the opposite direction, my girl's opponent doesn't reach the ball.

Cata gets the break.

I'm on my feet, clapping for her as soon as she wins the point. Charlie is beside me, cheering for her, too. The entire stadium is. Cata has a way of being the fan favorite wherever she goes, and it's no different here in Italy.

"That's it, *mariquita*," I call out, and she screams in victory for a moment, finally allowing her emotions to come to the surface.

Her next service game is an easy win. Cata's serve has been so strong, and she proves it by not losing a single point in her service game. The break between the games lets her take a breath, lets her refocus for the next game, which she doesn't have to win. She doesn't have to get another break. She is leading five games to two in the third set, so even if Hallin gets her next game through, it wouldn't be bad for Cata. She would simply need to win her service game to win the match.

My little rain cloud has never been a big fan of doing the bare minimum, though.

No.

She takes Hallin's service game, sealing the match. I feel pride coursing through every single part of my body as she wins the tournament for the second year in a row.

Catalina's racket drops to the ground as she sinks into a squat, covering her face with her hands. It takes her several seconds until she's composed enough to drop her hands and face the crowd, waving to them as she makes her way to the net to shake Hallin's hand. Then she shakes the umpire's.

Finally, Cata turns back to the crowd and waves to them, throwing kisses to them and placing her hands on her face when they scream even louder for her. I know I'm not anyone in the crowd of people for her, but I cheer for her in the same way because she deserves it. If I could, I'd lose my voice for her, to make her feel as loved as possible in the sport she shared with her mother.

The sport that connects her to the one person she misses more than words will ever be able to describe.

And when she makes her way to where Charlie, the rest of her team, and I are waiting for her, I feel my heart palpitating even harder because she's running to *me*. To her team that I am a part of, and when she reaches us, she kisses *me* for the whole world to witness.

*I love you, Catalina.*

The words almost escape my lips. They're the hardest truth I've ever had to hold back, but this moment isn't about my feelings for her. It's about her victory, and I'll never do anything to take that away from her.

So, instead, I say, "You did amazing. I'm so proud of you," which makes her kiss me again, this time harder and with a smile on that perfect mouth of hers.

# CHAPTER 37
## CATALINA

SANTI HAS TAKEN ME to Zakynthos in Greece.

After my win in Italy, he told me to pack my bags because we were going on a trip. He didn't tell me where, only that I should bring lots of bikinis and summer dresses, shorts, light tops, and anything else I'd need on a beach vacation. He promised me it'd be only for a few days since I can't be slacking off this close to the second Grand Slam of the season. I have to train every single day, and he assured me he'd even find courts there for us to play for a few hours a day if it made me feel better.

It did.

So, we packed our bags, made our way to Greece, and I haven't asked him why we're here once. I could have looked up what there is to do here, but Santi clearly has plans for us, and I don't want to ruin the surprise.

Plus, I love surprises.

Not the people jumping out at your birthday and scaring the shit out of you kind of surprises.

But the thoughtful gestures that a partner does for you to make you happy.

Santiago has perfected those kinds of surprises over the last half year that we've been doing this whole fake/real dating thing.

I haven't spoken to him about what the hell we are yet, but it's a conversation that lingers on the tip of my tongue every single time I'm near him. Uncertainty is one of my worst nightmares, but at the same time, I can't bring myself to start the conversation.

Our reputations have been cleared.

We are *the* couple of the world of tennis.

Most people love us together, and so do I. I love us together so much, I'm scared that when I start asking him what he wants for the long run, it won't be me. That he'll want more, or to get back to his life. Before this whole charade we put on, Santi loved partying. He loved going out and fucking a new person whenever he wanted.

*What if he'll want to get back to that as soon as he's free at the end of the season?*

*What if I'm just a way for him to get sex?*

*What if I'm not enough for him?*

As much as I try to logically stop myself from thinking such irrational things because I know how deeply he cares for me, these doubts attack the vulnerable part of my brain that harbors all of my insecurities like piranhas attack a piece of meat.

"*Mariquita*," Santi says, and I snap out of my thoughts, turning my head to look at him abruptly. "What's wrong?" he asks and cups my face, rubbing his thumb along my cheek in soothing motions.

"I hate how well you see through me," I whisper, fighting back the panic crawling into my chest.

"No, you don't. You're a romantic who needs your partner to be able to pick up on the little things." He traces my bottom lip with his thumb, and I inhale deeply, taking in his scent, something that reminds me of pure sunshine, just like the man who emanates it. "And I want to be your partner, Catalina. I want to be your partner in everything, not just while we train. Is that a worry you need to have soothed? Because I'll say it again. I'll say it in every language you know until you believe me."

The car we're taking to the location Santi didn't tell me a lot about, hits a bump in the road that has me moving closer to Santi, our breaths becoming one as he leans down to close the distance between us even more.

"What are you? A fucking mind reader?" I ask with a frown, but Santi merely smiles at me before he kisses the corner of my mouth softly, gently, and oh so sweetly.

"I'm simply a man desperately in love with the woman he's known most of his life. I can read your thoughts in the same way you can read mine, *cariño*, because that's how well we know each other," he says, sending tears straight into my eyes because a love declaration was the last thing I was expecting right here and now. "It was bad timing when I told you that you're my favorite person, but it was true. It *is* true."

He doesn't give me a chance to respond as he takes a deep breath and repositions himself, clearly gathering more courage.

"Catalina, you are everything to me. You are the very reason I look forward to getting out of bed in the morning, even on the mornings when I have a hard time doing so. You are my strength, my courage, my dream, and everything else in my life that keeps me going. I love you so much that life seems brighter now when I think about it. I love you so much that the only thing I ever faked with you was the contempt I thought I held for you. It's why I thought I was dreading it at the beginning of this, but really, I was just terrified my feelings for you would grow and you wouldn't feel the same way I do."

As much as I try to fight my tears, they roll down my cheeks during the most romantic speech anyone has ever given me in my entire life. Santi is careful as he wipes them away, always so gentle with me, like I'm the most precious person in the world to him, which I'm slowly understanding that I am.

"What about your life before? All the parties and people? Aren't you going to miss that?" I ask, my heart sinking at my words, but it's also still beating more rapidly than ever before. His amber eyes are on mine as he answers without hesitation.

"I don't miss it. I don't miss any of it. I haven't since we started this. You've kept my head so occupied with any and all thoughts of you, and I don't need anything else, Cata. All I need is you," he says, and so many of my worries finally subside, replaced by the certainty that Santiago loves me.

He loves me more than anyone has ever loved me before.

He loves me even though he's seen all of my ugly sides.

He loves me even though I hated him for so long.

"Santiago, I—"

"We're here," the driver of our taxi says, interrupting me. Excitement blooms on Santi's face, and he kisses me before handing the driver some cash and rushing over to my side to open the door for me.

My head is spinning, but I take his hand and let him pull me out of the taxi, right against his chest. My other hand is clinging to the bag we brought, but Santi doesn't force me to say anything back to his love declaration. He simply kisses me three more times, melting against me when I wrap my arms around his neck and pull him closer.

"Let's go, *cariño*. This is a bit time sensitive," he says, placing one last kiss on my forehead and then pulling me toward where a small boat is waiting for us.

The sun is blaring down on us, but I welcome the heat and the scent of saltwater as I follow behind Santi. My flip flops get lost in the sand with every step, but it's too hot to take them off, so Santi and I end up lifting our knees higher and laughing at ourselves for how funny we look doing so. That is, until I curse when my feet get burned, and he scoops me into his arms so it doesn't happen again.

"Will you tell me what we're doing here yet?" I ask, smiling because of how light I feel.

It's a wonder what a healthy dose of communication can do for an overthinking mind, especially when the reassurance comes from the person you desperately need it from.

And I love Santi even more for never shying away from telling me how he feels.

As soon as we're not in a rush anymore, I'll allow myself to be as vulnerable as he was with me.

"Not yet. But we've almost made it," he assures me, offering me another one of his smiles.

My favorite smile in the entire world.

Once we arrive where the boat is, the person there speaks to Santi in hushed voices, and I do my best to relax my face because my cheeks are burning from how much I'm grinning.

"Perfect," is all I hear Santi say before lifting me into the boat.

Santi gracefully gets into the boat too before the short man with brown hair, hazel eyes, dark skin, and a kind smile finally starts the boat and makes our way to our location.

The wind is warm as it blows my hair around, and Santi chuckles as I try to get it back under control. He takes my hair tie from me to twist my hair into a bun at the back of my head, placing a kiss on my lips as soon as he's done. I nuzzle against his side, the view of the ocean and the land beside us almost as wonderful as Santi's words that continue to bounce around in my head.

*Catalina, you are everything to me.*

*I love you so much.*

*All I need is you.*

Over and over as I study the waves the boat makes. As I let the sun heat my skin. As I take in all of the smells around me, my favorite still being Santi's. I inhale it with every breath, his arms firmly wrapped around me.

It's a short boat ride, and I wish it was longer because I adore the way Santiago holds me. He holds me like he's never held me before. He holds me like I'm the very reason he lives. He holds me like I'm exactly who he said I was.

His everything.

"We've arrived," the boat driver says, pulling me back into reality and out of the fantasy land that Santi drags me into whenever we're together.

"Arrived where?" I ask Santi, and he untangles his arms from me.

"To swim with sea turtles," he says, pulling me off the seat with him to move to the edge of the boat where I see several sea turtles swimming in the water.

More tears flood my eyes, and my hand lifts to my tattoo instantly.

"You said you wanted to find a way to feel closer to your mamá before the next Grand Slam," he explains, and I cover my mouth with my hand as I study the majestic creatures swimming around in the ocean.

"You brought me here so I could feel closer to Mamá," I repeat, unable to process the information, but Santi is patient.

He simply says, "Yes," and rubs my arms to comfort me.

The man in the boat turns out to be one of the instructors who bring people here to swim with them, so he spends the next little while explaining everything we have to know before we're allowed near them. Stay at least three meters away from them unless they approach you. Only approach them from the side. Don't make any abrupt movements. Don't touch them. He explains several more things, but then Santi and I make our way into the water together.

I do as the man instructed, keeping my distance from them. I'm slow in my movements, waiting for them to approach, if they choose to do so. Considering sea turtles are docile unless they feel threatened, and these ones are used to people in their habitat, they waste no time investigating Santi and me. A rather large one approaches me, swimming against my legs and then toward the man I love. He smiles brightly, and I let out a small laugh when an expression of awe covers his features.

The same big one that approached me first keeps returning, swimming with me and even moving against my stomach and back as if it can't quite sever itself from me. The same awe that crossed Santi's face fills me from top to bottom.

"That one's name is Veronica. She's the one that likes people the most." I look at the man on the boat right as he tells me something that has my heart stopping entirely. "I was there the day she was born eleven years ago." Santi looks at me at the same time I look at him, at the same time the sea turtle nudges my leg again.

"What day?" Santi asks, voicing the question I don't have the power to force from my lips.

"March 20th."

It's a coincidence.

I know it's a coincidence.

It can't be anything else because I don't believe in any of that stuff, rebirth and such. At least I didn't, not until that sea turtle that loves people and was born on the same day my mother passed eleven years ago, swims with me through the water, never leaving my side.

*It's a coincidence*, I try to tell myself over and over.

"Don't overthink it, Cata. Let what you feel be," Santi says, and damn him, I allow that feeling of connectedness I was looking for to spread through me.

I allow the tears to fall.

It's not her, but maybe it's her, and I'm too heartbroken and lost without her to fight it. So I let it be.

I welcome the proximity of the sea turtle as she follows me around as if it is enough to assure me my mother is here and telling me I'm going to be just fine.

And once it's time for us to leave again, I do so with a heart that may feel heavier but also more healed than it has in years.

It's when Santiago hugs me to his chest and lets me cry it out that I know no matter where in the world she is, a part of her will always live inside me and be with me.

"We can come back whenever you want to," Santi says once my sobs slow and the peaceful sound of the waves fills my ears.

"I love you, Santiago," I say against his chest, all of my emotions too much for me to hold back the words. "I'm in love with you," I add, feeling him tense and then untense as he processes my words.

"You don't have to say that because of what I said in the car earlier or because I brought you here," he says, but it's not in a condescending way. I know him well enough to sense that it's fear making him say these things, and that won't do at all.

I lean back and grab his face in my hands, tilting it down to make sure he pays close attention to my next words.

"That's not why, Santi. If it was, that would make things so much easier, but they're not easy. I don't want them to be. It wouldn't feel real to me if they were because you and I have always been complicated, but that isn't a bad thing. On the contrary. To me, working for something to have it makes it that much sweeter. It means more than if things simply flew into my hands."

He leans into my left hand, kissing the palm of it as his eyes close.

"You've become my favorite person, too, Santi. A day I don't spend with you is a day I don't see the sunshine that I so desperately crave," I say, and he pulls me close, capturing my mouth with his.

"I love you, *mariquita*," he says, taking my mouth before I have a chance to respond, and I don't mind.

I've finally shared my feelings with him.

I just hope neither one of us makes me regret it.

# CHAPTER 38
## SANTIAGO

Catalina and I are both in the quarter finals of Roland Garros.

She's been strong all tournament long, a new sort of determination coursing through her veins since we went to Greece, where we potentially found her mother's sea turtle incarnation. I know a lot of people don't believe in those sorts of things, but I do. I always have, and ever since we were there over a week ago, I believe it even more. I know Cata never did, but there is no denying her renewed view on life. She's practically glowing every single time she's on the court, something that hasn't happened since her mother passed away.

It's a glorious sight, and I have a hard time not staring at her every time we practice together. She's smiling a lot. She finds the joy in tennis she had lost for so long. Cata has always had a passion like no other. Goals to achieve. Dreams to reach. But she approached them logically so often. Win this, close the gap. Lose this, widen the gap. Win this, become number one. With Layla still unable to participate in tournaments due to an injury, this Grand Slam win is all Cata needs. And while that is the logical thing she's told me, she also told me how excited she is to be playing on the clay courts again. I don't blame her. She's magnificent on them.

She's magnificent on any court.

"Come on, Cata. Push," Charlie calls out, and I stand at the net on the practice court, studying my woman's playing.

She's doing footwork right now, running around the cones that Charlie put at the baseline for her. Her feet are so quick, never losing their rhythm. Her quarter-final is in a few hours, but I have no doubt she'll win it. She's playing against the number seven player, Akiko Yamamoto, and as amazing as her opponent plays, she is no match for my Catalina.

"Faster. Get under the ball, then follow through," Charlie says, and I throw them a smile when Cata starts cursing them out for making her run so much.

"This is supposed to be a warm-up," she complains, but her coach and best friend doesn't look like they give a shit.

"It is whatever I make it. Now move your ass and run," they call back, and I chuckle fully as I turn my head to look at Cata running back and forth.

Papá and Charlie have a lot in common when it comes to beating our asses during training. They both love pushing us to our limits, but Charlie isn't overdoing it today. They push Cata far enough to make her complain, but not too far that she'll be too tired later.

"Alright, Santi, let's go," Papá says, clasping my shoulder in his hand as he guides me toward our own court. "You're playing at the same time as Catalina, so you need to warm up, too." My eyes catch Manu as she appears beside our father, a bright smile covering her face.

She's been looking much happier since everything happened with the woman whose name we won't speak, and I wrap an arm around my sister, pressing a kiss to her temple.

"Did you know that I love you? Like a lot?" I tell her, but she pushes me away and scrunches her nose up in disgust.

"Enough, Santiago, you know I'm not good with the whole feelings talk," she says with a little chuckle, her amber eyes glowing with happiness as she looks at me. "Love you too," she mumbles, shaking her head when I grin at her. "Let's train," she announces, bouncing around on the court in excitement.

I look over my shoulder at Cata one more time to admire her, but she's too busy to pay me any mind, so I turn back around and follow my family to our court.

I have a match to get ready for.

And while Catalina won't be there because she has her own match, I want to make her proud no matter what.

I'm playing against Renjun Choi, my biggest competition in the world of tennis. After taking a break for two tournaments to play doubles with Catalina, Renjun managed to take a chunk out of the point-distance between us in the rankings, but since I've come back, I've been unstoppable, increasing the distance all over again.

My seed as the number one in the world is safe for as long as I can continue participating in matches and win them.

The score is currently one set to nothing for me, and we're taking our break between sets to drink and potentially take a bite of either a banana for me or whatever Renjun is eating.

Papá is in the box where coaches and family members go, and I look at him for an update on Catalina. He lifts up one finger. One set for her. Zero fingers. No sets for Akiko. Two fingers. Two games for Cata. One finger. One game for Akiko in the second set.

I nod several times to acknowledge the standings, pride blooming in my chest for *mi mariquita*.

"Time," the umpire says, and I'm on my feet and running toward the baseline to prepare to return Renjun's serve seconds later.

I kick my knees high, almost touching my chest, to get them ready for another set after sitting for about a minute or even longer. Renjun doesn't bother, walking straight toward where he puts down his towel before grabbing the balls to serve from the ball person.

I take a deep breath for concentration.

I shake out my shoulders as I wait for my opponent to prepare to serve, getting in position to start this second set of the day. Confidence rolls through me, adding to my determination.

He misses his first serve, so I move closer to the baseline, anticipating his second, slower one. My return, unfortunately, isn't great, and I hit it straight to his feet, allowing him to easily make me run to the other side of the court as he hits it back. I barely manage to get it, sliding across the clay court. It takes a lot of my strength to stand upright and run back to the middle of the baseline to prepare for him to hit the ball to me again.

But right as I try to run, I roll my ankle.

A sharp pain goes through my foot and leg, and I collapse to the ground, barely catching myself with my hands as it happens.

The crowd gasps, but there is nothing I can do but lie there and give myself over to the pain because fuck, it hurts. It hurts more than any other injury I've ever had in my life.

"Santiago," I hear Papá calling out, and I try to lift my head to respond. The only thing I manage to do is tug my leg to my chest and wrap my fingers around my ankle, which is now pulsing from pain.

"Calling medical timeout," the umpire says, the entire stadium silent as I writhe in pain. I roll my lips to keep the scream and burst of swear words from escaping me, but from the way no one utters a single word, I might as well have let it all out.

"Hey, are you okay?" Renjun asks, and I realize he made his way over to me. I open my eyes to see his genuinely concerned expression.

"No, man. I think something's seriously wrong with my ankle."

# CHAPTER 39
## CATALINA

I SERVE AN ACE, securing myself the win of the match and a spot in the semi-finals. My heart pounds in my chest, happiness consuming every part of me. I'm in the semi-finals. I played so well, I won the match in two sets with little struggle. This feeling inside my chest, this certainty that I am going to win this tournament, makes me feel invincible.

But that feeling dissipates as soon as I see Charlie's worried expression, their hand covering their mouth as they talk to someone over the phone.

My heart drops.

I move over to the umpire, looking up at her as I wait for her to finish speaking on the phone, too, to ask the one question I don't want to ask because I already know whatever it is, it can't be good. Waiting for her to finish talking to whoever she's on the phone with is torture, but I do my best to take the time to even out my breathing.

Technically, I *know* nothing for certain yet. There is no need to jump to conclusions except... I can feel it deep inside of me.

"What happened with Santiago?" I ask her as soon as she's done speaking on the phone.

"Santiago injured himself during his match. He's with the doctor we have here right now," she explains, making my heart sink even further.

"Please tell the interviewer and fans I'm sorry," is the last thing I say before grabbing my tennis bag, slinging it over my shoulder, and running out of the stadium.

The fans will understand.

The interviewer will understand.

Charlie will understand.

Getting to Santiago is my top priority.

It doesn't matter if my body is exhausted, adrenaline is coursing through my veins. It's pushing me further and further until I reach the room Santiago is currently lying in with an ice pack wrapped around his ankle. Relief only resides in my chest briefly because at least it's only his ankle, but then the realization of all of the horrible things that could be wrong with his ankle set in, and worry returns tenfold.

"How bad is it?" I ask as I burst into the room. Santi's head shoots up, his eyes flying open as he takes in the sight of me.

"Hi, *cariño*," he says, throwing me a sheepish smirk.

"Don't do that. Don't pretend you're not in pain. Don't give me that smirk." I move to his side, and he grabs hold of my hand, placing it on his cheek.

"I can't help it. Seeing you makes me happy, even in the worst of times," he replies, and as much as I wish it would soothe this ache in my stomach, it multiplies by the second at the sight of his elevated foot with the ice pack on it.

"What happened?" I ask, rubbing his cheek with the pad of my thumb to soothe him.

"Your boyfriend isn't as young as he used to be, that's what happened," Carlos says, placing a hand on my shoulder as he appears beside me.

"Shut up," Santi mumbles, but I welcome Carlos' lightheartedness. It eases some of my worry.

"He rolled his ankle," Carlos explains right as Santi's eyes close when I trace his left eyebrow.

"How bad is it?"

"Not great. We're going to have to take him to the hospital to do some tests. It might either be a partial tear or a full one, but let's hope it's only partial because otherwise Santiago won't be able to play in tournaments for the rest of the season." Carlos might have made his voice sound as emotionless as possible, but I see the tension around his mouth and eyes.

And there comes the concern again.

"Stop talking, Papá. You're worrying my Catalina," Santi says, his eyes on me.

"My worry should be the least of your concerns," I argue, but Santi shakes his head.

"Your feelings are more important than a stupid injury." He repositions himself, grunting in pain, just so he can face me better. "Speaking of which, tell me you won," he says, taking my hand in both of his and bringing it to his chest.

I can feel his racing heart instantly.

"I won," I reply, making Santi squeeze my hand and Carlos my shoulder.

"Good job, Lina," Carlos says with pride. "I'll give you two a second," Carlos adds before leaving the room.

"Cata, can you flip the ice pack around, please?" Santi asks, so I move to do so.

A gasp almost escapes me at how swollen his ankle is. Tears fill my eyes because I can't imagine how much pain he is in or what this might mean for the rest of his season.

"Come here," he says, holding out his hand for me right as the tears fall.

"I'm sorry. I know it doesn't help to see me cry, but I love you so much, and I'm so sorry this is happening to you halfway through the season," I rant, covering my mouth to keep more words in.

"Don't be sorry. Knowing you care so much for me is heaven on Earth," he replies, wiggling his fingers to get me to come closer. He places his hand on my cheek to wipe my tears as soon as I'm beside him again. "You're in the semi-finals," he says with excitement in his voice, but I shake my head at him.

"It doesn't matter," I whisper, doing my best to stop crying, to be strong for him.

"Yes, it does. *Mi mariquita*, this season was never about me. It was always about you and your goals." I'm about to protest when he keeps talking. "Don't argue with a man in pain."

"I'm not arguing with any man. I'm arguing with you," I defend, but Santi merely smiles.

"Why don't you kiss me instead?"

It's hard to fight with him when his season might be over and he's prioritizing me over everything else, proving once more how much he loves me.

I press my mouth to his, but we're interrupted by Carlos coming back into the room with Alana and Manuela.

Everything happens in a blur after that. We take Santi to the hospital and, after his adrenaline washes off and the exhaustion of the day sets in, he sleeps for most of the drive with his head on my shoulder.

He doesn't go anywhere without me in the hospital if he can take me with him, and we sit in the waiting room for hours after the tests, waiting to hear about his results. His head is in my lap, letting me massage it as he continues sleeping. I sift my fingers through his hair, praying to whoever might listen that his ligaments aren't fully torn.

No athlete wants to miss an entire season because of an injury. He says this season was about me, but his dreams and goals are important to me, too. I used to hate him for being the number one player in the world, but that was pure jealousy and envy. Now that we're not fighting every step of the way, that we've fallen in love, knowing he could lose his number one seed makes me sick to my stomach. He could lose all his progress. His goal to win more Grand Slams and set new records will be put on hold indefinitely.

"Everything will be fine."

"Stop reading my mind," I reply through gritted teeth, but Santi simply chuckles.

"Then stop thinking so loudly."

In some of my fantasy books, the main characters can actually talk to each other in their minds, which I always found fascinating because I think if Santi was constantly in my head, I'd knock him unconscious so he'd stop every once in a while.

Then again, apparently, this man knows me well enough to look inside my head without any magic in play.

"Why don't you get your ereader out and read something from your book to me? It'll calm both of us," he says, and with a suggestion as good as his, it's hard to argue.

Another hour passes while I read to him. Manu listens too, and Carlos and Alana are sitting together on the other side of the seating area. Carlos has his arm around his wife while she speaks to him, and he watches her with his heart in his eyes.

I realize Santi looks at me the same way.

Like I'm his present, future, and all the good things yet to come wrapped into one person.

"All this waiting is driving me up the wall," Manu says, standing up and running her hands through her hair.

"You can go back to the hotel, Manu. You don't have to be here," Santi says softly, making sure she knows he doesn't mean it rudely.

"Shut up, Santi," she replies, looking at him with a stern expression. "I'm going to find a doctor and demand they tell us what is wrong with your gigantically swollen ankle." She walks away, and I do my best not to burst into laughter because it's so inappropriate, but I should have known Santi would find her comment hilarious.

"Gigantically swollen ankle," he repeats and laughs, his whole body shaking on top of me.

It dies out as soon as the nurse we met earlier approaches us, Manu standing beside her.

"The doctor will see you now," she says, gesturing toward the room we were in earlier. I help Santi up, handing him the crutches we were given so he doesn't have to put weight on his ankle.

Carlos, Alana, and Manu move toward the room, too, making me hesitate.

"What's wrong?" Santi asks, not moving either because I have stopped.

"You have your family with you. I'll wait out here," I say, but he furrows his brows at me like he doesn't understand a single word I'm saying.

"But then a big piece of my family would be missing," he replies, and my heart melts into a little puddle. "Please come with me. I need you," he adds, delivering the killing blow to my chest, except the thing that dies is the remaining doubts about his feelings for me.

Not that there were many.

Perhaps there weren't even any, and I simply needed the reassurance that I'm not barging in where he doesn't want me.

I should have known Santi wants me everywhere with him.

We settle down in our seats across from the doctor, who barely looks away from her computer to acknowledge our presence.

It takes several tense moments, filled with dread and hope, until she finally turns to us.

"Well, Mr. Castillo, I think you'll be very happy to hear it's only a partial tear. That means lots of resting, icing the sore area, compression, and elevation. Then, after a few weeks, you can start physiotherapy. I'm confident you'll be back to playing matches in approximately two months," the doctor says, and the sense of relief that floods my chest is mirrored by Santi's shoulders dropping.

"Thank you for the good news, doctor. I'll go rest, ice, compress, and elevate now so I can watch my girlfriend win her first Grand Slam in a few days."

I think Santi is taking this all too well, but when I open my mouth to argue, he turns to me and kisses me instead.

"It's the only thing keeping me from falling apart right now. Let me focus on you entirely so I don't think about what this means for my season," he begs, and my argument dies on my tongue.

"Okay," I say, and he gives me a relieved smile. "I'll win," I promise him, and he kisses my lips softly once more.

"I know you will."

# CHAPTER 40
## SANTIAGO

My ankle is killing me.

As relieved as I am that it's only a partial tear that'll heal in a month or two, it's still a fucking pain that my season is on hold for as long as it'll take this stupid injury to heal.

But even so, with all of that happening, I can't help focusing entirely on Catalina. She's made her way into the finals, and I flew her family out to France so they can watch her win her first Grand Slam today.

Because she will win.

There is no doubt in my mind.

Ori, Sami, Hernanda, and Felix, her father, are here, and while I didn't tell Cata that I've arranged for them to be at another one of her games, I know she'll be happy to see them. It's added pressure, yes, but it's also the kind of comfort she may need on the biggest day of her career.

I don't think Cata will survive losing another Grand Slam with her heart intact.

"She's got this," Ori says from her seat beside mine.

"Are you trying to reassure me or yourself?" I ask, my heart racing. The tall woman with the same color hair as Cata, as well as the same nose and eyes, doesn't even look at me as she replies.

"I'm trying to convince the universe so it doesn't take it from her again."

"I thought you're a scientist. Do you even believe in that sort of thing?" I ask with a nervous laugh, but Ori looks as serious as always. It reminds me a lot of Cata's expression.

"I believe because she believes. And she believes because of the trip you took her on," Ori explains, scanning my features for something. "I want to go there one day, too. See what Cata saw." I place a comforting hand on her shoulder and offer the smallest of smiles.

"I'm sure she'd love to go there again. We can make it a family trip. I'm sure Sami and Hernanda would love to go too." That finally makes her smile, but it's the kind of sad smile a child in pain wears when thinking about the loss of a parent.

Cata never speaks to me about her siblings' grief because she said it isn't her pain to share with anyone they wouldn't be comfortable with. Seeing it so plainly on Ori's face makes me understand why. I don't think any of them have truly dealt with the extent of their grief yet. A big step for Catalina was our trip, but her siblings haven't had the kind of closure or healing experience as their sister.

I make a plan in my head then and there to find a way to take them all to Greece.

Our heads snap in the direction of the entrance of the court where the players come out as soon as Catalina's name is announced. The crowd starts screaming her name, and pride surges through me at the sight of her. I didn't get to see her for long today before she disappeared with Charlie, preparing for the match, but she did kiss me thoroughly before telling me she loves me, so I can't complain.

I'm a very lucky man.

Catalina looks determined, fierce in the skirt and top combination *Spin* put her in, and absolutely breathtaking as she prepares for the match. She's listening to music as she places her bag down, letting it comfort and calm her as well as put her in the zone. Her opponent is Frederica Udo, the number three tennis player in the world.

Past match statistics between them show that they're about evenly matched when it comes to match wins against each other. That means this one could end with either of them on top. But I believe in Catalina.

She's got this.

It takes her several more minutes until she finally spots her family in the box for her team, but when she does, the tension that resided in her shoulders finally leaves.

Tears fill her eyes as she waves at us, and Charlie, Ori, Hernanda, Felix, Papá, Mamá, Manu, Vanessa, Sage—who should still be recovering but was too stubborn to miss the match—and I stand up simultaneously to show off our shirts.

They have "Catalina is our #1" written on the front.

She covers her mouth with her hands, shaking her head as she takes us in while we cheer for her. Catalina throws us kisses, and I do my best to ignore my stupid ankle to keep upright. It helps that I'm not putting any weight on it, but it's not exactly pleasant either.

After they go through all of the pre-match procedures and warm up, it's finally time for the start of the match.

Frederica wins her first service game. It's very clear that Cata is still warming up, but she secures her service game minutes later.

They look so evenly matched that I stay at the edge of my seat from the second service game Frederica takes. Catalina struggles in her next one a little before, eventually, making the score two games to two.

This back and forth continues all the way until it's six games to six.

Nerves have wrapped around my throat, making it impossible to breathe properly.

"Oh God, I hate tiebreaks," Ori says beside me, and Hernanda and Sami give agreeing nods.

Playing them is easier than watching them for me, so I almost tell them that I agree, but my words die on my tongue as Frederica positions herself to serve. It's an advantage to start serving in the tiebreak, which is annoying considering I want Cata to have all of the advantages, and so far, she's had none in the match.

Frederica serves an ace, getting her the first point in the tiebreak. One out of seven to win.

Catalina doesn't look rattled in the slightest, but I know my woman. She's getting nervous.

She wins one of her service points, but when she loses her second service point before it switches back to Frederica, I see her confidence crumbling.

She loses another point.

Then another.

It's four points to one, and Catalina's hands seem to be shaking as she picks up her towel to wipe her face.

She loses both of her service points.

It's six points to one for Frederica.

My heart stops beating when I realize it's a set point and not for Catalina.

"What the fuck is happening?" Ori whispers to me, and as much as I'd love to reply, I don't have an answer.

I wish I did. Cata thinks I can read her mind, but I only know what she's thinking sometimes because of how well I know her. No matter how long I've studied her playing, it's hard to look into her head during a match.

But I know for certain that right when she misses the next point, giving Frederica the first set, that her heart drops into her stomach in the same way mine does inside of me.

Fuck.

# CHAPTER 41
## CATALINA

I'VE LOST THE FIRST set.

I'm losing the second set four games to zero.

All Frederica needs is to win two more games, and the title is hers.

It's a good thing I have my emotions under control, otherwise, I'd be bawling my eyes out on the court right now. I'm frustrated with myself. The way I'm playing? I don't deserve the title. I don't deserve to become number one. I don't deserve—

"Catalina," I hear my older sister call out as I wipe my face on the towel. "You have nothing left to lose. Take risks. Play the lines. Forget what's at stake. This is for fun," she says, and it takes another piece of strength to keep the tears at bay because that's exactly what Mamá would tell me.

She'd urge me to forget everything and rediscover why I fell in love with the sport in the first place. I fell in love because it made me feel happy. It brought me the kind of joy I had never found in anything else, and losing was never meant to take that joy away. Mamá always told me there is beauty in losing, too, in learning from your mistakes so you can be better next time.

And yet, the words that come out of my mouth are, "*No puedo.*"

"*Sí*, Catalina. *Tú puedes. Puedes hacer todas las cosas que quieres,*" my father says with his thick English accent butchering the words, and the tears finally spill into my eyes.

"You got this!" Sami chimes in.

"We believe in you, Lina," Hernanda adds.

"The score doesn't matter. Focus on every point," Charlie reminds me.

"You can do it," Ness calls out.

"*Vamos*, Catalina," Sage cheers.

"You *are* the best, Cata. You don't have to win for that to be true, but you will anyway," Santi says, but I have no time to linger.

Breaks between games when the score is an even number are very short, and I'm the one serving. I don't want to get a time violation.

So, I let my family's words bounce around my head as I grab the balls from the ball person. It's impossible to win this, no matter what my family says, but for them, I'm going to give it my all.

I'm not a quitter.

I won't give up until the match is truly lost.

Which it isn't.

Not yet.

*Dig deep,* mi amor. *Find the strength.*

Mamá's words stay with me, too, the ones she told me countless times. I almost wish she was here with me in my head, but that would mean she isn't already, which isn't true. Part of her lives on in me. In Samuel. In Hernanda. In Ori. In Dad. She's here. I can feel it.

The first serve of my next game goes straight down the middle of the line, and Frederica barely returns it. Her shot lands near the service line, so I approach it, then attack it, sending it cross-court at the highest speed I can muster.

"Fifteen-love," the umpire says.

I roll out my shoulders, ignoring the slight pinch in my back.

My next serve is an ace.

"Thirty-love."

I nod to myself several times.

Frederica and I battle over the next point. Forehand, backhand, forehand, backhand. She does a drop shot that has me sprinting toward the net, but I manage to get it before the second bounce, hitting it back to her a little awkwardly. I have no time to see where it's going because I'm making my way to the center line, preparing to volley the ball back to her.

It doesn't get to me again.

"Forty-love," the umpire says, sending a wave of confidence I desperately need through my system.

I win my game with another ace.

The crowd explodes into cheers so loud, my heart overfills with love until it's spilling onto my face in the form of a smile.

It's a small victory to win my own service game, but it's one I needed after losing so many.

It's four games to one for Frederica, but maybe there is still a chance for me.

After the break between an uneven number of games, it's time to go back to battling against Frederica, and battling is exactly what I'll have to do to get back the two breaks and even out the score before taking the set for myself.

The next game is the longest one out of the entire match so far, but I win it. I win the game, making the score four games to two.

"*Vamos*, Cata," Santi calls out, and I place my finger to my temple, letting him know I'm locked in.

No one can stop me anymore.

Not even myself.

My next service game is as easily won as the previous one. More determination courses through me.

"*Un juego más*," Santi says when I get back to the side of the court where they're sitting.

One more game until I've evened out the set enough to take at least a small breath. One more game, and she won't have an advantage over me anymore. One more game, and I can win the set.

I stand at the baseline, lowering myself enough to get in position. I spin my racket several times as I wait for Frederica, who looks truly rattled. It gives me an advantage.

My first return is a winner that has the crowd exploding into cheers.

"Love-fifteen," the umpire calls out, but I don't celebrate. I simply move to the other side of my half of the court to prepare.

The next point is difficult, and I end up losing it by hitting the ball into the net. I don't let that get me down or demotivate me. I still have a chance.

I attack the next return, hitting it into the corner on the opposite side of where Frederica is standing. She manages to get it, but she lobs it over my head after I've run to the net.

"*Ah*," escapes me as I stumble backward, running as fast as I can to get to the ball. It lands deep in the court, and the only way I manage to return it is by hitting the ball between my legs.

A tweener that lands inside the court, but Frederica is on it and hits a forehand right down the other side of my court. The only thing that allows me to get it is the fact that I took a fifty-fifty chance and started running that way before her racket strings even touched the ball.

I send it cross-court, getting the point.

"Fifteen-thirty," the umpire says, but her voice is drowned out by the sound of the stadium cheering for me. For this incredible point.

I win Frederica's service game in two more points.

More cheers erupt as I finally let out a "COME ON" so loud, it sends the crowd into a frenzy.

It's four games to four games.

"You beautiful badass," Charlie says as I wipe my face on the towel. "You're so close," they add, and I nod several times.

"Two more games to win the set," I mumble, more to myself than any of my family members.

Because I'm so consistent with my serves at the moment, I win my service game easily again, making it five games to four for me. I've just won five games in a row, which isn't unheard of in the tennis world, not at all, but it *is* fucking impressive.

One more game.

One more game and it'll be one set to one.

One more game and I'll have proven my doubts wrong.

That I do deserve this.

Frederica's first serves weren't consistent before I started catching up. They most certainly aren't now that she's rattled because of the score, and her second serve isn't strong when I play well. When I get my shots in.

The set is mine within five minutes.

My eyes catch Santi as he jumps up from his chair, clapping for me. Charlie is beside him, doing the same.

I form my hand into a fist and punch the air, letting victory take over.

But it's not until I win the third set with ease, until I hit a winner that secures me the win of the match and the title of the Grand Slam, that I sink to my knees and cry into my hands. A wave of relief floods through my chest, but it's soon overpowered by the feeling of victory and accomplishment.

I've won my first title.

I'm the number one women's tennis player in the world.

I did it.

After shaking Frederica's and the umpire's hands, I do what Santi did after every tournament he won with me as his fake and then real girlfriend. I run to him. I run to my family. I run as fast as my legs can carry me while they feel like jello.

Security people and the crowd help me climb all the way up to get to my box.

My team hugs me first, but only because they're standing closest to me. Then follows Dad, Hernanda, Ori, and I lean down to hug Sami too. Charlie pulls me into their arms next, and I feel Sage and Ness pat my back, congratulating me on winning a game that I almost lost.

If I were anyone else except the daughter of one of the most famous tennis players in the world, I would have, but I'm not. I was always meant to follow in her footsteps, and even when I didn't feel like I would ever be worthy of it, today I've taken a major step into accomplishing everything she did.

"I'm so proud of you. You deserve this more than anyone, Catalina. You worked so hard for it, and it has finally paid off," Charlie says, but it's their next words that have me crying even harder. "Your mother would be so, so proud of you."

I'm crying so hard a sob leaves me, and that's when Charlie turns me to Santiago, who's been patiently waiting for me. He's putting his weight on his healthy leg, and I'm careful as I fling myself into his arms, welcoming the way his very presence settles me. The tears keep running down my face, but I doubt they're going to stop anytime soon.

"What a fucking match, Cata. I think my heart hasn't found a way to beat evenly since it started, but it's so worth it," he says with a little chuckle, making me laugh against him.

"I won my first Grand Slam," I whisper against his shoulder, and he nods several times.

"You did, and you did so gloriously," he replies, and I lean back to place my mouth on his.

He kisses me as fervently as I kiss him, the heat of the moment making me forget we're surrounded by people for a moment. It's only when I hear Dad say, "Okay, okay," with a little laugh that I lean away again.

"I love you, *mi corazón*," I whisper to Santi, who presses his forehead to mine, a tear streaming down his face as more run down mine.

"I love you so much, *mi mariquita*," he replies, kissing me softly before he smiles against my lips. "Now, go get your trophy."

The brightest of smiles covers my face before I go to do exactly that.

And as I hold up the trophy, my eyes drift back to my family where they're sitting in the box, cheering for me. For a moment, I think I even see Mamá standing behind them, but when I blink, naturally, she isn't standing there.

But I know she's here, watching me accomplish something so major in the sport we shared.

My fingers lift to the necklace she gave me, wrapping them around the charm. *This one is for you, Mamá.*

# EPILOGUE

*Catalina*

BREATHING HAS BECOME EASIER than it has been in years.

After winning Roland Garros and losing the German Open, I went on to win Wimbledon, too. Layla and I were in the final together, and I won it in two sets.

It was amazing.

Santi's ankle has been doing much better, and he's planning on going back to playing tournaments after a couple more weeks of physiotherapy.

The season is still long, but three Grand Slams are already done, which means the last one will be the US Open and a few more WTA tournaments, ATP for Santiago.

My boyfriend and I have been doing really well together, too. More than well. Being with Santi is Earth-shatteringly incredible. In every way. Emotionally and physically. He fulfills all of my needs in a single breath, and I can't help but glue myself to his side whenever we're together, which is easy considering he's never more than a step away from me when I'm close to him. He gives me space if or when I need it, but otherwise, he's not ashamed in the least to show everyone that he could spend all of his time with me without ever getting bored.

I'm happy.

Every part of my life has found a rhythm I'm truly content with, and while I know it won't last forever, some things always fall out of balance, I won't worry about that. Life is all about living in the moment, not to miss the little things.

Or the big things like meeting Valentina Romana and doing hot laps with her around the Monaco circuit, only a couple of days before she's racing in the Monaco Grand Prix.

Ever since she got a seat in F1, the Monegasque has won her home Grand Prix every single year in a row. She's my favorite F1 driver, a complete badass, and a role model to every little girl who wants to make it in racing. She even opened her own driver academy with Formula One legend Leonard Tick to give kids who aren't born with privileges a chance.

"Your hands are shaking," Santi says, and I tilt my head to the side and back to look up at him.

"Well, I'm about to meet the woman I used to have the biggest crush on, who also happens to be my favorite athlete of all time. It's a lot," I explain, and Santi starts grinning at my response.

"I don't blame you. I also used to have a crush on her. Her and her brother," he replies, and I nod in agreement because I get it.

But then again—

"She's my celebrity crush. Mine," I tell him, pointing my index finger at him warningly. Santi grabs me by the hips and pulls me into him, kissing my lips firmly before responding.

"Don't worry, *cariño*. You're my celebrity crush. You're my everything crush," he says, and I hate that I'll never get tired of hearing him be so sweet to me. That my body will forever melt into his at the words.

"We've come such a long way," I point out with a little chuckle, and Santi smiles brightly.

"All thanks to a stupid fake dating agreement set up by our managers," he says, nudging my nose with his in a soft, tender gesture. "Thank you for following through in faking this relationship with me," he adds, brushing his mouth over mine.

"Thank you for being mine," I reply with a wicked grin.

"Always."

His mouth moves back onto mine, but we're in a rush, so neither one of us lingers. We're making our way through the paddock. There are only a few people here, nothing like how it would be during the race weekend, and I find myself enjoying the privacy of the moment.

Santi's and my relationship has been so public from the very beginning, it's nice when people aren't constantly watching our every move. When we get to have these quiet moments when it's just the two of us.

I step on my tiptoes to press a kiss to his jaw as we walk, bringing a full smile to his handsome face.

The sight of Valentina Romana leaning against a bright red Velocità Rossa sports car with sunglasses and a charming smile on her face has my breath hitching a little. This woman exuberates power, and I feel my feet cement themselves to the ground. Santiago keeps walking and tries to pull me with him, but I'm immovable.

"Cata, what's wrong? She's right there," Santi says, and I nod several times, swallowing hard.

"I know she is. That's why I can't move," I explain as I study her long, curly, dirty-blonde hair. She's accomplished so much. Broken down so many barriers.

"She probably can't wait to meet you, Cata. You are also famously known for changing the world of tennis, you know?" he says, placing his hand on my cheek and rubbing comforting circles with his thumb.

"Yeah, you're right," I say, looking up at him and nodding even though I don't feel confident at all. I just feel nervous. "I did do that. I'm cool, right?" Santi chuckles softly, his thumb still tracing circles.

"The coolest person I know, yes," he replies, so I shake out my arms and take a deep breath. "*Vamos*," he says, taking my hand again and leading me to Valentina.

Her face lights up at the sight of me.

"*Hola*, Catalina. *Es un honor a conocerte*," she says in flawless Spanish, and I can't help but let out a nervous laugh as I shake her hand.

"I'm so sorry," I say and cover my mouth, but she simply shrugs off my apology.

"You're all good. I'm touched you're so nervous to meet me. To be honest, I was the one who was nervous about meeting you. You just won two Grand Slams and became the number one tennis player in the world. That is incredible," she compliments me, and I feel my mind leaving my body for a second.

"I think I just passed out a little," I admit, making Valentina laugh again, a sound I think angels would make.

"Hey, Val, do you mind telling me where you put Nevaeh's other camera bag? She's looking for it," another familiar voice says, and I turn my head to see Adrian Romana approaching. He looks exactly like his sister, only much taller and with sharper features. Beside him is Gabriel Biancheri, who is paying me no mind as he smiles at his wife, Valentina, and honestly, I can't blame him.

"It's in my room, on the chair in the corner," Val tells her brother, who finally shifts his attention to me.

His face widens in surprise.

"No way! You're Catalina Sanchez. Oh my God, please wait here. I have to get my wife," he says before running the opposite way.

"Sorry, he's always all over the place, but Nevaeh would really like to meet you. She's a huge fan," Gabriel explains, and Adrian's excitement about my presence finally settles my nerves.

"Nevaeh Fuchs, right?" I ask, feeling Santi's hand slip onto my hip before he pulls me against his side.

"Yes, do you know her?" Val asks, lifting her sunglasses off her face to show me the excitement in her eyes.

"I used to play with her and told Catalina about her," Santi explains, and I nod in agreement.

Minutes later, Adrian is walking beside his very pregnant wife. He's practically holding her stomach while she continues to swat his hand away. He looks happy and worried at the same time, and the sight makes my heart swell because I know one day, if Santi and I both want it, it'll be us.

"Adrian, I won't break apart, I promise. She's fine and I'm fine," Nevaeh assures her husband, placing her hand on her swollen stomach. He doesn't look any less concerned, but he lets her approach Santi and me by herself. "Santiago, it's so nice to see you again. And Catalina, I'm a huge fan. I watch every single one of your matches," she says more calmly than I greeted Valentina, but she's probably used to meeting celebrities she likes and having to stay calm.

As a journalist, it's part of her job.

"I've read all of your articles," I reply, which finally brings a blush to her face to let me know maybe she is affected by my presence after all.

"Not to rush you all, but I have a few places I need to be today, one of those being my academy to meet with Estrella and James, so let's get this show on the road," Valentina says, tilting her head in the direction of the car.

We move through the procedures of the pre-hot laps, people telling me it'll be filmed and helmets being put on our heads—mine by Santi, and Valentina's by her husband, even though I know she doesn't need help—before we get to sit in the car.

Valentina wastes no time driving onto the track. Or more accurately, flying across it. I barely hold back my amazed screams as she drifts into the corner. Adrenaline and fear go through me in tidal waves, but I welcome the odd sensation. The F1 champion beside me even starts talking to me to distract me, and we end up having an easy, genuine conversation about our careers.

"You know, I may drive three hundred-something kilometers on the track, but you actually serve... about a hundred and seventy kilometers on average?" she asks, and I smile as awe settles in my chest because she's right. The speed of my serve is fucking impressive when comparing it to the speed of a sports car.

"Yeah, that's my average. My fastest ever was two hundred and twenty," I reply, grinning when she lets out a whistle.

By the time everything is done and I get out of the car, happiness has consumed every part of me. I run straight toward Santi, without whom this would have never happened, and I kiss him deeply, fully, until I'm sure I've shown my gratitude through my kiss.

Then I add, "Thank you so much for the best birthday present ever." He kisses me again, lingering longer than I did.

"The best for now. I'll outdo myself next year, and then the year after, and then the year after," he promises, pressing his forehead to mine.

"A lifetime full of you outdoing yourself every year sounds perfect to me."

"A lifetime with you by my side sounds perfect for me," he adds, and I melt fully against his body as he presses his mouth back onto mine and wraps his arms around me.

"I love you, *mi corazón*."

"I love you, *mi mariquita*."

***The End***

# Translations

Mijo - My son

Mi amor - My love

Papá, por el amor de Dios, dimelo sin el drama, por favor.
-
Papa, for the love of God, talk to me without the drama, please.

Mi enemiga - My enemy

Cabrón - Asshole

Mariquita - Ladybug

La reina - The queen

Juntos - Together

Joder - Fuck

Guapo/hermoso - Handsome

Bebé - Baby

Mi corazón - My heart

Eres mi mariquita - You're my ladybug.

La vida de una tortuga marina es una vida libre.
-
The life of a sea turtle is a free life.

Lumière des Étoiles - Light of the star

Bruja - Witch

Pendejo - Asshole

# Translations

Mi pequeña villana. - My little villain.

Baila conmigo, cariño - Dance with me, darling

Dolcezza - Sweetness

Vamos - Let's go

Yo sé que a ti te encanta el sonido de tu voz, pero no necesito tus palabras.
Necesito silencio
-
I know you love the sound of your voice, but I don't need your words.
I need silence

Enfocate, Santi - Focus, Santi

Ya sé - I know

Tú puedes, cariño. Respira y concéntrate
-
You can do it, darling. Breathe and concentrate.

No puedo. - I can't

Sí, Catalina. Tú puedes. Puedes hacer todas las cosas que quieres.
-
Yes, Catalina. You can. You can do everything you want to.

Un juego más. - One more game.

Hola, Catalina. Es un honor a conocerte.
-
Hello, Catalina. It's an honor to meet you.

# ACKNOWLEDGEMENTS

Thank you to everyone who got me here. To the people who support me unconditionally. To the friends I've made online. To the readers who read every single word I write. Thank you to those who've been on this journey with me from the very beginning, and to the ones who just discovered me too.

Words will never be able to express how grateful I am for every single one of you. Without you, I wouldn't be where I am today. I wouldn't keep writing the stories you all love so much.

So, thank you. For everything.

# About the Author

Bridget L. Rose is a queer author currently located in Toronto, Canada. She was born in Germany and is half-Italian and half-German. During her teenage years, she was fortunate to live in Singapore and the USA as well.

Bridget fell in love with books from a young age, and soon discovered her passion for writing as well. Over the past two years, Bridget has written and self-published ten books. She writes contemporary romances, most of them set in the world of Formula One, as well as cowboy and tennis romances.

In her books she aims to be inclusive because of her own experiences of being queer and living with mental illnesses. Even nowadays, people still make assumptions and use stereotypes about queer people as well as people with mental illnesses, which she experiences daily as well. Bridget is passionate about changing the narratives on these subjects, especially in the romance market.

When Bridget is not busy writing, she loves to read and spend time with her family, including her two furry children JJ and Diego.

# Books by Bridget L. Rose

## *The Pitstop Series*

**Jump-Start**

**The Last Championship (Novella)**

**The Inside of a Rainbow**

**The Other Sider Of Her Storm**

**Rush: Part One & Two**

**Chase: Part One & Two**

**Reserved**

**Diffuse**

**Straight to the Chapel**

**A Romana Christmas**

## Silver Creek Ranch Series

## *From Angels to Devils Series*

**To Pluto & Back**

**From Devils to Angels**